NOW YOU ARE MINE

AMANDA BRITTANY

B
Boldwood

First published in Great Britain in 2024 by Boldwood Books Ltd.

Copyright © Amanda Brittany, 2024

Cover Design by JD Design Ltd

Cover Photography: Shutterstock

The moral right of Amanda Brittany to be identified as the author of this work has been asserted in accordance with the Copyright, Designs and Patents Act 1988.

All rights reserved. No part of this book may be reproduced in any form or by any electronic or mechanical means, including information storage and retrieval systems, without written permission from the author, except for the use of brief quotations in a book review.

This book is a work of fiction and, except in the case of historical fact, any resemblance to actual persons, living or dead, is purely coincidental.

Every effort has been made to obtain the necessary permissions with reference to copyright material, both illustrative and quoted. We apologise for any omissions in this respect and will be pleased to make the appropriate acknowledgements in any future edition.

A CIP catalogue record for this book is available from the British Library.

Paperback ISBN 978-1-83617-176-8

Large Print ISBN 978-1-83617-175-1

Hardback ISBN 978-1-83617-174-4

Ebook ISBN 978-1-83617-177-5

Kindle ISBN 978-1-83617-178-2

Audio CD ISBN 978-1-83617-169-0

MP3 CD ISBN 978-1-83617-170-6

Digital audio download ISBN 978-1-83617-173-7

Boldwood Books Ltd
23 Bowerdean Street
London SW6 3TN
www.boldwoodbooks.com

In memory of Sue Allen
One of the strongest women I've ever known

PROLOGUE

TWENTY-SIX YEARS AGO

Sheer adrenalin enables me to lift the body into the waiting wheelbarrow and push it round the vast, inky lake. Halfway to my destination a limp arm, as though trying to stop me from moving forward, flops from the barrow and drags along the hard earth. But the wind is on my side, powerful against my back, pushing me onwards, whispering, *They deserved to die. They brought this on themselves.*

Following an exhausting walk, I drop the corpse into the World War II bunker. It lands face down, arms and legs bent awkwardly at the bottom of the steps, like one of those murder-victim outlines you see on TV. I wait some moments, catching my breath, before heading back for the second body.

And the process begins again.

Before loading the next corpse, I rest, taking deep breaths, my hair clinging to my skull, damp patches under my arms, wondering if I'm doing the right thing. Maybe I should report what happened. No. It's too late for that.

Once the second body is down in the bunker, I return to Lakeside House, scrub blood from the driveway and wheelbarrow, my odour none too pleasant, my breathing erratic. Then I go into the house and type a suicide note on the computer, print it off, and pin it to the front door against the flaking paint. It will be a while before anyone comes here. Visitors are rare at Lakeside House. But, if they come, they will believe the suicide note, of course they will. *The couple were odd,'* they will say.

In time, the house will become derelict. Nobody will know what happened here. Nobody will care.

Dashing towards the car, I glance back just once, sickness churning my stomach, bile at the back of my throat threatening to choke me. *Yes,* the whispering wind reminds me, *they deserved to die. They brought this on themselves.*

1

POLLY

Polly drives her car onto the cobbles in front of Lakeside House and kills the engine. Taking a deep breath, she picks up the framed photograph from the passenger seat and studies the forlorn young woman in the picture. Polly has known it's her mother since she was old enough to know she was adopted, but only recently, since her parents moved abroad, has she noticed how her biological mother's eyes are a reflection of her own and felt the need to know more about her.

She looks up at the sign for Lakeside House etched into the brickwork above the front door – the same sign is in the photo. She's got the right place, there's no doubting that, and her stomach flips.

She slips the photo into her canvas bag, opens her car door, swings her legs round and steps into the oppressive heat, unusually hot for early September. Stretching her arms above her head and rotating her shoulders, she attempts to shift the aches from the long drive from Oxford.

Greek-style pillars flank the doors to the brilliant-white building. Green lawns hug the uneven land, lazily sprawling into the distance towards breathtaking views of the rugged Cumbrian mountains. Polly wishes for a moment she was here for different reasons. To absorb herself in the beauty and tranquillity of this stunning part of northwest England, to walk in the invisible footprints of Beatrix Potter and William Wordsworth and wild swim in the lakes would go a long way towards repairing her shattered nerves.

Her gaze moves across the pretty borders that frame the driveway, landing on a double garage, one door open to reveal a shiny, blue minibus. An austere-looking woman in, at a guess, her mid fifties, with a sharp blonde bob, sits on a shaded bench nearby dragging on an e-cigarette as she reads from a Kindle, a decrepit, rusty wheelbarrow overflowing with decaying cuttings abandoned beside her.

Four cars are parked on the drive: an electric Fiat 500 plugged into a charger, an old Volkswagen camper van with blacked-out front windows and checked curtains tied back at the rear with faded ribbons, a red Vauxhall Corsa and an SUV.

Tugging her suitcase free from the boot of her car, Polly makes her way towards the building, sun burning her neck where her floral cotton dress dips at the back. It's a humid heat, well into the thirties – the kind that makes her blonde curls frizz, her pale skin freckle. She's grateful for the air-con as she steps into the silent, stunning lobby.

The floor and furnishings are marble, the ceiling high and ornate. A blue vase stands on the reception counter, white lilies giving off a musky scent. A cosy, cushion-filled sofa is wedged into a bay window that looks out towards the drive, a low round table in front of it, glossy art magazines displayed on its glass surface. You could fit the apartment she'd shared with her best friend Nicky into this area alone. Not that she'll ever go back there – to *that* apartment. Not after what happened. Thank God her brother cleared out her stuff so there's no reason to return. She grips the necklace around her neck. She'd had a ring made for Nicky with the same stone about a year ago, and the gesture was returned on Polly's twenty-sixth birthday six months later. A green teardrop peridot stone on a gold chain. '*For everlasting friendship,*' Nicky had said, and they'd hugged. Happy with their lives. That was before everything went wrong.

Polly approaches the counter, rings a bell and turns to admire the paintings by artists she recognises from a recent trip to an art gallery in London. She'd hoped to gain some knowledge so as not to appear too ignorant when she arrived here. Not that she needs to be an artist to attend. The website deemed the course suitable for anyone from newbies to experienced artists wanting to brush up on their skills or experience a different style or art form.

High on the walls are the vivid colours of a Cecily Brown abstract, a Vincent Van Gogh, an Henri Rousseau and a Henry Hopper. Copies, but even she can appreciate them in their heavy frames. Her eyes fall on the painting that had made the new owner of Lakeside, Xander Caldwell, rich: *New York in Spring*. Again, a copy. The original sold at auction two years ago for three million. There's no doubting this place is amazing. Xander and his wife Tara have done a fantastic renovation. It looks so different to how it appeared in the photograph taken in the eighties that Polly found online.

'Hello. I'm Tara Caldwell. Welcome to Lakeside.' This beautiful blonde woman in black shorts and a white lacy top seems to have appeared from nowhere, her eyes now fixed on Polly. 'I hope you had a good journey?'

Polly presses the palms of her hands against her hair, trying to tame curls that seem determined to fly away, conscious of the creases in her dress and her exhausted appearance. She's not normally worried about how she looks, but this place is posh, and this woman in front of her is pretty much perfect.

'There were a few jams on route,' Polly says. 'Especially in the last five miles.'

'Flash flooding?' Although the woman's smiling, there's a slight tremble in her voice. She seems uneasy as she brushes lily pollen from the counter, staining her fingers yellow.

'Yes. A tree was down. I had to take a diversion.'

'The weather's been erratic lately.' Tara glances towards the window and back at Polly. 'But hopefully it will be a sunny ten days.'

'I hope so.' She tugs at the collar of her dress. 'Though perhaps a few degrees cooler.'

Tara taps tanned fingers across her laptop keyboard and looks at the screen. 'You must be Polly Ashton.'

'Yes, that's me.'

As Tara continues to look at the screen, Polly spins round, absorbing more of her surroundings. A grand staircase curves towards what must be the guestrooms. Across the lobby, double doors stand open giving a view of an elegant lounge, and French doors at the far side lead out towards a stunning lake.

'Kendalmere,' Tara says, and Polly returns her gaze to the woman behind the counter. 'The lake, it's called Lake Kendalmere. It stretches to the far edges of the retreat.'

'It's beautiful. How big are the grounds?'

'The furthest reaches are about two miles out.'

'Wow! I hadn't realised the size of the place.'

'It's a stunning walk, takes about two hours there and back, with plenty of wildlife. I've seen red squirrels and ospreys, and a family of otters took up residence in the lake earlier this year. Not that I got too close – they might be cute to look at, but I read on Facebook they're one of the top predators in the country.' Tara holds out a gleaming key. 'Room Six,' she says. 'It's gorgeous, you'll love it. Looks out over the lake. So relaxing.'

'Thank you.' Polly takes the key and turns it over in her hands. Truth is, she's not sure she can relax, not after everything that's happened. How can she come to terms with the fact a stalker invaded her home, her and Nicky's lives? She shakes away her intrusive thoughts. She's not here at Lakeside to relax anyway, or paint for that matter. She'll have to give the art sessions a go, she knows that, but she's here in search of her family history, her blood relatives – to transform her mother from the Jane Doe who died giving birth to her to something tangible. A real person. And she's certain the answers lie here.

Tara hands Polly a suitcase label with 'Room Six' written on it. 'Please tie this to your luggage and put it with the other cases. Ralph will take it up to your room.'

There's a pile of cases in the corner. Polly ties the label and lifts the handle of her case.

'Xander and the other guests are in the lounge.' Tara points to the double doors as the sound of soft voices reaches Polly's ears. 'There's a glass of bubbly and nibbles waiting.'

'Thank you.' Polly rolls her case across the marble tiles and stands it with the others. When she turns back, Tara is disappearing through a door behind reception.

2

POLLY

Polly enters the lounge, anxiety rising, not a fan of meet and greets.

She recognises Xander Caldwell from his website, standing in the far corner surrounded by a handful of guests. He's tall, good-looking, his ice-blue eyes startling, even from a distance. The website described him as a successful artist who owns a gallery in London, although he's only had the one huge success. His subsequent work has sold, but nothing on the same scale as *New York in Spring*. According to the About Us section, he and Tara – also an artist – met eighteen months ago, and, after a whirlwind romance lasting just five weeks, they got married on a beach in the Caribbean.

At a guess, he's around forty. His dark hair is swept back from chiselled features, and he's dressed in a trendy checked suit, a crisp white shirt open at the neck.

He catches Polly's eye as she approaches, lifts his chin. 'Hi there. You must be Polly.' There's a hint of an American accent.

'That's me,' she says, sitting down next to a woman who looks to be in her sixties, with short grey hair and a wonky, short fringe. She's wearing denim knee-length shorts, and a pink, fluffy sweater despite the humid weather, and peers at Polly over gold-rimmed glasses, a small fan whirring in her hand close to her flushed face.

'Is it hot in here, or is it me?' she says, as the fan hits her nose and makes a painful buzzing sound.

'It is hot, yes. Though the air conditioning helps.'

'Janice Hardacre.' The Scottish-sounding woman offers her hand, fingers together, her handshake sweaty but firm. 'Lovely to meet you.'

'Polly. Good to meet you too.'

Xander gestures to a tray of bubbly-filled glasses. 'Help yourself to Prosecco, Polly.'

'Thanks.' She picks one up, takes a gulp, then another, before scanning the other guests.

There are three.

Sitting on the other side of Janice is an attractive red-haired woman in her mid to late thirties, wearing a turquoise kaftan dress and flat black sandals laced up her long legs, gladiator style. Beside her is a man of around forty, legs crossed, an A4 sketchpad resting against his thighs, a pencil in his hand. He sports a goatee and a bald head, and his dark green polo shirt and chinos give him a smart-casual vibe. And finally, a straight-backed spectacled man – who looks to be of a similar age to Kaftan Woman, with a red waistcoat and matching bow tie – stands by the French doors, arms folded.

'It doesn't look as if our sixth guest, Marsha, will be joining us,' Xander says, 'so I'll crack on.' He pauses for a moment, his eyes skittering across the expectant faces. 'I'd like to say a huge welcome to our first ever art retreat at Lakeside House. I hope you are as excited as we are to be here.' He smiles, his teeth super white. 'I've called this little meet and greet not only for you to introduce yourselves and tell us what you hope to gain from the course, but also for my wife and I to tell you a bit about the art course and Lakeside.'

Tara's sudden approach from behind the row of chairs startles Janice, who leaps up and shoots her drink from her glass, snorting as it splashes her face and goes up her nose.

'And here's my beautiful wife,' Xander says, ignoring the incident and reaching for Tara's hand as Janice regains her composure and sits back down, mopping her face with a tissue.

'Hello again, everyone.' Tara pins on a rigid smile, still seeming uneasy. 'I hope you all enjoy your stay with us.'

'Indeed.' Xander continues to hold her hand. Tight. 'And now let me tell you all about Lakeside Art Retreat.'

Kaftan Woman moves to the edge of her seat and runs slim fingers over a tattoo on her wrist: the letter D entwined by a rose.

Bald Man snaps closed his sketchbook and lays his sharpened pencil on the low table in front of him, then curls an index finger over his top lip, pressing a thumb under his chin, as though contemplating.

Bow Tie Man turns towards the window, giving the group his back.

Xander releases Tara's hand and lowers himself into a leather chair, crossing his long legs, and Tara stands by his side, a hand on his shoulder. They look like royalty.

'I bought Lakeside House eighteen months ago, after my darling wife found the details of the auction online.' He glances up at her. She doesn't meet his eye. 'The building had been unclaimed for over twenty years. Run down and abandoned, it needed so much work. Dilapidated didn't begin to cover it. And now look.' He casts his eyes across the high, ornate ceiling, his voice full of pride. 'We've transformed the place.'

'Wasn't there a suicide pact here years ago? A couple in their early forties?' It's the woman in the kaftan, her lips twitching as the smile drops from Xander's face.

The man with the red bow tie tears himself away from the window, narrowed eyes focused on Xander. 'I heard that too.'

Polly knows about the suicides. When she realised she may have found the house in her mother's photograph she went on an Internet search, finding a 'mysterious happenings' website that focused on the Lake District. There she'd found an article about the previous tenants, Esme and Stephen Frampton, taking their own lives, along with the photo of Lakeside from the eighties. She shudders. Were the couple connected to her mother? However beautiful this place is, tragedy lingers here.

'Their bodies were never found,' the woman goes on. 'All very strange if you ask me.'

Xander flicks his hand, agitated, dismissive, and rises once more, resting one arm along the high mantel of an open fireplace. 'But, as you say, it was a long time ago. We don't dwell on the past here. The future is where we're heading.'

'I must admit, the place has a weird atmosphere,' Bow Tie Man says.

'Well, I've never felt it.' Xander taps his fingers, a sheen appearing on his tanned face. He forces a smile.

'I bet it's haunted.' Janice giggles, which feels untimely.

'Of course it isn't.' Xander's smile disappears, his tone defensive.

'I thought I heard a ghost once,' Janice goes on. 'Heard this terrifying scream in the middle of the night. Turned out to be a wee fox in my garden. Gave me quite the scare, as you can imagine. I'm not saying they don't exist – ghosts, not foxes. I know foxes exist. There was one in my garden—'

'What a great story, Janice,' Xander says, stepping forward. 'But I must cut in as we've so much to get through.'

'Yes, we have lots planned for you here at Lakeside,' Tara says. 'You'll adore the surroundings. I'm certain they'll lend themselves to your art and grab your imagination.'

'Nobody knew much about the couple, did they?' Kaftan Woman twirls a long strand of her red hair around her finger. She's not about to let the subject drop.

'And this is just the beginning for the Lakeside Art Retreat.' Xander's clearly ignoring her, not meeting her eye. 'We're drawing up plans for two self-contained holiday cottages on the far reaches of the grounds, for those who enjoy more privacy, and there will be a further art studio. So, when you return in the future, which I hope you will, you'll have even more choice.' He places his arm round Tara's shoulders.

'We're a small but proactive team here,' Tara says, flashing a look at her husband and pushing her hands into the pockets of her shorts. She clears her throat. 'Presently, we have two members of staff but hope to employ more as we expand.'

Xander nods across the room to where a tall, grey-haired man with a look of George Clooney leans against the bar, his age difficult to judge. He could be anything from fifty-five to early sixties.

'Ralph is our jack of all trades.' Tara smiles over at him 'There's not much he can't turn his hand to.'

'And if you have any questions about the area,' Xander says, 'Ralph is your man. He lived in the nearby village of Marplethorpe many years ago.'

'We don't know what we would do without him,' Tara says, and Ralph raises his hand in a wave and throws the gathered group a friendly smile. 'Then we have our new chef, Lorcan, who came to us from a Michelin-starred restaurant in London and is now busy in the kitchen preparing a magnificent feast for this evening. All our vegetables are fresh, grown here at Lakeside, and everything else is sourced locally.'

'And now it's your turn to tell us a bit about yourselves,' Xander says, smiling at his wife and caressing her back. They really are stunning. Beautiful, rich people. Then why does Tara seem so tense? Why does her smile look forced?

'Can we start with you, Polly?' Xander asks.

Her stomach churns with unease. She's confident with people she knows, but seems to have lost faith in strangers since she and Nicky were stalked – since the cameras were installed in their apartment; since their every move was filmed. She reassures herself that nobody will really be listening to her spiel anyway, all busy rehearsing what they're going to say in their heads.

'Well,' she begins. 'I'm Polly, and I'm twenty-six.' *True.* 'I would love to be good at art and read somewhere that, given the right tuition, I could be.' *Lie.* She opens her mouth to carry on but is cut off by Xander.

'Thanks, Polly. How about you?' Xander looks towards the man in the red bow tie, who turns out to be Harry Hampton, a serious, pale man with a quiet disposition and a floppy dark fringe he constantly flicks back.

'I've been painting since I was nineteen,' he says, pushing his red-framed glasses further up the bridge of his nose. 'My go-to is Gothic – macabre paintings that represent the destruction of our world. Something I feel passionate about. But I'd like to give other styles a go – I recently dabbled in pottery and would like to develop my skills there, too.'

'Excellent.' Tara tilts her head. 'You look familiar, have we met?'

'Not that I'm aware of.' He turns back to the French doors. 'I think I would have remembered you.'

The woman in the kaftan speaks up next. 'I'm Beatrice and I

specialise in graphic design.' She's softly spoken, and there's a slight quiver in her voice. 'I hope to get a feel for more traditional art forms while I'm here.' She pauses, presses her hand against her chest, her chin crinkling as if she's about to cry. 'Please excuse me if I seem a bit wobbly at times.' She breaks off, flaps her face with her hand and dabs a screwed-up tissue to her nose. 'My husband died twelve months ago, and I'm still coming to terms with it.'

'I'm so sorry,' Polly says, leaning forward to see past Janice, who is pulling at a thread, unravelling the cuff of her jumper.

'Yes, how truly awful,' Tara agrees. 'Let's hope the retreat helps you work through your grief. And please know that my husband and I are here should you need us.'

'Thank you.' The woman – Beatrice – shoves the tissue into the pocket of her kaftan.

Janice tells the huddled group that she's taken up art since retiring as a schoolteacher and mainly paints dogs in jumpers, and, though nobody seems particularly interested, she tells them how she collects biros from everywhere she visits, bringing out a handful from the bottom of her large handbag. 'Have you got one I could have, Xander?'

The bald man with the goatee, William Doyle, well-spoken and a little aloof, tells them he's been an amateur artist for some time and hopes to pick up lots of tips that might help him branch out professionally.

'Wonderful!' Xander claps his hands. 'I'm so looking forward to seeing all your artwork.' He pauses for a moment before picking up a pile of glossy pamphlets and starts handing them out. 'We have so much to fit into our ten days together and I, for one, cannot wait to get started. I hope you are all ready for what is going to be a fabulous experience at Lakeside Art Retreat.'

It's as he's handing out the pamphlets that Polly glances outside, her heartbeat quickening as she glimpses a figure in the distance. A tingle crosses the back of her neck. There's something about the way they're walking, stooping as though not wanting to be seen. The way they're dressed head to toe in black. She turns to Xander. Should she mention it? But then it's probably the chef or the other guest, and the last thing she wants to do is come across as paranoid, even though that's exactly how she feels at times. She's certainly let what happened back home shatter her confidence – her feeling of safety.

If only Nicky hadn't had that one-night stand a few months back. It was clear, after trying to cool things off, it had been a terrible mistake. The doorbell would ring in the middle of the night. A shadowy figure lingered in the darkness of the church graveyard opposite their apartment. Bunches of flowers arrived at the apartment, and at the company where Nicky worked. Then came the abusive texts.

Later it became clear someone had been in the apartment while they were out. One of the front door keys had gone missing a few weeks before and they'd had a new one cut, thinking nothing of it. But when odd things started happening, they realised the stalker must have the key – must have taken it the night Nicky stayed over.

The first thing they noticed was one of Polly's dresses – a pretty blue one with tiny white daisies – had disappeared, as had the peridot stone ring Polly bought Nicky. Next, a pink teddy bear was left on her friend's bed, a pair of scissors plunged into its stomach, upsetting them both.

'We need to get away from here, Nicky,' Polly had said in floods of tears. 'I'll go stay with my brother. You need to drive down to your parents. Work from there. At least until we can find somewhere else to live.'

Then they'd found the hidden cameras – a flashing red light between the books on a shelf alerting them. And not just one:

there were cameras hidden in every room, and they had no idea how long they'd been there.

They called the police, but despite them checking out the address where Nicky had stayed the night, it was hopeless. The house had been a holiday let, and officers struggled to track down the person who'd rented it out that week.

Nicky packed and left immediately, and Polly moved in with her brother and his wife, just a few streets away. Neither wanted to set foot in the apartment ever again.

Now Polly turns back to the window to see the figure disappear from view. If only she had seen the stalker. Not knowing what they looked like is hard. Nicky's description of short dark hair and blue eyes could be almost anyone.

But whoever they are, they surely couldn't be here. Whoever was out there by the lake just now can't have anything to do with what happened back home. Polly knows she must keep a check on herself – keep herself grounded, concentrate on why she's here. Here at Lakeside. The place where the photo of her biological mother was taken.

She rises, a hint of a migraine encroaching. She needs to be alone with her thoughts. Adjust to being here. 'Well, it was good to meet you all, but—'

'I was going to go through the itinerary.' Xander hands Polly a pamphlet.

'I'm afraid I'm going to have to pass. I have a bit of a headache.' She flicks through the pages. 'Is everything I need to know in here?'

He nods. 'Well, yes.'

'Then I'll see you all later.' She lifts her hand, turns, and walks away, the sounds of Janice asking Xander where the toilets are and Tara calling after Polly again that she'll love Room Six fading into the background.

* * *

Tara is right, Room Six is amazing. And although her case hasn't yet been brought up to her room, the bathroom shelves are stuffed full of fluffy white towels and laden with expensive shower gels and body lotions. She pops two painkillers and wastes no time in stepping under the luxury waterfall shower, enjoying the way the hot water pulsates against her neck, her head, her body.

Once showered, and the pain relief has kicked in, she starts to feel better. She pulls on a complementary robe and makes her way past the beautiful bedroom furnishings, running a hand over the marble surfaces, as she moves towards the window.

She stands next to a heavy wooden easel laden with canvases, paints and brushes she'll never use – something Xander and Tara put in all the rooms, according to the website – her gaze taking her through the full-length window and out across the immaculate gardens in full bloom. The shimmering blues and greens of Kendalmere are breathtaking. She blinks away the sun. Someone's out there again. Further away this time – but she's sure it's the same person. Narrowing her eyes, she steps closer to the glass, but whoever they are they're moving deeper into the surrounding trees. Annoyed at her stupid anxiety, Polly turns and makes her way towards the queen-sized bed and drops onto it, sinking into the super-soft pillows, dozing for a few moments, before pulling herself up and resting her head against the headboard.

She takes the picture of her birth mother from her canvas bag and studies it through the scratched glass of the old frame. The young girl looks to be about sixteen – a sprinkling of acne across her chin giving away her youth, and she's wearing a loose-fitting ankle-length grey dress. Her blue-green eyes are large – so like Polly's – yet perhaps more soulful.

Her parents gave her the framed photograph when she was

young and simply told her it was a picture of her 'biological mother', that they didn't know who she was. That they would always
love her.

Polly never asked questions. As a child she worried the
answers would reveal that her biological mother hadn't wanted
her – had abandoned her. In fact, she created stories in her mind
that her mother was a warrior princess who left her to save the
world. Later she didn't need to know the truth – her parents were
amazing and had been there for her always. Her years growing up
were rich with trips to the zoo and the seaside and simpler things
like sharing her mother's joy of gardening, following her around
as she told her the names of all the plants in English and Latin.
She recalls pulling the flowers close to her nose, smelling their
delicious scent. There had been no place in Polly's world, growing
up, for the woman who'd abandoned her.

But more recently she'd wanted to know more. Perhaps the
trigger was her parents deciding to up and move to Provence. She
would miss them. Their absence would leave a void. Or maybe it
was because she felt if they lived hundreds of miles away, she
wouldn't hurt them by looking into who her real mother was. Just
before they moved, Polly had found the courage to ask her mother
if she knew anything at all about her biological mother. Surpris-
ingly, her mother was forthcoming, didn't seem to have a problem
with Polly wanting to know.

'All I can tell you is that she was found on the streets of West-
minster, in labour. That she was rushed to hospital where she died
giving birth to you.' She'd touched Polly's face then. 'She had no
identification on her, only the photo. I'm sorry, my darling.'

So, whoever Polly's biological mother was, it seemed she
hadn't abandoned her after all, and Polly found herself travelling
down a rabbit hole, determined to find out who she was. The
photo, the house name etched into the wall, was her only clue.

She looks around the vast bedroom. Had her mother lived here at Lakeside, or was the fact she was photographed on the doorstep incidental? Was she connected to the suicide victims, Esme and Stephen Frampton? And who is the figure roaming the grounds?

3

ESME

Forty-Two Years Ago

I'm pregnant.

I wish I wasn't.

But I am.

It's not that I don't want a baby. I do. I used to dream when I was in my late teens that I would meet the perfect man and we'd have two children, a boy and girl, and call them Lila and Edward. But now, at twenty-five, and married to a monster, I fear for my unborn baby.

Of course, I will love the child with all my heart, will breathe in the smell of its soft newborn skin, will pour affection onto my tiny boy or girl like liquid gold. But the thought of Stephen as a father fills me with dread. He doesn't know how to love, only how to hate.

I can and I will protect my child from its father, I tell myself. *I won't let any harm come to my baby.* But I'm not sure I'm equipped to keep my baby safe. The man locks me in the pantry when I annoy him, despite knowing I'm claustrophobic. He strikes me often. And once he left me outside in the snow in my nightdress for hours. What if he does it to baby Lila or baby Edward?

I haven't told Stephen I'm pregnant, afraid of his reaction. I'll wait until I've seen the doctor. He doesn't need to know. Not yet.

I saw Perdita Brook in Marplethorpe Village Shop earlier. I pinned her in the corner by the cheese. The Red Leicester was on offer. I love Red Leicester. I didn't buy it. Stephen hates it.

Perdita was the only person I could tell my secret to. She'll be my midwife. She had to know sometime.

'You must share the good news with Stephen, Esme.' Her eyes were bright with excitement, her shiny dark hair resting prettily on her shoulders. 'He'll be so happy, you'll see.' But she doesn't know what he's like.

Perdita thinks she's pregnant too. 'Early days,' she said, placing a hand on her stomach. 'I'm sure it's a boy. I can sense it.'

'But you're not married.' I don't doubt I sounded like a naïve fifties teenager, as though I believed it was impossible to get pregnant out of wedlock.

She laughed, rested her hand on my arm. 'You're so old-fashioned, Esme,' she said, her smile wide and warm. 'I may get married at some point, but it's OK these days—'

'To live in sin?'

She laughed again at that. She's right. I am old-fashioned. I was brought up to believe you shouldn't do rude things with boys until you are married, and even then only when *he* wants to. *'Never initiate, Esme,'* Stephen said once, when I tried to kiss him, telling me I was no better than a whore. Stephen would certainly be shocked to hear about Perdita's loose behaviour. I won't tell him.

'I may not have a ring on my finger, Esme,' Perdita went on. She's truly beautiful is Perdita. She could have any man. 'But I'm in love, and that's all that matters.'

I wonder now who she's fallen in love with. He's an artist, she mentioned that much, and apparently he works on the fairground that comes to Marplethorpe. I wonder, too, what that feels like – to be in love, and for someone to love you back. It must feel incredible. I read romantic novels when Stephen's not home. Hide them under the mattress when he returns. I imagine being in the arms of a man I truly love, who truly loves me. It feels magical to enter that fantasy, even though I can never stay long.

I wish I could leave Stephen, but the truth is I'm scared to. He told me once that if I ever leave, he will find me, and I'll regret it.

I met him when I was an assistant at a garden centre in Ambleside. I loved my job. I miss it. Stephen was a customer, looking to buy a wheelbarrow. He chatted with me, said I was pretty, which I'm fully aware I am not. I suppose I'd never had much attention from the opposite sex – well, from anyone really – and fell for his greasy charm.

I blame my upbringing, to some degree, for my desperation to be loved. Mother and Father were good enough people, I suppose, but when my younger brother Edward died from a rare blood disease when I was seven, they were never really the same. They were old-fashioned in their thinking long before Edward died, but it got worse. They were too protective of me in some ways – feared I might die too – but neglectful in others. Hugs and kisses, which had been two a penny when Edward was alive, dried up, becoming a peck on the cheek when it was my birthday, if I was lucky. They're dead now, my parents. Died of a broken heart, I suppose. I miss the people they once were, but not the faded, bitter replicas they became. But I'll never get over the loss of my little brother; he'd been my everything as a child.

I'm the first to admit my looks aren't my greatest asset. My mother once called me Plain Jane, which was silly as my name is Esme. But I thought Stephen saw something in me. I was a fool – stupidly thrilled when he invited me out for a meal. It was nice.

The meal, I mean. I had scampi, I remember. Scampi and chips in a basket with tartar sauce. I'd never had it before. He was such a gentleman that day, and I couldn't believe he liked me. Well, as it turned out, he didn't. His attention soon evaporated after we got married, like moisture on wet clothes drying in the sun. I'm not sure why he wanted me in his life, except perhaps to control me.

I'll go and see the doctor next week when Stephen's at work. Or maybe I'll go tomorrow when he's in Windermere. He's started collecting war memorabilia, though I'm not sure why. He saw an advert in the newspaper. A man called Giles Alderman is selling some medals. He's heading to meet him. Perhaps if he gets a hobby, he'll leave me alone.

4

POLLY

There's a sharp knock on the bedroom door. Polly rises and makes her way across the room, picking up on the tinkling sound of music out in the hallway.

'Hello!' she calls, pressing her ear against the door. The tune is 'Polly Put the Kettle On'.

She looks through the peephole at the cone-like shape of the hallway. There's nobody there. The music has stopped.

Heart thudding, she places her hand on the door handle, waits a moment, then gingerly opens up. She pokes her head out, looking left and right down the hallway of closed doors. There are no windows, the lighting low, the area silent. 'Hello? Is there anybody there?'

She tries to convince herself she imagined the sound, that it was a kind of ringing in her ears – after all she's tired, has driven a long way. But surely she didn't imagine the knock? She's about to step back into her room when a shadow crawls along the wall at the end of the hallway, growing bigger. Someone is down there, just round the corner, out of sight. An icy prickle runs down Polly's spine. She leaps back into her room. Slams the door.

For goodness' sake. What's wrong with her? The looming shadow could have been anyone coming up the stairs. Why was she so stupidly afraid to check it out? But she knows why. Why she's always on edge. It's since the stalker invaded her home.

Within moments there's another knock on the door, and her heart speeds up once more. 'Who is it?'

'It's Ralph, Ms Ashton.' The shadow? It must have been his.

She opens the door once more to see the man who was standing behind the bar at introductions, still wearing a white polo and black trousers. His skin tanned, his grey hair neatly styled.

'Good afternoon, Ms Ashton,' he says, flashing dark eyes, her suitcase at his feet. 'May I come in?'

She nods, opens the door wider for him to enter, and he wheels in her case, turning immediately to make his exit.

'Thank you,' she says. 'And please call me Polly.'

He turns as he reaches the door. 'Dinner will be served from seven, Polly,' he says with a smile.

She goes to close the door once he's stepped back out into the hallway. 'Just one more thing before you go,' she says. 'Did you hear music when you came up the stairs?'

He furrows his forehead. 'No... is everything OK?'

'Yes, all good.' It's far from the truth. 'I don't suppose you saw anyone on your way up?'

'No, I'm afraid not. Are you sure you're OK?'

'I am. Yes.' She smiles and he heads away down the lush hallway in his shiny shoes. Perhaps she did imagine the music, after all.

* * *

Polly sits opposite Janice at dinner, watching as she devours her starter of beetroot bonbons. Beatrice, wearing the same turquoise kaftan as earlier, is sitting at a table with William. Harry is alone in the corner. There's no sign of Marsha.

'So, you enjoy art?' Polly says, feeling she should make polite conversation.

'I do, I do.' Janice covers her mouth, continuing to chew. 'Since I retired from teaching, I've been painting regularly.' She swallows, puts down her fork and pulls her phone from her handbag, though how she found it amongst the chaos of used tissues, biros and till receipts is a mystery. She shakes the phone as though it's an Etch A Sketch, seemingly trying to wake it up, then thrusts the small screen a little too close to Polly's face. The blurry images of pugs, dalmatians and every kind of oodle are scrolled past her eyes, all wearing brightly coloured jumpers, rather like the one Janice is wearing. They're good, Polly supposes, if you like that sort of thing.

'It humanises them, don't you think?' Janice smiles, beads of perspiration lying above her top lip, her face glowing red. 'I'm hoping to branch out to cats. Though they tend to get a bit scratchy.' She leans forward, runs her hand over the shoulder of Polly's floral summer dress. 'Such a lovely frock, by the way.'

'Thanks.' Polly's eyes drift to Beatrice and William, Beatrice seeming to be talking at him rather than with him. He looks uncomfortable, keeps stroking his hand over his bald head, crossing and uncrossing his legs.

'I'm learning to play the trumpet, too.' It's Janice again, breaking into Polly's thoughts, her fork back in her hand, suspended in the air. 'It's harder than it looks.'

'I'm sure it is.'

Once the five courses have been eaten, Polly lays her napkin on the table, feeling far too full and a little braindead after listening to Janice for so long.

'And to cut a long story short,' the woman is saying now, 'the postman said I'm to put circulars into my recycle bin, *not* back in the postbox. Well, I said to him – nice boy, wears shorts in all weathers – well, I said—'

'Sorry to interrupt,' Polly says, rising, 'but I think I'm going to have an early night. I'm pretty tired. It's been a long day.'

'OK, dear. Well, I'll see you tomorrow then.'

Polly turns away from her and dashes across the dining room and out through the door.

The lobby is cooler. A clock on the wall behind the plush reception desk chimes ten. She should go to bed. Try for a good night's sleep. But nobody's about, and this place is calling to her to be explored. Had it once been her mother's home? The scene of a double suicide?

She makes her way across reception towards a sign that points down a small flight of stairs to the swimming pool, gym, art studio and an emergency exit. At the bottom she finds a long, silent hallway lit by low spotlights. It could be the air conditioning, but she feels a chill, and goosebumps rise on her arms. She stands for a moment listening, about to turn back when she spots a photo display charting the development of Lakeside from abandoned decaying property to the incredible art retreat it is today.

Footsteps on the stairs behind her make her jump. She looks over her shoulder to see Tara.

'Everything OK, Polly?' Tara says, reaching her side. 'You look a bit... worried.'

'I'm fine, just tired. I should probably hit the sack.'

When Polly doesn't immediately move, Tara gestures towards the photographs on the wall. 'It was very different when Xander bought the place.'

'I can see that.' Polly moves closer to the pictures. 'It's incredible how much it's changed. Must have been such hard work for you both.'

'It was. But Xander is the kind of man who gets what he wants, whatever the cost.' She bites down on her lip. 'I mean that in a good way, of course.'

'Of course.'

Tara touches her throat, glances about her. 'If I'm honest, this place was strange when we first arrived. Creepy really, as though the walls held secrets. Ghosts. Not the spooky kind, but the kind that leave a dark residue.' She shudders, shakes her head. 'The Framptons let the place run into the ground. I mean, how they lived like that at the end is beyond me.'

'And then they took their own lives?'

Tara frowns. 'Supposedly. Though it's quite the mystery. It seems most people accepted it was suicide, including the police, but I'm not so sure. No bodies were ever found.' She shudders again, glancing along the hallway. 'I shouldn't be talking about this. Xander would kill me if he heard me, says it will put the guests off.'

'Well, I'm not put off,' Polly says with a smile, wondering how far she can push the conversation. Wondering if this couple were connected to her mother. 'Do you know if they had any children?'

'The Framptons?' Tara shrugs. 'I don't know anything about them, I'm afraid.' Her voice has a slight tremble, her eyes moving down the hallway once more. 'All I know is this place was much better once the staff from Marplethorpe Emporium came in and cleared out everything belonging to the couple, and the decorators moved in.'

'Marplethorpe Emporium?'

'Yes. They called Xander when he first bought the place, gave us a good quote. They were efficient, got everything done while we were living down in London.' She smiles. 'One of our more successful days.' She goes to step away. 'I really should get on. Is there anything at all I can help you with?'

'No. Thank you. I'm about to head to my room. Busy day tomorrow.' Polly turns, as though intending to go back up the stairs. 'Goodnight.'

'Sleep well.' Tara raises her hand in a wave as she hurries away, disappearing into a room to the right.

Once the woman is out of sight, Polly returns her attention to the display and scans the pictures of Lakeside, studying how the Framptons had left the place when they vanished. Images of the dark and dingy rooms, peeling wallpaper, dirty paintwork – the crushing sadness of Lakeside House makes her heart feel heavy. It's hard to believe it's the same place she's standing in now. She shudders at the thought that her mother may have once lived here. Prays it turns out she was merely visiting, the day the photo was snapped. That she wasn't brought up in such a depressing place.

'I don't like it, Xander.' The distant, distressed voice filling the hallway from the room is Tara's. 'I don't know how much more I can take.'

'Whoever they are, they'll get bored eventually.' It's Xander, his tone dismissive. Hard.

'Will they? They haven't yet. And now we're open, and they said—'

'For Christ's sake, calm down. Everything will be OK.'

'We don't know that.'

'Oh, come on, Tara. What the hell can they do? Let's face it, they've made ridiculous, empty threats telling us not to open, or else – and here we are open, and they've done sod all except drop silly notes through our door. You really need to calm down, or you'll scare away our guests. Let's go to bed. We'll talk in the morning.' There's silence for a moment before Xander speaks again, softer now, 'If you care about me and the retreat – if you love me – you'll keep your paranoia in check, and your mouth shut.'

The couple appear from the room: Tara rubbing tears from her cheeks; Xander, shoulders back, an arrogance in his stride.

Polly darts round the corner, out of sight, her heart kicking her ribs. The way Xander spoke to Tara goes some way to explain the woman's unease. *What a dickhead!* And what the hell were they discussing?

Peering out slowly, she watches as they make their way in the opposite direction, his arm firmly around her shoulders. They turn the corner at the far end of the hallway, and, once they've gone, Polly lets out a breath.

Is someone threatening them? Does the answer lie in the office?

After a brief hesitation, her common sense telling her to go to bed, she creeps along to the room they vacated, her heart still hammering against her ribs. The door has a frosted glass panel, the words *Xander Caldwell's Office* in gold lettering. She tries the handle, surprised when the door clicks open. The couple's disagreement must have made Xander lapse, he hasn't locked up. Polly looks about her before stepping in, the door creaking closed behind her. The blind is up, letting in a dim light from outside, and she can make out a desk at the far end, a portrait of Xander and Tara hanging on the wall behind it.

She flicks on her phone torch and moves across the room, noticing a smaller desk with a computer and what looks like CCTV equipment on it. There's a map on the wall of Lakeside House and grounds – over a thousand acres of land surround the property.

A noise. *Crap!* She spins round, clutches her chest, but it's only the retraction of the floorboards.

A piece of paper lies on the otherwise empty desk. She picks it up, eyes scanning the words in the torchlight:

I warned you.
    The Stranger

So, someone *has* been threatening the Caldwells. And the question is, why?

5

POLLY

The door creaks open. A full moon shines through the window glinting off a silver blade. A figure in black moves fast, long strides, as though flying. A sudden weight against her chest, a knife to her throat.

Polly wakes from the nightmare, clammy with sweat, a pea-like pulse in her neck. The digital clock tells her it's 2 a.m. and she knows she's going to struggle to get back to sleep, not helped by raucous rain hammering against the windows.

She drags herself to a sitting position and rests her head back against the headboard. Presses her hands against her face. She's been having the same awful night terror since finding the cameras at her and Nicky's apartment. The chilling invasion of their lives, the fact that someone had a prime view of them for over a month, someone watching as they made breakfast, watching them getting ready for bed – showering – has left a lasting imprint on her nerves.

And now she's at Lakeside where someone is threatening Tara and Xander. Maybe she should leave. But then Xander didn't seem worried, and surely, whatever the dispute is, it has nothing to do with her and the other guests. No, she must stay. She's here to discover who her birth mother was.

After a restless hour filled with chaotic thoughts, she dozes sitting up, waking at half six and flicking on the bedside lamp, her neck aching.

She swings her legs round and climbs out of bed before searching the room for cameras, something ingrained in her now.

In the shower she raises her face towards the cascading warm water, pushing the note in Xander's office to the back of her mind.

She towel-dries her body and hair before opening her case, absently searching for her blue dress with the white daisies before remembering, with a sinking feeling, that it was taken from her apartment along with Nicky's ring. Taking a breath to calm herself, she pulls on a floral tunic top, leggings and trainers before leaving her room. She takes the stairs two at a time towards the dining room, desperately needing to concentrate on why she's here at Lakeside.

'Good morning, Polly.' It's Tara, standing behind reception, her hair scooped into a high ponytail, her face perfectly made-up. She seems more self-assured than she was last night, and her smile is more natural than the first time they met. 'I hope you slept well. That your bed was to your liking.'

'It was good, thank you.' *Apart from the nightmare.* Should she mention the letter? If she does, Tara will know she's been snooping.

In the dining room, sunbeams throw light through the open French doors, a light breeze moves the crisp, toothpaste-white tablecloths on the veranda. The view of Lake Kendalmere is mesmerising.

Ralph is pouring juice from a carafe for William, who is sitting in the corner. Beatrice, dressed in a pearl-white kaftan, is several tables away, her red hair flopped forward, covering her face.

'Good morning.' Polly raises her hand in a wave as the aroma of coffee and freshly baked pastries makes her stomach gurgle.

William doesn't look up, but Beatrice raises her head, smiling as she twirls a tendril of hair around her finger. 'Morning, Polly. Did you sleep well?' she calls across the room.

'I did, thank you. You?'

Beatrice shakes her head, her lips turning down at the corners. 'I haven't slept well since David died.'

Polly's neck tingles as she tries to find the right words. She lands on 'I'm so sorry. I hope things get better for you soon.'

'I hope so, too.'

'Morning, Polly,' Ralph calls. 'Please take a seat. I will be with you in a moment.'

Janice, wearing a paisley long-sleeved blouse tucked into stretch-topped jeans, her grey hair neat, her glasses slipping down the bridge of her nose, is sitting on the veranda, a plate full of pastries in front of her.

Needing coffee before she can cope with the woman, Polly finds a table out of Janice's eyeline and sits down.

All the guests are to meet at ten o'clock at the outdoor artists' pods – a row of individual wooden buildings enclosed on three sides with glass roofs, the fourth side looking out directly over the swirling greens and blues of the water – a place where they will find all they need to paint their landscapes.

'Would you like juice? We have orange, apple and grapefruit,' she hears Ralph say to Janice.

'Sounds lovely, dear.'

'A choice, rather than a mixed drink, Ms Hardacre. Well, unless—'

'Oh, yes, of course... silly me. Orange will do nicely, and do call me Janice, everyone does. Well, except for my next-door neighbour. She shortens it to Jan. Jan is all very well for some, but it doesn't suit me at all, but I keep schtum, nothing worse than falling out with a neighbour, is there? Even if she does leave her wheelie bin out for several days at a time.'

Moments later, Ralph approaches Polly, holding a pad and pen. 'What would you like, Polly?'

She glances at the menu. 'Coffee, and eggs Benedict, please.'

'Excellent choice.'

He's about to leave when she says, 'Would you mind if I asked you something?'

'Of course, anything.' His smile brightens his eyes.

'Were there any objections?'

'Objections?'

'To the renovations here at Lakeside.' *Someone who might send letters. The Stranger.* She's getting distracted from why she's here. She knows that. But then, she tells herself, she wants to know everything there is to know about Lakeside.

He glances around. 'I believe a few people objected on environmental grounds. Destroying habitat with the extension, that kind of thing. Claiming extra footfall to and around the retreat would have a negative impact on wildlife, but nothing came of it, and the council gave planning permission to go ahead anyway, as you can see.' He shrugs. 'Maybe ask Tara or Xander if you want more information. They will know better than me.'

'Yes, of course, thank you.'

'Will that be all?' He goes to walk away once more when Polly reaches out, touches his arm. Xander had said Ralph lived in Marplethorpe many years ago. Had he known the Framptons? Her mother? But she has to be careful. Take it slow.

'Sorry to be a pain,' she says. 'But I wondered, have you been here long?'

He waits a moment before saying, 'At Lakeside?'

'Mmm.'

'Six months, that's all. I did most of the landscaping.'

'Do you know the area well?' She knows he does.

He clicks his pen. 'I know Marplethorpe well, from years back.' He runs a hand over his chin. 'Then I moved down south, became a landscape gardener, kept in touch with friends up here, visited occasionally. I think I always intended to return at some point. I love the Lake District.'

'What's not to love?'

'Exactly. Anyway, a friend told me Lakeside was having a makeover, so I put in a bid to landscape the gardens. I decided if I got it, it would make my decision to move back. The idea of working at an art retreat appealed.'

Polly smiles. 'And you got the job.'

'I sure did.' He nods. 'Xander and Tara took me on, liked my work, offered me a permanent position and accommodation, and the rest is history. I now do pretty much everything they don't have time to do. Though I don't cook – we want to keep the guests alive.' He laughs, nods towards the open kitchen door, where Polly catches sight of Lorcan hurrying across the kitchen in his chef whites, grabbing a box of eggs. He looks to be in his sixties, average height, average build. 'That's the newbie's department.'

'Well, he looks happy in his work.' She brings her gaze away from Lorcan and back to Ralph. 'And so do you.'

'I am. I've fallen on my feet here. Grateful to the Caldwells for that.' He's glancing around the dining room as though hoping someone will call him away. 'Anyway, I'd better—'

'Do you remember the Framptons?' So much for taking it slow. 'From when you lived here before?'

He shakes his head, his smile fading. 'Not really.' He looks about him once more. 'To be honest, it's not a subject we talk about at Lakeside.' He's clearly irritated now. 'Will that be all, *Ms Ashton*?' he says, walking away without another word.

'Yes, sorry to keep you,' Polly says, feeling as though she's crossed a line.

6

TARA

Tara stands on the patio, the morning sun warm on her back, taking a long drag on her cigarette. The nicotine eases her anxiety as the letter she received last night plays around her mind. Xander doesn't seem at all bothered by the threats, even when she told him she'd seen someone in black hanging about. Could it be The Stranger? He said she was imagining it. That she was paranoid. That she should take her diazepam, maybe up the dose. This man, who she fell in love with just eighteen months ago, is now almost a stranger himself.

As the smoke spirals upwards, her mind drifts to the stressful events leading up to the opening of the retreat.

Environmentalist campaigners had appeared most days with their banners. OK they kept to the edge of the property, were silent, but it was unnerving all the same. The way they congregated, some wearing animal masks, staring at the house. They were angry. Angry that Xander had commissioned plans to extend Lakeside further.

They haven't been back for a week or so, but in truth she doesn't feel safe here. But she can't leave. Where would she go?

She walked out on her wrecked past life, deserting friends. Signed a prenup that says if they break up, she gets nothing. In fact, the only way she would get anything is if he died.

She takes another drag on her cigarette. Flicks ash into her hand. She thinks about this place, its past, the disappearance of the Framptons all those years ago. Could the notes be connected to that?

Glancing back at the house, her eyes flick across the windows, her gaze lowering to the apartment she shares with Xander. This is where she lives now, ensconced in luxury. She should be happy here. '*You're lucky,*' that's what Xander tells her often. '*Many would give anything to live in paradise.*'

And she is grateful. Of course she is.

So why is she unhappy?

The ground floor extension, built to Xander's strict specifications, is stunning. The forty-foot lounge has four soft leather sofas, several white units laden with expensive ornaments, a contemporary grandfather clock with a polished chrome finish and gloss-white dial. There's an expansive kitchen with every appliance you can think of, though she's not sure when she'll ever use an egg cuber or a strawberry stem remover. The dining room has an oak table to seat sixteen – though nobody visits. She left her friends behind when she met him, her parents are dead, and Xander doesn't speak to his.

There's a wet room, too, a home cinema – not that they ever watch films together – two bathrooms, two bedrooms.

The perfect man. The perfect house. The perfect life.

There's also a door leading through to the art retreat's lobby. Xander had insisted it be put in. '*It will allow us to respond quickly to our guests' needs,*' he'd said. '*Visitors can press the bell on the counter, and it will ring through to our lounge.*'

The *ding, ding, ding* is already grinding on her frayed nerves.

Eighteen months ago, Tara was a twenty-four-year-old wannabe artist. OK, she had addiction issues, and shared a dingy flat in East London with what Xander described as 'the wrong sort' – and, to be fair, he was probably right. But she had high hopes. Big dreams.

She met Xander when she took her artwork into his gallery, hoping he would like it. She's still not sure if he ever did. But he liked her. Made her feel beautiful. Rescued her from her troubled start in life. She owes him everything. That's what he tells her. *Often.*

There's no doubting he's an incredible man. His transformation of Lakeside is amazing. He gets what he wants, not caring about the damage he causes along the way. He told her when they first arrived at Lakeside that the walls would be filled with her artwork. But that never happened. *'It makes more sense to use artists people recognise to inspire our guests, Tara. I think you know that, deep down.'*

'Hey,' Xander says now, and she turns to see him heading through the French doors and onto the patio, a fluffy white towel tied around his waist, his naked chest tanned and toned, glistening with droplets of water. He's been down the gym for his workout, followed by a swim. His morning ritual – it never changes. It pays off. He looks good, there's no denying that.

She throws the cigarette and ash over the wall. Hopes he won't smell the smoke. She hasn't got time to use her breath freshener or to spray herself in perfume. *'It's a weakness, Tara.'*

He approaches, grips her waist, pulls her close and kisses her neck. He feels warm, smells fresh, of citrus shower gel. She doesn't resist. He wouldn't stop even if she did, and there's still a part of her that's attracted to him, melts under his touch. She hates that part.

She wants to bring up the notes from The Stranger again.

Whoever they are, they've tormented them since Xander bought the place. But he'll dismiss it, as he always does. He's never been fazed by the letters. *'If I was put off by threats, I wouldn't have got as far as I have.'* It's true. He's been the victim of online trolling a few times over the years, most recently on X, when someone calling themselves @NYIS222 started commenting on his art page, saying he was a fake, a phoney, that he needed to own up to what he'd done. Xander simply blocked the profile and moved on, claiming he had no idea what the troll was talking about.

'You've been smoking,' he says, releasing her. 'I can smell it.' He looks down at her hands, grabs them, studies her yellow-tinged fingers.

'It's lily pollen,' she says. 'Not—'

'You think I was born yesterday.' He's angry. She hates it when he's angry. 'Fuck's sake, Tara, go shower.'

She pulls her hands free, steps away from him. 'Shouldn't you be at the pods? It's almost ten.'

'Damn. I've lost track of time.' With long strides he makes his way towards the French doors. 'Get that shower, Tara,' he says dropping his towel as he steps inside, revealing taut, tanned buttocks.

'I hate you,' she whispers under her breath.

7

POLLY

Polly, in a pink straw sunhat, walks towards the seven wooden buildings, a squelch beneath her trainers from a downpour in the night. The sun is hot, though ominous black clouds drift across the blue sky like bruises.

The pods are positioned to take in Kendalmere Lake, the surrounding trees and an abundance of wildflowers and tangled hedgerow. Ducks and swans glide across the rippling water, and a worn wooden jetty stretches into the lake, a motorboat and pastel-blue rowing boat moored against it, bobbing on the water.

Polly considers including a nearby ageing oak tree in her painting, though she knows it probably won't look anything like it. She loves ancient trees – likes to imagine the history they've witnessed, events they've seen – and wonders what this tree has seen at Lakeside. Does it know what happened to the Framptons? Had her biological mother climbed its branches as a child?

She pulls out her phone and snaps a few photos to use while painting. That's what they do on TV. Though, to be fair, it's normally an iPad. The last time she tried her hand at drawing was at school, at around fourteen. But she's watched a lot of YouTube videos over the last two weeks, and a whole series of *Landscape Artist of the Year*.

Beatrice, in an apple-green apron embroidered with the Lakeside Art Retreat's paintbrush and palette logo, her sunglasses pushed back onto the top of her head, is engrossed in sorting through her brushes. She looks dreamy, in her own world, red curls falling about her pale face.

Harry, in a white straw trilby, is in the pod at the far end, putting tubes of paint into a neat line. He's wearing his own apron: black and white vertical stripes. He lifts his hand in a low wave.

'Can we pick any pod?' Polly calls to him.

'I have. They're all the same, so...' He shrugs.

She steps onto the decking of the nearest one, lifts an apron from a hook and puts it on. Peeling clear plastic from a couple of canvases, she lays one against an easel, then sorts through the brushes.

Xander struts across the lawn in a tight white polo and cropped trousers, showing off tanned ankles and bare feet in beige loafers. He's with Janice and William, and some way behind is the woman who was sitting on the bench reading when Polly arrived – Marsha?

'Good to see you guys have started without me.' Xander scans the pods through dark sunglasses. 'Can we gather at the table before you begin painting?' He points to a long wooden bench with a red parasol and continues towards it. 'I would like to run through a few tips and suggestions you might find helpful.'

Polly puts down her brushes and follows him towards the table, needing all the help she can get, and sits down between Janice, in a pale blue apron with the logo 'Trust me I'm an Artist' printed on it, and William, whose arms are folded so tightly across his chest he looks as though he might stop the blood flow getting to his lower body.

A rumble of thunder crosses the sky in the far distance. Janice shudders, seizes Polly's arm and, leaning in close, says, 'Sounds like a storm's brewing – more flash flooding imminent, I expect.'

'I hate storms.' Beatrice looks out over the lake, trancelike. 'Lightning can kill.'

'So! Let's begin.' Xander gives Beatrice and Janice a warning look as though they're chattering schoolgirls. 'First, I would like you to try to create a focus for your painting—'

William raises his hand.

'Can you let me finish, please, Mr Doyle? I'm more than happy to answer any questions then.'

'It's like being back at school.' William drops his hand and runs it over his bald head. 'I never liked school.'

'I'm sorry you think that. It's really not my intention.' Xander takes a deep breath. 'So, there are three types of landscape painting: abstract, impressionistic and representational.'

Harry rolls his eyes. 'I know that already, Xander.'

'The point is, Harry, our guests are at different levels, and some may need a little more guidance than others.' He's trying to sound pleasant, charming, but it's clear he's getting agitated.

'I'm more of a portrait artist, myself,' Janice says. 'Happy for any advice on landscape painting.'

'I wouldn't mind some tips too,' Polly says, trying to ease the tension.

'Perhaps those who would like to listen to Xander can stay, and anyone who feels they are experienced enough can set up in their pods.' It's Marsha, her American accent rich and confident. 'I'm sure you'd be OK with that, wouldn't you Mr Caldwell?' She doesn't wait for a reply, simply rises and, sunglasses in hand, marches across the lawn towards the pods, her strides long, her wide-bottomed trousers flapping against her legs, arms whipping her sides. She reminds Polly of a cross between Joanna Lumley and the formidable head teacher at the senior school she attended.

Harry rises too, jogs to catch her up.

The four guests remaining stare at Xander.

'Well, more fool them,' he says, before running through some tips, a twang of irritation in his tone.

Finally, he gets to his feet and leads Polly, Janice, William and Beatrice to their pods. 'There is no strict time limit,' he says, dragging a hand through his hair. 'But we estimate about three hours, and during this time I'll be moving through the pods giving you any help you might need. Following that Tara and I will move the paintings to the art studio to dry. Good luck.'

8

ESME

Forty-Two Years Ago

'I'm pregnant.' It's taken so much courage to say those words to Stephen. Every part of me trembles as I look into his vacant eyes. But I had no choice, my stomach is swelling, he would know soon enough. Would have been angry if I'd kept it from him.

He is silent for a moment before turning his back to me and sitting down at the dining room table.

I wait and wait for his reaction, but he's hunched over the Nazi medals he bought from Giles Alderman a week ago, laying them out in an obsessively neat line. I wonder if he even heard my confession – because that's what it felt like: a confession, as though Stephen had nothing to do with my condition. Yet, he forced himself on me. He always forces himself on me.

I hear a long deep breath, and he glances over his shoulder, looks me up and down, and smirks. 'Is it mine?'

I wrap my arms around my stomach. 'Of course it's yours.' *I wish it wasn't.*

He laughs. 'I'm joking. Nobody else would have you.'

'You don't have to be so unkind.' But he does. It's a need in him. He can't function unless he's cruel.

He turns back to his medals. 'I'm going to invest in more memorabilia,' he says, as though the topic of my pregnancy is too boring to continue. 'Giles Alderman is going to get it for me. I like the man – he has the same views and ideology as me.'

'I know. You said.' I hate Stephen's views, and wish I'd known about them sooner. Wish I'd never married him. I hate everything about him. I have dreams about picking up a kitchen knife and plunging it deep into his neck, imagining myself laughing as I watch him die.

'Giles has come across an original pistol issued to officers who patrolled Adolf Hitler's bunker. How crazy is that?'

I don't care. I hate you.

'It's a lot of money, but worth every penny.'

I don't care. I hate you.

The excitement in his voice makes me want to throw up. Not helped by the swirl of morning sickness in my belly. He'll buy the pistol and more, I know he will. He has money – lots of it. He inherited Lakeside House and several million from his parents five years ago. Some of it is in bundles of cash stashed around the house in hiding places he thinks I don't know about.

Why couldn't he invest his money in something uplifting instead of the awful Nazi stuff? To look at the way we live – the way *I* live – you wouldn't think we had a penny to our name. I've suggested many times that we should decorate Lakeside, that I'd be happy to work on the house while he's at work. Brighten it up. He's not interested. He spends his fortune on what *he* desires. Sadly, money poisoned him long before I came along. His parents lived at a time when status and money had power (perhaps it still does) and their beliefs and ideals rubbed off on Stephen, making him the man he is today.

'Can we talk about the baby?' I ask, taking a couple of steps back towards the door.

'Are you keeping it?' He doesn't look my way.

I could grab a knife right now. He'd be gone in seconds. I run a hand over my stomach, wanting to protect my unborn child from him. But if I end up in prison, what will become of my baby?

'Yes, I'll be keeping our baby, but if you don't want to be involved, I can—' *Escape.*

'Why wouldn't I want to be involved?' My heart sinks. A tiny part of me had hoped he would kick me out, force my hand, set me free.

'When's it due?'

'February.'

'If it's a boy, he'll need to be tough, Esme. No fussing over him.' He still doesn't look my way. 'My father taught me how to be a real man, and I'll teach our boy in the ways he taught me, with a firm hand.'

I turn and leave the room, unable to listen to him further.

'Please be a little girl,' I whisper, a feeling of doom washing over me.

9

POLLY

Polly makes her way along the hallway, past Xander's office where she'd snooped yesterday evening, heading towards the art studio, keen to see the finished landscapes by the other guests. The smell of paint hits her as she steps into a large room with a high ceiling and white walls. Floor-to-ceiling windows let in streams of sunlight, and on the far side are seven potter's wheels. Outside, through a glass door, is a pretty garden area and a large brick-built kiln.

Six canvases are propped on easels, and Polly approaches. Harry's Gothic painting of a woman with pale skin and dark sunken eyes emerging, slimy, from the lake, her long, dark hair clinging wet to her skull, is disturbing yet incredible – he's clearly talented. The surrounding trees and wildflowers are dead or dying, the paints used are murky greens and shades of grey.

She spins round, hearing a noise behind her. Harry is standing in the doorway, arms folded across his lanky body, his face unreadable, his blue eyes piercing through the lenses of his glasses. 'It represents the damage being done to the environment,' he says, flipping back his heavy fringe.

'It's a brilliant painting,' she says with a smile. 'If a little depressing.'

'I don't care what you or anyone else thinks of it,' he says. 'What I care about is the fact we'll soon have no world left to paint. People need to listen. But they never do.' He pushes his glasses further up the bridge of his nose, then turns and takes off as quickly as he came, leaving a dark atmosphere in his wake.

Polly moves her eyes to Marsha's brilliant landscape; it's clear she's extremely talented too. Beatrice's painting is OK considering that, as a graphic designer, traditional art is new to her, and William's is an abstract, made up of blocks of primary colours. Polly tilts her head left then right in the hope she'll understand what it's meant to be, but no, she really doesn't get it. Janice's effort is average, though a swan on the pastel-blue lake is way out of perspective, the dense trees in the background like giant balls of green wool.

Polly moves across the room towards the final easel, knowing this must be her own mediocre effort. As she reaches it, she lets out a gasp, covers her mouth with her hand.

Someone has added a corpse hanging by the neck from the ancient oak tree.

'Christ!' she mutters, reaching out a hand towards the painting, touching the addition with her outstretched finger, black paint coating her skin. The body has no features. It's painted crudely, like a hanged man from the word game – and it's far too big for the tree.

She looks about her, spotting a CCTV camera high on the wall.

'Everything all right in here?' It's Xander, wearing a pinned-on smile, his forehead furrowed.

'Not really, no.' She's cross at the tremor in her voice. 'There's been an addition to my painting.'

'Sorry?' His smile disappears. 'What do you mean, addition?' He moves across the room towards her, bringing a cloud of expensive aftershave with him.

'There,' she says, pointing at the faceless figure hanging from the tree, her heart thudding. Had someone deliberately targeted her painting?

'You didn't add it?'

She shakes her head. 'Of course not. Why would I?' She points up at the camera. 'But you need to check who did.'

He looks up. 'Yes, we'll get to the bottom of it. Don't worry. In the meantime, why not spend some time tinkering with your painting, return it to its former glory.'

Polly opens her mouth and closes it again. She doesn't want to cause a fuss, and Xander's tone is assertive. But whoever did this, for whatever reason, Xander must take it seriously. 'Shouldn't we tell the other guests?'

'Why?'

'Because if there's someone here prepared to ruin a painting—'

'It's hardly ruined. You can put this right with the flick of a brush.'

'But it's the fact there's someone here who—'

'Look, Ms Ashton... Polly. The truth is, I wouldn't want to worry the other guests over something and nothing.'

'Something and nothing?'

'It's probably someone's idea of a joke.'

'A joke?'

He smirks. 'Do you make a habit of repeating people's words?' He lets out a fake laugh, then with a serious tone adds, 'Listen, Polly, I'm sorry this has happened to you, but please can I ask you to keep it quiet, at least until I've watched the CCTV? We wouldn't want to ruin everyone's stay, would we?' And with that he disappears through the door before she can argue.

She pulls out her phone and snaps a photo of her artwork before settling down reluctantly to paint over the chilling addition.

It's as she's leaving the art studio and heading back down the hallway that she sees William staring up at the display of the renovation photos. He seems oblivious to Polly's approach, bringing out a magnifying glass and studying the pictures through it. She's tempted to tell him about her painting but thinks better of it. She'll give Xander a chance to look at the CCTV footage first, however much it's unsettled her.

'Hi William,' she says, reaching him.

He starts, shoves the magnifying glass into his pocket. 'Polly. I didn't see you there. I hope you're having a pleasant day.'

'Yes, thank you.' She glances up at the display. But before she can comment further, he dashes up the stairs. *Was it something I said?*

She follows, but by the time she reaches reception he's gone.

A flash of lightning brightens the area, followed by a crack of thunder, and within moments rain hits the bay window.

'More flash flooding, I expect,' Tara says from where she's sitting behind the desk. 'Let's hope it clears up soon, or we'll end up stranded at Lakeside.'

10

POLLY

After breakfast the following morning, Polly makes her way across reception and down the stairs leading to the art studio, for the life drawing session.

Janice is pacing the hallway, shoes squeaking, her phone pinned to her ear.

'Please stop worrying,' she's saying, her tone anxious. 'I'll be home in a few days, I promise. And you've got Sarah there with you.' She stops, stares at Polly for a moment. 'Listen, I must go,' she continues down the phone. 'Love you.' She ends the call, shoves the mobile into her pocket, and, without offering an explanation, hurries towards the art studio. 'I wonder who our victim is?' she says, reaching the door, Polly right behind her.

'Victim?'

'Who we are drawing today.'

'Ah, I see. Tara perhaps?'

'I'll be shocked if it is. She doesn't look the type to take her clothes off in public.'

They enter the room just after nine o'clock, and make their

way past the other guests towards the easels, getting their answer immediately: Ralph is posing discreetly naked on a chaise longue.

Tara appears through the door, approaches a free easel, and smooths the paper with a delicate hand. 'I realise some of you have done life drawing before,' she begins. 'But for those who haven't, I'm sure it can be a little overwhelming, so I wanted to do a demonstration, and hopefully it will give you some ideas on how to create lines and shapes that make up our model a.k.a. Ralph.' She smiles, and with flowing pencil, she continues to talk, describing what she's doing, suggesting tips. 'I find the hands and feet the hardest,' she says, though she's creating them perfectly. 'My favourite part is the face.'

The final picture is brilliant, despite taking less than ten minutes. Tara is a skilled artist, there's no doubting that.

'As before, take as long as you need.' She puts down her pencil. 'I will be here to answer any questions and give you advice as you draw.'

Time goes quickly, and Polly is enjoying the process. It feels therapeutic losing herself in art. Forgetting for a short time why she is here, and the stalker firmly at the back of her mind. Finally, she puts down her pencil, her drawing complete, and looks about her. The majority of the guests have completed theirs too. Only Harry and Beatrice are adding final touches.

Harry clearly sees Ralph as a decaying zombie, which must be another attempt to link his art to the problems with the world and environment.

Marsha's study is incredibly lifelike, and William is drawing another abstract interpretation of what's in front of him: squares, oblongs, ovals. Janice is limiting her picture to Ralph's head, her face flushing if her eyes dip below his shoulders, and Beatrice hums as she draws, her pencil strokes wild and flowing.

'You sound happy, Beatrice,' Polly says to her.

'I am. My boyfriend called last night.' Her voice is bright, loud enough for the room to hear.

'You have a boyfriend?'

She nods. Puts down her pencil. 'And I love that he checks in on me. Wants to be sure I'm OK.'

'Can we have some quiet please, ladies?' Harry's frown deepens a line in the middle of his forehead. 'There will be plenty of time to share your romantic stories later. I'm trying to concentrate.'

'Fuck off!' Beatrice shouts, her anger in complete contrast to her previous brightness, taking Polly aback. 'Just mind your own business, Harry. You've no idea what I've been through.'

Harry rolls his eyes dramatically. 'Charming. What part of Crawled from Under a Stone do you come from?'

'Just round the corner from your latest residence: Fuck You Avenue,' she spits.

Polly glances at Janice, whose eyes are wide behind her glasses, her mouth forming a small 'O'.

Tara just stares, taken aback, but Marsha waltzes over. 'Enough!' she cries, her voice firm.

Beatrice grabs her bag and storms from the studio.

'Absolute attention seeker, if you ask me.' Harry drops his pencil and steps back to admire his picture. 'Perfect,' he says.

'What was that all about?' Tara says, watching her go.

Ralph picks up his robe and puts it on. 'Don't worry your head about it.' He touches her arm gently, like a father might comfort his daughter. 'It's all good,' he says. 'No worries.'

Tara looks at her watch. 'For those who are interested,' she says, 'it's time to go into Marplethorpe for lunch. Xander will be waiting in reception.'

* * *

Polly reaches the top of the stairs and spots Beatrice standing by the French doors in the lounge, her back to everyone. Unsure whether to leave her be or check she's OK, Polly freezes. Beatrice was pretty aggressive towards Harry, and she doesn't really want to stir her up further, and yet she knows the woman is grieving the death of her husband. She takes a deep breath and makes her way across reception and through the doors into the lounge.

'Are you OK?' she says, reaching the woman's side.

Beatrice turns, shakes her head, her eyes filling with tears. 'I made a complete fool of myself, didn't I?'

'If anyone did, it was Harry. He started it.'

'Yes, but he didn't act like a complete potty mouth. My mother would be horrified. Always said the F-word was sent by Satan himself. She was quite the tyrant.'

Beatrice is certainly one for sharing.

'Well, I think you can forgive yourself, Beatrice. You've been through a lot.'

Beatrice looks down at the tattoo on her wrist – runs a finger around the letter 'D' and circles the rose. 'But it's not like I'm alone any more.'

'So, you've met someone?' Polly says.

Beatrice nods. 'Yes, recently. He's amazing, so caring. I can't help hoping things will work out between us. Nobody could ever replace David, but, well, who knows what the future will bring?' She sighs. 'I really have no right to be temperamental. Life is getting better.'

'Well, that's good.' Polly touches the woman's arm. 'I'm happy for you.'

Beatrice looks into her eyes. 'It's nice of you to come and find me, Polly. I appreciate it. You're a good person.'

'No problem at all.' Polly turns to see Xander in reception, jiggling a set of keys, then returns her gaze to Beatrice. 'Are you coming into Marplethorpe?'

There's a beat before she replies. 'I think so. Yes, why not? If Harry comes, I'll bite my tongue.'

Once in reception, Polly and Beatrice approach Xander, who smiles, and within moments, Janice appears, wincing and holding her stomach, her face screwed up in pain. 'I'm afraid I'm going to have to cry off,' she says, whizzing past them, heading for the curving staircase. 'I've come over quite poorly.'

'What a shame,' Xander says, clearly attempting sincere, but not completely pulling it off. 'Hope you feel better soon.'

Janice blinks, gulps and moves a hand to her mouth. 'I think it must have been something I ate. Don't get me wrong, Lorcan is a superb cook, but all this rich food doesn't agree with me, however delicious. I keep wondering if I'm glutton intolerant.'

'Gluten?' Xander says.

'No, definitely glutton.' She laughs through her obvious discomfort and takes the stairs slowly, one at a time.

'Get better soon,' Polly calls after her.

'To be honest, I'm a bit relieved she's not coming,' Beatrice whispers from behind her hand so only Polly can hear. 'She's OK in small doses, but she caught me earlier to tell me about the problems she's having with her boiler. Impossible to get away from.'

'She means well, I think,' Polly says, not wanting to be unkind, though Beatrice does have a point.

'I'm afraid I won't be coming either,' Marsha says, following Janice up the stairs. 'I only landed in Heathrow a couple of days back. Still can't shift this damn jetlag.' She lifts her hand in a wave. 'But you guys have a great day now.'

'Excuse me, Xander.' It's William. 'Where are we heading for lunch?'

'The Red Lion in Marplethorpe. A great pub. Changed hands about a year ago. The food is good – pub grub, but tasty.' In fairness to Xander, he's putting all his efforts into being friendly and charming. 'I thought it would be a chance for you all to get to know each other better and get a feel for the area – stimulate those creative juices.'

William stares at him for a moment, brushes a hand across his bearded chin as though deliberating whether he can be bothered to join them, then shakes his head. 'Nope, not for me, I'm afraid. I much prefer a gourmet lunch.' He turns and makes his way up the stairs towards his room, leaving behind an awkward silence.

Harry comes out of the gents' loos and glares at Beatrice as he approaches.

'Let's call a truce, shall we?' she says, still clinging onto Polly's arm. 'I'm sorry for my outburst, and happy to forget it happened.'

Harry stares at her, as though he's taken an irreversible dislike to the woman. 'If you like,' he says.

'*OK*, then.' Xander claps his hands and pins on a limp smile. 'It might be worth getting your raincoats from your rooms. I'll meet you back here in five.'

11

POLLY

Once everyone is back in reception, Xander turns and makes his way into the porch, where he lifts the hood of his rain jacket. 'If you need an umbrella,' he says over his shoulder, 'help yourselves to one from the rack.'

Polly, Harry and Beatrice lift their hoods too and follow, Polly self-consciously observing that she's wearing the same green jacket as Xander.

They dash past the camper van and Fiat 500, the hammering rain almost soaking them through in moments, and climb aboard the minibus Polly saw when she first arrived.

'As it turns out, we could have used the car,' Xander says, starting the engine and pulling away and out onto the road. 'I felt sure more of you would want to come into Marplethorpe.'

Polly sits between Beatrice, who's staring down at her hands, picking at her dark blue painted nails, and Harry, who is deep in thought as he stares out of the rain-speckled side window at the passing countryside. There are a few strands of silvery grey in his thick dark hair. He's handsome in a Tim Burton character kind of way: pale, aloof, blue-eyed, tall and slim. He doesn't seem to feel

Polly's eyes on him, seems determined not to enter into conversation.

After several detours, to avoid the worst of the flash flooding, they reach their destination.

'Marplethorpe won village of the year on several occasions,' Xander says, breaking the heavy silence. The only sounds for miles have been the wipers pounding the windscreen and rain hammering on the roof. 'Such a pretty village,' he goes on as they pass a row of stone cottages near a duckpond. He glances over his shoulder at the tense-looking guests, possibly to see if anyone is still alive in the back, then returns his eyes to the road. 'And I heard through the village grapevine that it was almost used for an episode of *Midsomer Murders* a few years back, though I don't know how true that is, so don't quote me.' He continues past a church, indicates and pulls onto the Red Lion's car park, tyres splashing through puddles. 'Of course, it's even better on a brighter day.' He drags on the handbrake. 'So here we are. One of the best pubs in the area. Well, the only pub in the area if you want to split hairs.' His laugh is loud and fake, and Polly's not sure what to make of this man, who hasn't yet mentioned her painting or whether he's checked the CCTV.

A fan whirs in the corner of the rustic bar, making little impact on the dense air. Polly shrugs off her damp jacket as they head for a heavy oak table with a reserved sign in the centre. The pub is busy. People chat over glasses of wine and pints of beer, eating hot pots, and ploughman's lunches with giant pickles and crumbly cheese. The ceiling is low, wooden beams stretching the length of the bar, which offers real ale and multiple kinds of gin, including Marplethorpe Rhubarb. The nose-tingling smell of home-cooked food is tempting, though Polly is far from hungry, breakfast still lying heavy on her stomach.

'Only four of us today, Pete,' Xander calls to the barman. 'If you want to move us to a smaller table—'

'No worries, matey,' a man with crazy white hair and a horseshoe moustache says from the far end of the bar, raising a large hand in greeting.

A long-coated Labrador sprawls near an unlit fire, and Polly bends to ruffle its head, glancing up to see an attractive young woman with shiny chestnut hair also serving behind the bar.

'Please pick anything you fancy.' Xander hands out clipboards with menus attached. 'I can recommend the lamb shanks.'

Polly rises. She wants to speak to the man with the horseshoe moustache while he isn't busy, ask him if he knows anything about Lakeside House. 'Won't be a minute,' she says, but nobody answers.

She leaves the menu on the table and makes her way towards the end of the bar where the man is drying a pint glass.

'Hi,' she says, with a wide smile. 'I'm Polly Ashton. I'm staying at Lakeside Art Retreat.'

'Pete Chester.' The man returns the smile, lines spreading from the corners of his eyes as he glances towards the table she's just vacated. 'I've heard Xander and Tara have done a great job on the place.'

'They have, yes.'

He puts down the glass. 'What can I do you for, dear lady?'

Polly smiles again. 'Well, I wondered...' She pauses, a tingle dancing on the back of her neck. She turns. At the other end of the bar, sitting near the loos, is a woman in a black ankle-length dress and battered black boots, her greying hair tied back in a long ponytail. She could be in her late sixties, perhaps older – it's hard to say. She's pale, her eyes appearing liquid black under heavy eyebrows. She's staring at Polly, a half-drunk pint of stout clasped in both hands. Polly pulls away from her uncomfortable gaze, her eyes back on the barman. 'Sorry,' she says, unable to shake the prickle of unease. 'I just wondered if you know anything about the history of Lakeside House.'

'Not much, I'm afraid. I haven't lived in Marplethorpe long. People have told me a bit, that the house was pretty run down towards the end of the Framptons' time there, that kind of thing. The former landlord of this place said it was a blessing when the couple disappeared. He's living in Spain now.'

'Who?'

'The old landlord. Loving it apparently. Can't get enough of the old Sangria.'

'Oh, I see. So, he didn't like the couple?'

Pete rubs a hand across his chin. 'Well, Stephen Frampton, by all accounts, was a nasty piece of work and so was his best mate. Glad I never met either of them, quite frankly.' He tweaks the end of his moustache. 'They used to drink in here, equally as bad as each other, so they say. Giles something-or-other – that was the other one's name. I know because the old landlord kept a list of everyone he barred. My wife found it when we were having a clear out, and we laughed when we read it. The strange reasons he would give for banning folks made us chuckle.' He leans forward, lowers his voice. 'One of the farmers from around these parts wasn't allowed in the bar because his sheep did her business in the snug.' He lets out a raucous laugh. 'He wouldn't let the fairground lot in either. Caught one of the young 'uns pocketing a pint glass, and that was that.'

'And he banned Stephen and Giles?'

Pete nods. 'Right enough, he did. They would get pretty loaded, the pair of them, apparently. Start banging on about Hitler being some kind of god, spouting their Nazi views about immigrants and gays – anyone who didn't fit their ideology. As I say, awful men by all accounts. And Giles's son was no better at the time, constantly trying to be like his father. Rumour has it he burnt down one of the fairground caravans. He was seen running from the scene.'

'That's awful. Was anyone hurt?'

'Thankfully not.' He wipes a cloth across the bar. 'Police couldn't prove it was him, but most people around here say he did it.' He shakes his head. 'This was years ago, mind you. He's now in his forties, keeps his head down for the most part. He owns the emporium across the way.'

Polly looks through the pub window at the row of shops opposite, the emporium nestled on the end. She brings her gaze back to Pete Chester.

'I don't suppose you have any idea if the Framptons had a child.' It's an important question, which leaves her stomach churning. *Was my mother their daughter? Were the Framptons my grandparents?*

He nods. 'Believe so, yes.'

'A boy or a girl?'

He sniffs, rubs a hand across his chin once more, before folding his arms across his wide body. 'No idea. I've heard Stephen was a rotten father – controlling, a bully – and Esme was overprotective of the kid, but I don't know if it was a girl or a lad, I'm afraid.'

'Any idea what happened to the child?'

He shakes his head, and Polly's aware she's darting him with too many questions and being far from subtle, but she's not about to stop now. 'What do you think happened to the Framptons?'

His eyes, pale grey under bushy white eyebrows, meet Polly's. 'Are you some kind of journalist?'

'No, not at all.' She shakes her head. 'It's just... well, the previous owners at Lakeside intrigue me, is all. I heard they took their own lives.'

'Yes, I guess they did. There was a suicide note, at any rate.' He presses his lips together and shakes his head. 'For what it's worth, I don't believe they topped themselves. Just my opinion, mind you. I mean who prints out their final goodbye?'

'Was it signed?'

Another shake of his head. 'Pretty sure it wasn't, though bear in mind everything I'm telling you is gossip carried down the years.' He taps the side of his nose. 'Secrets. Rumours. That's all. In fact, some say the Framptons had millions in the bank.' He scratches his head. 'Though for the life of me I can't remember who told me that. Apparently, the money is still sitting there untouched.' He shakes his head again. 'The thing is, dear lady, gossip has a habit of spreading, even if it's a pack of lies. My guess would be that they set up new identities somewhere remote – maybe in the Australian outback. You can hide there and no bugger will catch up with you.' He laughs. 'Seriously though, I reckon they're alive, and hiding from something or someone. Having said that, it doesn't explain why they left all that money behind.' He takes a long breath before adding. 'If you want to know more about them, why not go and see Cathy Tipton? Word has it she befriended Esme for a while. She lives in one of the cottages on the green, behind the duck pond. The one with the wooden porch.'

'Pint of your Cumberland Golden Bitter, please, mate,' says a man approaching the bar.

Pete shrugs and heads towards the customer. 'Coming right up.'

Polly returns to the table, avoiding looking over at the strange woman in black, though she feels her eyes burning her back.

'What will you have to drink, Polly?' It's Xander, on his feet, waving a credit card. 'The first drink is on me.'

She's tempted to ask for a large glass of Pinot, or a double gin, in an attempt to get her money's worth, but she needs to stay alert. 'Lime and soda, please.'

He makes his way to the bar, towards Pete Chester, and Polly looks quickly down at the menu. She's really not hungry. Decides on a prawn sandwich.

'How are you enjoying the break so far, Polly?' It's Harry, his elbows on the table, hands holding up his head. 'What do you think of Lakeside?'

'It's a beautiful place.'

'It is, isn't it.' He moves, leans back against his chair and pushes his glasses further up the bridge of his nose. 'The best part is the lake and surroundings, don't you think?' he says. 'The habitats of so many animals and birds, there's so much beauty there.'

She nods. 'I saw a red squirrel earlier,' she says. 'You don't see those down south.'

'Exactly.' He fiddles with a silk scarf hanging around his neck. 'They need to be protected.'

'It's a wonderful venue though, isn't it? All that marble.' It's Beatrice, sitting a little too close to Polly, her perfume musky, distinctive, a little cloying. 'I think it's going to be a lovely break, even with the spasmodic rain showers.'

'Time will tell,' Harry says, his tone serious. He flips back his floppy fringe, glances at Xander at the bar and, reducing his voice to a whisper, adds, 'Though something's not right at the retreat. You must have felt the undercurrent running through the place.'

Polly thinks of the note from The Stranger, the creepy addition to her painting, the weird tune she heard through her bedroom door, and a chill runs down her spine. She imagines her mum telling her to leave, Nicky being angry that she's ignoring the weird happenings. But Polly knows the notes are nothing to do with her, and she's convinced herself the tune was her imagination. *But what about the painting?* Xander will be able to explain that soon enough.

Xander plonks a glass of lime and soda down in front of her.

'Actually, I need the loo,' she says, rising. 'Won't be a sec.'

She's relieved to see the strange woman has gone – an empty glass, a layer of creamy froth in the bottom, the only proof she was ever there. Polly glances out of the window – the rain is lighter now. The woman is drifting, ghostlike, towards a copse, her head down. Polly freezes, unable to move. Mesmerised. And as though sensing Polly's stare, the woman stops. Not turning. Just still.

Polly shudders, thaws, and makes her way into the ladies', her heart racing. Was the woman a ghost? *Of course not.* She tells herself to stop being ridiculous – it was just a woman minding her own business. How had Polly made her into someone – something – to fear? 'Control yourself, Polly,' she mutters, as she flies into one of the cubicles. 'Don't let the paranoia get to you.'

As Polly's washing her hands she senses someone behind her. She looks up and into the mirror. Beatrice's frozen reflection is there. She's standing right behind her.

'Jeez,' Polly cries, still a little jumpy, and presses a soapy hand against her chest. 'I didn't see you come in.'

'Sorry.' Beatrice moves forward. 'I didn't mean to startle you. It's just—'

'Is everything OK?' Polly rinses her hands as Beatrice stands beside her at the sinks, staring at Polly in the mirror.

'You were so kind earlier, thank you,' she says, eyes shimmering. 'I felt you were someone I could talk to. Someone I could confide in about David, share how I feel about my new boyfriend.' A tear rolls down her face. 'I didn't mention before, as I feel I'm all doom and gloom, but I lost my father too, six months before David died.'

'Oh, how awful. I'm so sorry.'

'Sometimes it's as though I'm watching my life unfold and I'm sinking with the tragedy of it all, scared the happiness I feel now will end, that I'm ill-fated.'

Polly touches Beatrice's arm with the tips of her fingers, unsure what to do. Taken aback by how intense the woman suddenly seems. 'It sounds natural to me,' she says, 'after everything you've been through. But there's no reason to think it will happen again. Maybe you should talk to someone.'

'That's just it. I hoped it would be you.'

Polly moves her hand, feeling awkward, and pulls a paper towel from the dispenser, dries her hands. 'I'm happy to listen, but worry I may say the wrong thing, and we don't know each other very well—'

The door swings open and the woman who was working behind the bar enters a cubicle, her chestnut-brown hair bouncing.

'It's just I don't get many chances to talk about it, not any more. People wanted to listen at first, but then they drifted away. It helps me to talk.'

'You can talk to me,' Polly says, although she feels, perhaps selfishly, that she might be taking on too much. She's here to sort out her own life, come to terms with the stalker, find out who her birth mother was.

Beatrice moves closer, grips Polly's hand. 'Thank you,' she says, smiling at their reflection in the mirror. 'I really appreciate it.'

* * *

The journey back to Lakeside takes over half an hour due to diversions, and by the time the minibus pulls onto the cobbled drive next to the camper van, Polly's ready to head to her room for some downtime, the hint of a migraine encroaching. Pete Chester's words about how horrendous Stephen Frampton was are playing in her head on repeat. She needs to lie down. But before she heads upstairs, and once Harry and Beatrice have disappeared to their rooms, she approaches Xander.

'Have you had a chance to look at the CCTV from the art studio?'

'Not yet, I'm afraid. But I will. I promise.' He walks away from her at speed.

Polly clenches her fists, races to catch him up. 'When exactly?'

'I'll look soon, I promise.' He stops. Turns. Touches her arm. 'We'll find out who did it, don't you worry. But please get it in perspective. It's probably someone messing about.'

Polly watches as he strides away once more. This arrogant man who she's beginning to dislike more by the moment. But if she causes a fuss, will he ask her to leave Lakeside? She can't afford that. She needs to stay. Find out as much as she can about the family who once lived here at Lakeside House. *Her* family?

12

TARA

Tara sits on the edge of the queen-sized bed, holding an unlit cigarette between her fingers, her anxiety levels off the scale.

Here. This place. It's getting to her. Perhaps she should leave. Take her chances out in the world. She could take a job – she must be capable of something – and she'd be free.

But she's isolated here. Miles from anywhere. Without any money. She doesn't even know where the car keys are. A victim of her own making. She's allowed Xander to tell her what to wear, how to style her hair, even what to eat. She's slowly lost her identity – the person she once was – barely noticing the changes tip tapping away over the last eighteen months. But she sees them now. What happened to the twenty-year-old woman who skydived for charity and dreamt of being a famous artist one day, the twenty-one-year-old who'd travelled the world with a rucksack on her back, the twenty-four-year-old who walked into Xander's gallery with her portfolio of paintings? OK, so she'd become a bit of a mess by then – but she was still *her*. The woman she quite liked being. The woman who is now buried under all this luxury, controlled by a domineering man.

She shakes away her thoughts. She should be grateful. Shouldn't she? *Yes*, she tells herself for the millionth time. *I should be grateful.* She reaches over to her bedside unit, picks up her box of diazepam, pops one free from the foil and swallows it down.

It has been a funny sort of afternoon. Some of the guests went to the pub with Xander, and Marsha and Janice spent time in their rooms. It was about two hours ago – after spending time in the home cinema, watching YouTube videos on the giant screen – that Tara had ventured outside for a cigarette. The rain had eased off a little, so she'd wandered along the back of the retreat, spotting William coming out of the wine cellar.

'You caught me,' he'd said, in his usual superior tone, barely masking the shifty look on his face. 'I was just exploring. I hope you don't mind.'

She did mind. The basement wasn't somewhere guests should go. There's expensive wine down there. But she couldn't be bothered to comment. Didn't want to get into an argument. Because there was something about William.

'Such a fascinating place, Lakeside,' he'd continued, striding past her and into the building.

She'd watched him go, sensing he was up to something. Or perhaps Xander's right, her anxiety is morphing into paranoia. She wouldn't be surprised if it was. The letters from The Stranger have got to her. The campaigners have got to her. This lonely life has got to her. Xander has got to her.

When Xander returned from the pub an hour ago, he began pacing the room, saying nothing, just huffing, puffing. Tara was silent too, watching him from the edge of the sofa. She didn't want to know about the trip into Marplethorpe. She didn't want to hear about their mixed bag of guests. And so, when he poured himself a gin and flopped onto one of the other sofas, dozing, glass dangling from his hand, she'd retreated to the bedroom.

And now Xander's heavy footsteps pace the lounge once more. She shoves her unlit cigarette back into the box and hides it in the bedside cabinet.

What's bugging her husband?

She rises, makes her way across the bedroom and into the hallway. Through the crack in the lounge door, she sees him striding up and down, rubbing a hand over his chin then his neck. It's as though he's on high alert, waiting for something to happen. She opens the door. He stops, turns.

'Tara.' His tone is sharp. 'I didn't see you there.'

'Are you OK?' she asks, as he makes his way towards her. 'It's just... well, you seem... agitated.'

He moves to within inches of her face, and with a dark intonation says, 'What's that supposed to mean?'

'Nothing.' She looks down, wishing she were a hundred miles from here – from him.

He places his hand on her cheek. 'I noticed you haven't cleaned the toilets in reception.'

'No, not yet.'

'And there are crumbs on the desk.'

'I had a sandwich—'

'And you didn't clean up after yourself?'

'I must have missed a bit.'

'Or perhaps you've been lazing around watching YouTube.' He removes his hand, yet it still feels as though it's there, sucking life from her. 'Tara, we need the place to look perfect for our guests.'

She watches as he heads for the door to the retreat. 'Where are you going?'

'I have something I need to do.' His face is rigid. 'Stay,' he adds, as though she's a dog he's training. He doesn't look back. Slams the door behind him.

Tara's not sure what makes her follow, but she does, despite knowing he won't be happy if he sees her. Perhaps there's still a bit of the old Tara left, after all.

* * *

As Tara comes through the door into the lobby, Xander is disappearing down the stairs towards the office and art studio. She keeps enough of a distance that he won't see her – hear the thudding of her heart. She tiptoes down the stairs to see him heading into the office and follows.

Through the crack in the door, she sees him sit down in front of the computer in the corner. Leaning back in the chair and stroking the back of his head, he watches black and white CCTV footage of an empty art studio.

Xander and Tara appear on the screen. They're bringing in the landscape paintings one by one and putting them on easels, their voices inaudible. She recalls how they were slightly amused by William's abstract. It was small talk. Something they rarely did. Eventually they leave the room.

Xander coughs, leans closer to the screen and fast-forwards the footage, stopping the recording when another figure appears in the art studio. Tara screws up her eyes, trying to see. Whoever is on the screen has their back to the camera and is wearing a black jacket with the hood up. They crouch down in front of one of the paintings and, with a brush and a small pot of paint, add something to the picture.

Tara's heart thumps. She places a hand on the door. It creaks. *Crap.*

Xander spins round on the swivel chair, gets to his feet and strides across the room. Tara wants to run, but freezes. Unable to move.

He flings the door open, and she stumbles forward, losing her footing and falling to the floor, her face crashing against the wooden floorboards.

'Tara?' he cries. 'What the hell?'

She struggles to her feet, holding her nose, blood wetting her fingers. He doesn't apologise as she scrambles in her pocket for a tissue and dabs her face. 'What's going on Xander,' she says, close to tears. 'Who was that on the screen?'

He glances back at the computer. 'I've no idea, but I'm guessing it must be one of the guests sabotaging another guest's painting, nothing I can't handle.'

'What was with their creepy outfit?'

'Hardly creepy. A hooded jacket, disguising who they are. They must have known about the CCTV as they kept their head down.' He briefly touches her arm, fingers cool against her skin. 'Keep things in perspective, Tara – please.'

She shoves the blooded tissue into her pocket. 'So, we're going with the old "you're paranoid" thing again, are we?' Tears burn behind her eyes. 'I'm not paranoid, Xander.'

'You do tend to overreact. Blow things out of proportion.'

She looks towards the screen. 'Who painted the picture that was damaged?'

'Polly Ashton, and unfortunately she's seen the addition.' He drags his fingers through his hair. 'But I can't have her thinking some hooded idiot tampered with her painting. It's better that she thinks it was one of the guests.'

'But you just said it *was* one of the guests.'

'Yes... well... I'm sure it is. It must be. But the last thing we need is—'

'Anyone thinking it's The Stranger?' Tara covers her mouth with her hand, blood from her fingers coating her lips. There's so much she wants to say, but for now she'll keep it locked inside.

He places a hand firmly on her shoulder. 'Now we're going to tell Polly that the CCTV was corrupted, and I've already asked her to keep quiet about what happened. Told her we don't want to upset the other guests. And she's painted over it. So, all good. The point is we could scare them all off, and any bad publicity could ruin us before we've even started.'

'But what if—'

'Do you want the place to fail? Eh?'

She shakes her head. Though in truth she couldn't care less any more.

He places a kiss on her cheek. 'I know you'll do the right thing, Tara. That you'll keep quiet for the sake of our future.'

Tara screws her hands into fists, knowing she has no choice – for now at least. 'OK,' she says, as he returns to the screen and, in front of her eyes, deletes the footage.

She stands behind him for a moment, wondering once more what life would be like without him, then turns and moves across the room, and out into the hallway.

'Hi there.' It's Marsha, standing by the display of renovation pictures, dressed in a loose-fitting embroidered tunic and wide-leg trousers, her blonde bob razor sharp, a swim bag over her shoulder. She looks at Tara, smiles, revealing a gold crown. 'Would you be so kind as to direct me to the pool?'

'Yes, yes, of course.' Tara takes a breath. Tears close. 'It's just down the hallway, turn left, and it's on your right next to the gym.'

'Thank you.' The woman moves down the hallway towards her, confident and straight-backed. A fit, strong woman. She stops when she reaches Tara, stares into her eyes then down at her blood-coated fingers, and as Tara moves her hands behind her back, Marsha whispers, 'He's an ass, honey. Only thinks about himself. Doesn't deserve you.'

'It's fine,' Tara says, taken aback. The woman barely knows Xander. Had she overheard everything? 'We're fine. Honestly.'

'There are options. You don't have to live like this, there's always a way out.' Marsha touches Tara's arm, and smiles. 'You should get your pretty little butt out of here and move on. Find yourself again – escape from that black cloud he's trapped you under. You don't have to get angry. Just step away.'

Marsha continues on her way, and Tara sweeps a shaky hand across her forehead. The woman's right, but things are never quite that simple.

13

POLLY

It's five in the afternoon when Polly enters the lounge. A half-moon of chairs surrounds a display of the guests' artwork. William and Marsha are already here, sitting together, Marsha clasping a glass of white wine. The gathering has been called by Xander to discuss the guests' artistic efforts so far, but Polly could do without it. In fact, she almost didn't come.

She makes her way across the room, glancing to her left through the gleaming glass of the French doors, taking in a darkening of clouds. More rain is on its way, though it's still warm outside.

As Polly approaches, William glances over his shoulder, narrowing his eyes when he sees her and rising.

'To be honest, I'm not in the mood for Xander right now,' he says to Marsha. 'I need some air. Perhaps we can grab a drink later?'

'I'd like that,' Marsha says, as he walks towards one of the French doors, nodding a stiff, half-greeting at Polly as they pass each other.

Polly reaches the chairs and casts her eyes over the landscapes propped up along the wall, and the life drawings on easels.

'How's the jet lag?' she says, sitting down next to Marsha, who takes a gulp of her wine.

'Gee, good now, thanks. Just had a pleasant chat with William. He's a bit uptight, but a nice enough guy. I wouldn't kick him out of bed.' She lets out a laugh that brightens her face. 'I'm joking. Far too young for me.' She's an attractive woman, and despite the age gap, it wouldn't take a big stretch of the imagination to see them as a couple – though why Marsha would be interested in him is a mystery. William isn't the most cheerful of men as far as Polly can tell.

'Between you and me,' Marsha whispers, as though they're not alone in the room, 'his paintings aren't very good.' She laughs again. 'I feel awful for saying it, and I obviously wouldn't tell him, but—'

'I admit I wondered about them,' Polly says. 'Though I don't know much about abstract art.'

'Well, take it from me, William doesn't either.' She leans closer.

'He said at the meet and greet that he's hoping to turn professional.'

Marsha laughs. 'Well, that'll never happen.'

'Maybe he's an imposter. Here to steal the family silver.'

Footsteps approach. It's Janice and Beatrice hurrying across the room, Janice muttering something about how unusual Beatrice's perfume is.

'Hello, ladies,' she says, plonking herself down next to Polly with a puff.

Beatrice lowers into the chair next to her.

'Feeling better?' Polly asks Janice.

'Much. Though I'm going to avoid the beetroot bonbons going

forward.' She leans forward, staring at Polly's necklace. 'How love-ly,' she says, clearly a flatterer.

Polly grips the green stone that Nicky bought her. 'Thank you. A friend gave it to me. It's a peridot stone, for friendship.'

'Beautiful.' She looks up, stares into Polly's eyes. 'And you have such lovely eyes, dear,' she adds. 'Has anyone ever told you that?'

Xander and Harry appear, and Harry stops near the window as Xander continues towards the display.

'Does anyone know if William is coming?' Xander asks.

'He's gone out for some air,' Marsha says. 'I don't think he'll be back.'

This is Polly's moment. She can put Xander on the spot. 'Have you had a chance to look at the—?'

'Can we discuss it later?' he cuts in, worried eyes darting across the other guests. 'I would like to talk about the artwork first.'

Polly rises, glares at him, wanting him to know she won't stop until she finds out who tried to ruin her painting. He turns to study the guests' artwork, giving her his back, and without another word Polly storms out of the room. She'll confront him another time.

* * *

At six thirty, Polly, in trainers, shorts and a T-shirt, steps out onto the patio. The air feels cooler, and the dark clouds have thinned, now tufts of smoky grey. A run before dinner might go some way towards getting her thoughts in order, dispel her anxiety. She sets off towards the artists' pods and lake, shoving in her ear buds and selecting her running playlist on her phone.

As she reaches the lake she sees someone on the far shoreline across the water. They are dressed in light clothing, too far away to make out their features, the low sun making the lake shimmer, the glare bouncing off her sunglasses. Whoever it is seems to be taking something from a wheelbarrow and throwing it into the lake a piece at a time. Maybe it's Ralph doing some work on the grounds. *It's nothing to worry about,* she tells herself, a flutter of unease in her chest.

Her gaze moves to a muddy path leading between high hedgerows. Taking a deep breath, she carries on running, the route taking her past fruit trees and raspberry bushes, several small greenhouses and a sprawling vegetable patch, leeks and sprouts growing alongside cauliflowers and sweetcorn and a multitude of other veg. The buzz of a bumblebee flitting around plump tomatoes accentuates the silence. This is where she saw that stooped figure in black on her first day at Lakeside. It must have been Lorcan collecting vegetables, or Ralph tending the vegetable patch. It may even have been Lorcan on the other side of the lake a moment ago with the wheelbarrow. Her tension lifts, though she still feels there's something odd about Lakeside.

She runs for thirty minutes before turning and heading back, hot and sweaty now, desperately needing a shower. The sun is setting as she passes the kitchen garden once more. Xander's voice echoes from somewhere in the bushes.

'I have no idea what you're talking about,' he's saying, his voice loud and anxious. 'And I suggest you stop these ridiculous accusations, or I'm going to have to ask you to leave Lakeside.'

Polly moves closer to the bushes, trying to see who Xander is talking to, but sudden footsteps pound towards her. She turns and runs, glancing back just once to see Xander, hands on hips, watching her go, leaving her wondering which guest the owner of Lakeside is threatening with eviction and why.

14

POLLY

Polly had sat with Beatrice at dinner, though the woman didn't stay for all the courses, deciding on an early night. And Janice had come down to dinner late looking flustered. She was still eating when Polly grabbed her glass and left – she didn't look up, seemed deep in her own world, which wasn't like her.

Now Polly steps onto the lantern-lit veranda, warm and over-full after another amazing five-course meal. She carries the remains of her glass of wine to a table and sits down, her heart leaping as she catches sight of the jagged, black shape of a bat whipping its way through the darkness.

Footlights glancing off the lake brighten the way to the pods, where Lorcan, in his chef's whites, stands, an orange glow of a cigarette in his hand. Polly takes a sip of her drink, watching as Marsha reaches him, stopping to say something before heading towards Polly, arms swinging by her sides. Marsha had left the dining room some time ago, saying she was going for a stroll, and as she continues towards the retreat, her head down, Polly wonders where the American woman has been.

Polly takes another sip of wine, her mind travelling to the half-conversation she heard as she completed her run earlier. Who had Xander been talking to? Who was making accusations that were so bad he'd threatened them with eviction from Lakeside? Was it one of the guests? Or had it been a member of staff?

'May I join you?' Marsha says, looming over her.

'Of course. Can I get you a drink?'

Marsha waves her hand dismissively, pulls out a chair and sits, gold bangles jangling around her wrists. 'No thanks. I won't be long before I head upstairs to bed. I'm pretty exhausted.'

They sit in silence for a few moments, enchanted by the sight of a red deer crossing the pathway and stopping to look at them before it goes on its way. Polly turns back to Marsha. 'Have you been painting long?'

'Since I was a child. How about you?'

Polly shakes her head. 'I'm a real novice, I'm afraid.'

'Then you are doing very well. I like your efforts so far.'

'You do?' Polly feels oddly chuffed.

'Don't act so surprised. We all have to start somewhere, and you do seem to have a creative flair.' She leans forward and, reducing her voice to a whisper, adds, 'Unlike one man we discussed earlier.' She looks around her. 'Have you seen him this evening?'

Polly knows she means William. 'No, he wasn't in the dining room earlier.'

'That's kind of strange, don't you think?'

'Mmm, I guess so.' There's a beat before she says. 'I love your paintings. You're very talented.'

'Why thank you, though my husband was far better than me.'

'Was?' Polly takes a gulp of her wine. 'Doesn't he paint any more?'

'He died over twenty years ago. A tragic accident.'

'I'm so sorry.'

'Thank you.' She's silent for a moment, then adds, 'He was younger than me. Couldn't read and write when we met, had had a rotten upbringing, but boy could he paint. I was teaching him to read when he died.' The woman lapses into deep thought, her eyes glistening. Polly's unsure what to say, relieved when Marsha begins again. 'It was a long time ago. You learn to live with these things. And joining the army helped. I was thirty-five at the time – retired in 2021, just after being evacuated from Afghanistan. I was diagnosed with breast cancer, had to call it a day.'

'I'm sorry.'

'Nothing to be sorry for. I'm happy enough. The cancer is under control. Though I miss the military. It was my identity for a long time after James died, carried me through his loss.' Another long pause follows before she says, 'So, what do you do, Polly, when you're not painting?'

'I work in a bookshop in Oxford.' It feels weak after Marsha's revelation.

'How lovely to be surrounded by books all day.'

'It is. Yes.'

They look out towards the lake for some time: the water like black ink, the silhouette of trees against the moonlit sky mesmerising.

'It's a lovely evening, isn't it?' Polly says eventually.

'It is, yes. Though there's more rain on its way, according to the weather forecast.'

'It doesn't surprise me, the weather's been so unpredictable.' Polly turns to Marsha. 'So, what part of America are you from?'

'Maine.' Marsha pulls her eyes away from the lake and meets Polly's gaze. 'Have you been?'

Polly shakes her head. 'No, but I hear it's beautiful.'

'Stunning. Come in the fall if you get a chance. And Acadia

National Park should be top of your list.' She smiles. 'Listen to me, I sound like a travel brochure.'

Polly laughs. 'So, are you just holidaying in the UK?'

'A vacation of sorts, I guess. I do love the Lakes.' She looks towards the water once more and pulls an e-cigarette from her sling bag. Drags on it a couple of times. 'I keep worrying about William. I know he's a grown man, but I expected to see him this evening.' She shakes her head. 'I'm sure I'm overreacting. It's the sleep deprivation.' She yawns, stretches her arms above her head, bangles crashing down her arm. 'I'll give him a quick knock before I hit the sack.' She rises, rubs creases from her tunic. 'Well, it was good to properly speak with you.'

'Good to talk to you too, Marsha,' Polly says, as the woman steps into the lounge and disappears.

Polly finishes her drink and is about to get up when Janice appears in the doorway, a gathering of crumbs at the corner of her mouth.

'I just wanted to wish you a good night, dear,' she says, 'before I head to my room and read a few chapters of my book. I've just got to an exciting part where the handsome hero is making a play for Chloe from the cattery. Silly girl is completely oblivious to his charms and flashing blue eyes, far too absorbed in her feline friends.' She laughs and lifts her hand in a wave. 'Toodle-oo then.' And with that she disappears, and Polly guiltily breathes a sigh of relief.

Two minutes later, Polly heads through the lounge and into the lobby.

'Ah, Polly,' Xander calls from behind the reception desk. 'I just want to reassure you that we are keeping the art studio locked from now on. If a guest wants to go down there, they will need to get the key from reception. How does that sound?'

'OK, I suppose,' Polly says. 'But I still think we need to find out who attempted to ruin my painting. The CCTV—'

'The tape was corrupted, I'm afraid.'

'Really? Well, maybe we need to talk to the other guests. Call the police?'

'That's a bit extreme, don't you think? Calling the police because someone painted—'

'A corpse, Xander. You must admit it's weird.'

'We need to put this behind us, Polly.' His voice is tense under his smarm. 'I'll be keeping a strong eye on all the guests, and that's all I can do.' And with an obvious dismissal, he turns and passes through the door behind reception.

Polly climbs the stairs, and on reaching her bedroom door, she rummages in her bag for her key, tipping the contents onto the floor: screwed-up tissues, purse, phone, brush... but no key. 'Crap.'

She scoops her belongings back into the bag and races downstairs. Rings the reception bell, not especially looking forward to seeing Xander again.

After a moment Tara appears, her face heavily made-up but not fully hiding a bruise across her nose, a darkness under one eye.

'Is everything OK?' Polly says.

Tara instinctively touches her nose. 'Walked into a door,' she says, her tone putting end to any more questions. 'How can I help?'

'I seem to have lost the key to my room. I'm so sorry, hopefully it will turn up, I can't think where it could be.'

'Don't worry, we have spares, but if you haven't found yours by the end of the stay, we will need to charge you, I'm afraid. Xander's rules.' She reaches under the counter and hands Polly a spare key.

'That's great, and not a problem.' She turns and heads back up the stairs. Flustered, she glances back at Tara watching her go. 'As I say, hopefully it will turn up.'

Back in her room, she starts to feel unnerved, and heavy rain clattering against the window isn't helping. Her rational side tells her she's simply lost her key, though she must have had it after her run, to let herself back into her room for a shower. But what if someone took it? What if they've been in her room when she's not there, or worse, when she is? Should she push the chest of drawers in front of the door tonight? Maybe she should go home tomorrow.

She decides to get into her PJs and robe. And as she climbs onto the bed, about to pick up her Kindle, a WhatsApp message pops up on her phone and she's excited to see it's from Nicky.

> How's it going? Was the photo of your mother really taken at Lakeside?

> > Yes, it was. But I've no way of knowing if she ever lived here. Not yet anyway. How are things with you?

> Better now I'm back with the parents. Though Mum's treating me like I'm ten. I'm just relieved to be as far away from that psycho-weirdo as I can be. Listen, the tenancy on our place is up in three weeks anyway, so I was thinking maybe we can look for somewhere else to rent together. In a bit anyway. I'm going to stay here for a while. Though I feel a bit ridiculous being so shook up by everything that happened.

> > Well, I'm shook up too, so don't be too hard on yourself.

> Thanks, Polly.

I'll take some photos of this place tomorrow and send them over – so you can see how amazing it is.

Sounds great! And Mum said, as you are in the Lake District, why not pop in on your way home? Pretty sure Blackpool isn't on the way, but Mum's insisting it is. They'd love to see you.

I'd love to see them again too. Will make a detour! Better go, will be back with pics asap. Take care. Love you x

Love you too x

Polly closes the WhatsApp chat, feeling guilty that she didn't tell Nicky the whole truth. She closes her eyes, rests her head, her mind drifting to the moment they first met at infant school. They'd lived in the same village, just outside Oxford, at the time. Nicky had been smaller than Polly and often walked about the playground alone. One day Polly approached the lonely child. 'Want to play?' she'd asked with a smile, reaching out her hand. They quickly became firm friends. Have looked out for each other ever since.

There's a knock on her bedroom door, and Polly jumps from the bed and heads across the room, tightening the belt of her robe. She peers through the peephole – Marsha – before opening up.

'Hey,' she says, not masking the surprise in her voice. 'Is everything OK?'

'I'm so sorry to bother you so late,' the woman says. 'And yes, probably everything is fine, and I'm being foolish.' She rubs a hand across the back of her neck. 'But there's nobody on reception, and I didn't want to ring the bell and disturb lovely Tara. I saw your light was on. So...'

'Come in.' Polly beckons her into the room, and Marsha enters and perches on the edge of the bed. Polly sits down beside her. 'What's happened?'

'Well, I'm worried about William, as I said earlier. I've knocked on his door a couple times and there's no reply. And he didn't come down for dinner. You said yourself you haven't seen him.'

'I'm sure—'

'I don't think he returned from his walk, and now it's raining again. Perhaps I'm worrying for nothing, but it's just that he suggested a drink earlier, so I assumed he intended to return.'

'I'm sure he's fine, Marsha. Maybe he's taken off in his car.'

'That's just it, I saw him arrive by taxi. I was reading on the bench out front when he was dropped off. And now it's pouring down out there. He'd have to be crazy to still be out walking in this, wouldn't he?'

Polly shrugs. 'He could be the kind of person who just takes off.' In fact, she wonders, he may have been the guest Xander was suggesting should leave.

'Yes, you're right. I know nothing about him.' Marsha rises. 'Sorry, I shouldn't have bothered you.'

'No, it's OK, honestly.' Polly rises too. 'If he's not back by morning, we'll send out a search party.'

Once Marsha has gone, Polly gets into bed, and flicks off the light. But she can't sleep for the rain hammering against the window, and what with the addition to her painting, and the notes the Caldwells are receiving from The Stranger, maybe she should be more concerned that one of the guests is missing.

15

POLLY

Polly had found the note pushed under her bedroom door when she woke at six thirty:

Meet me in the basement at 8 a.m. It's the red door at the back of the house. I need to talk to you alone. I know who sabotaged your painting.
Marsha

And it's now five to eight, and Polly is walking through the deserted lounge, glancing towards the dining room as she goes, a waft of bacon and the aroma of coffee making her tummy rumble. But still she hurries onwards, all thoughts of going home pushed from her head.

The tranquillity of the area outside hits her as she steps through the French doors into the still morning air, the promise of a hot day ahead lingering in the atmosphere, an early sun burning away last night's rainclouds. She makes her way along the path towards three concrete steps leading down to a weathered red door. With a turn of the handle, it swings open, emitting a soft creak from well-worn hinges.

'Marsha,' she calls. 'Are you down there?'

She bends her head to enter, wondering for a moment why Marsha never mentioned, the night before, that she knew someone had sabotaged her painting and why she's chosen such a creepy location to meet up. Though, Polly guesses, the woman probably doesn't want anyone to hear their conversation. She hesitates, looking down the steps. Feeling around on the dank wall, she finds a light switch, flicks it, and a bulb comes on, so weak it barely lightens the area below. She turns on her phone torch and makes her way down, flashing the thin beam around her. The main area of the basement is square and bigger than she'd imagined, with tunnels leading off in two directions at the far end. Goosebumps rise on her bare arms, and a shuddering chill dances on her neck. 'Marsha?'

She stands at the foot of the steps, taking in the racks of wine, some layered with dust, others in boxes as though just delivered. A light hum rings in her ears. A chest freezer stands up against one of the walls. *Basements and chest freezers aren't a great combination*, her imagination shrieks, and there's a drip, drip, drip coming from somewhere down one of the tunnels. She should probably leave.

'Marsha? I'm going to go back outside.' She flashes her torch beam around the basement once more, just to be sure.

She's about to head up the steps when the door above slams shut. She spins round, heart thudding, dropping her phone to the ground. 'What the—?'

She steps backwards, feels the sense of someone in the shadows. 'Marsha? Is that you?'

A figure glides through the darkness at the other end of the basement and into one of the tunnels. Polly blinks. Is she imagining it?

Seconds later there's a noise above her, someone is opening the door, and as light beams down, a scurry of footsteps disappears into the darkness.

Polly grabs her phone from the floor as someone descends the steps.

'Who's down there?' It's a man's voice, Irish, and Polly aims her torch up the steps, to see a flash of white.

'Lorcan!' She presses her fingertips against her chest, feeling her heart race. 'You almost gave me a heart attack.'

'You didn't do much for my heart either, young lady,' he says, his weathered face bursting into a smile. 'In fact, you scared the bejesus out of me.' His cheery face is a welcome sight. 'Now what would you be doing down here?'

'Marsha asked me to meet her here.'

He runs his fingers through his thick grey hair, his blue eyes holding a twinkle, telling Polly he was probably a charmer in his younger days – or might be even now.

There's a sudden bang above them, and they both look up. The door has slammed shut once more.

'It has a habit of doing that,' Lorcan says, picking up a bottle of red from the rack. 'You have to prop it open with a rock. Good thing I wasn't carrying this beauty when I saw you. Wouldn't have wanted to drop it. Worth forty-five pounds, so it is.' He steps towards the freezer and throws it open, takes out a bag of hash browns and some frozen sausages. 'It's a great house, don't you think?' he goes on. 'And this basement, with its tunnels, can certainly bring out the Indiana Jones in you.'

'Do the tunnels lead far? It's just I thought—'

'Haven't a clue. And I've no desire to check them out. Truth be told, there are rats as big as penguins down here, and spiders that will eat you for breakfast as soon as look at you.' He huddles his wine and frozen goods to his chest, a cheeky grin on his face. 'Are you done here?'

She nods, and together they head up the steps and out into the warm air.

'So, what made an Irishman come to the Lake District?' she asks, genuinely interested, as they walk along the path.

'I haven't been back to Sligo since I was eighteen,' he says. 'Came to London wanting to be a chef, started at the bottom and worked my way up. It was a perilous journey at times. I've got burn scars in places you wouldn't believe.' He holds open the door, and Polly steps into the lounge. He follows. 'I decided it was time to slow down. I'm getting on a bit in years now, I'm sure you've noticed—'

'Not at all. I thought you were in your thirties.'

He laughs. 'I'll pay you later,' he says with a smile. 'Anyway, I saw an advert online for the job here. I thought, why not? I started a couple of weeks back.' He taps his forehead in a salute. 'Well, I'll love you and leave you, young lady – better get on with what I'm paid to do. 'Twas nice talking to you.'

And as he veers across the dining room, hurrying towards the kitchen, clasping his wine and hash browns, she hears Marsha's muffled voice in reception. 'About time,' she's saying. 'I've been ringing this damn bell for hours.'

16

POLLY

'Marsha!' Polly calls, hurrying towards her, bringing the note from her pocket.

'Polly, I—'

'Did you write this?' She shoves the note into Marsha's hand.

'What?' Marsha looks down at the note. 'No. This isn't my handwriting. What's this about?'

'Are you sure?' Polly's aware she's coming across flustered.

'Of course I'm sure.' She returns the note and swings round, staring at Tara who's wrapped in a flimsy, silk robe, looking younger without makeup – the bruising around her nose and eye still red, her blonde hair sleep ruffled.

'But if you didn't send it, who did?' Polly goes on.

Marsha looks back at her. If she's noticed Tara's bruising, she doesn't mention it. 'Watch my lips, dear girl. I did not send it. And I have no idea where the basement is, nor, for that matter, that your painting was even messed with. I would ask what that's about, but I have more pressing things on my mind, right now. William is still missing.'

Polly shoves the note into her pocket, she'll have to work out who sent it later. 'He's still not in his room?'

Tara yawns and stretches.

'I'm sorry, Tara,' Marsha says. 'Am I keeping you up?'

'It's not a problem,' Tara says, clearly not picking up on her sarcasm.

Marsha rolls her eyes, taps her hands on the reception desk like a drum. 'The thing is, I've been knocking on William's door all morning and most of yesterday evening, and there's no reply. He didn't come down for dinner yesterday, and hasn't yet been down for breakfast. I'm concerned about him.'

'He's probably sleeping,' Tara offers.

Marsha stops tapping. 'He surely would have heard me knocking, if that was the case.'

'He may have ear plugs in, or possibly he's listening to music with headphones.'

'Goddammit, I'm simply asking that we check in on him, make sure he's OK. Is that too much to ask? He could be in there dead, for all we know.'

Tara huffs and picks up a key and, as though it's all too much trouble, comes out from behind the counter, her feet bare, toenails painted pink.

Marsha and Polly follow her up the stairs and huddle outside Room One. Tara thumps on the door with a clenched fist. 'Mr Doyle?' she calls. 'William! Are you in there?'

Marsha joins in, hammering harder. 'Open up, William. We need to know you're OK.'

After a few moments, Tara unlocks the door, and they pile inside the room. William's bed is neatly made, as though it was never slept in. The heavy floral curtains are open, the view to the lake vivid.

'It doesn't look as though he slept here last night,' Polly says, scanning the room for the man's luggage, her eyes falling on an open case near the window, a neatly folded pair of tartan PJs and several pairs of socks on the top.

'I'm sure he's on the premises somewhere,' Tara says looking about her, now clearly flustered. 'Or maybe he's gone home for something. I remember him saying he didn't live far from here when I spoke to him on arrival. Maybe he's just decided to leave—'

'Maybe,' Marsha says. 'But wouldn't he have taken his luggage?'

'I'm guessing he didn't check out?' Polly asks Tara.

'No, but if he left, he wouldn't have needed to speak to me or Xander. All payments for the retreat were taken up front, as you know. In fact, William paid in cash a few weeks ago.' She pauses for a moment, heads for the door and holds it open. 'Have we finished here?'

'But surely he would have handed in his key,' Marsha says.

Tara shrugs. 'Perhaps he forgot.'

Polly's eyes move across the bedside table, landing on an old black and white photo. 'What's that?' She makes her way over, picks it up. It's of a room filled with Nazi memorabilia: medals, a flag with a swastika symbol, a military jacket, and an old-fashioned pistol lying on a heavy wooden table. She turns it over, reads out loud what it says. '"Memorabilia. Stephen Frampton, Lakeside House."'

Tara lets the door close once more and walks over. 'I've seen this photo before,' she says. 'It was in a battered shoebox full of photos mainly of Stephen Frampton's ancestors. It was taken away by the clearance company.'

Polly's eyes skim over the picture. The room is dark and dingy and doesn't appear to have windows.

'Interesting.' Marsha points at the pistol on the table. 'Now that's got a be worth an absolute fortune,' she says. 'Millions, in fact. It's a rare World War II German Luger. Maybe the Framptons pretended to take their own lives and took it with them, sold it and now they're living in luxury somewhere with new identities.' She pauses for a moment then gives a little laugh. 'Listen to me, going all Columbo on you.'

'But why would they do that?' Polly says. 'What possible reason could they have for wanting new identities? And how did William get the photograph? Why would he have it here at Lakeside?'

'Who knows?' Marsha says with a sigh. Which isn't helpful at all. 'Well, thanks so much for looking with me, ladies. Though I can't say it's put my mind at rest. It still doesn't explain his sudden disappearance.' And with that she heads for the door.

Tara and Polly follow her out of the room, Tara closing and locking the door behind her. 'I'm sure he'll turn up,' she says, but there's concern in her eyes.

Marsha enters her room, and Polly follows Tara down the stairs. At the bottom Tara swings round, meets Polly's eye and, with her voice lowered, says, 'The thing is, it's not the only weird—'

'Tara!' It's Xander, his hair combed back from his chiselled face. He's standing behind the reception counter, his eyes dark. 'Good God, woman, you're in your sleepwear.'

'Yes, I—'

'Get dressed, for Christ's sake.' He suddenly spots Polly and, quickly changing his tone, adds, 'You need to get ready for the portrait session, darling, and I'm sure Polly wants her breakfast.'

'Yes, of course, sorry.' Tara hurries away, not looking back, pulling her robe tightly around her.

Polly wonders if the woman had been about to confide in her about the letters. Or was there something else?

* * *

Polly arrives at the art studio after breakfast. The easels are ready. And, apart from William, all the guests have arrived. There is something about this morning that makes her feel determined not to be scared away. She intends to go back to Marplethorpe to see Cathy Tipton, in the hope the woman can tell her something more about Esme Frampton. The roads might be flooded in places, but she needs answers about her mother, and she isn't getting any here at the retreat.

Xander strides into the studio and informs everyone that they are to paint either Ralph or Tara, who are sitting on a raised platform in wingback chairs: Ralph in jeans, a white T-shirt and black boots; Tara, looking far more glamorous than when Polly saw her earlier, dressed in a green silk top, flowing skirt and heels, her blonde hair swept over one shoulder, an emerald necklace hanging around her neck. Polly goes to grip her own necklace, the green stone Nicky gave to her for her birthday, but it isn't there. She must have forgotten to put it on after her shower.

'You have three hours to complete your portraits, as we are taking a boat across the water for a picnic at twelve thirty,' Xander says. 'Consider what angle you prefer to paint. You may choose head and shoulders, full length or a bust image, which is—'

'We know what a bust is, Xander,' Marsha cuts in. 'Not that I have much of one myself.' She lets out a laugh, and Janice giggles.

Xander glares at Marsha for a long, cold moment and the room falls quiet, the atmosphere awkward. He clears his throat. 'Or you may consider a half-length portrait,' he says. 'Think about your background, the lighting and whether you choose acrylics, oils or pencils. I will be here throughout the session to help and advise.'

Polly picks up a pencil, casting her eyes around the room, wondering who might have sent her the note luring her down to the basement, her gaze landing on Harry. He looks up, narrowing his eyes, making her uneasy.

Her eyes then drift to Beatrice. She looks pale and troubled, strands of red hair falling about her face, a pencil in her hand. She remembers how the woman accosted her in the loos at the pub. How she'd said she wanted to talk to Polly, yet she hasn't mentioned it since.

She notices Ralph glance towards Tara. 'You OK?' he mouths, and she nods. He seems to really care about her, though Polly feels it's more as a father might care for a daughter, rather than anything romantic.

The three hours plod slowly, with Xander moving in and around the paintings.

'You seem to have a lot of teeth there, Janice. Consider showing only a few.' 'Perhaps blur the hairline into the background, Beatrice. It will make it appear softer.' 'Beautiful brushstrokes, Harry.'

Polly attempts to draw Tara, and by the end of the session her arm aches, and she's not sure the picture even resembles a human being, let alone Tara.

Marsha's painting is amazing once again. And Harry's – a Gothic study of Tara's head decaying like a rotten apple – is brilliant yet disturbing.

Tara rises and stretches her hands above her head, her top rising to show her toned, tanned midriff.

'Brushes and pencils down please, everyone,' Xander says. 'Excellent work this morning. Now for those who want to come out on the boat, we're meeting on the jetty in half an hour. A picnic will be provided. Please bring your pads and pencils as there will be an opportunity to do some sketching.'

'Are you going?' Janice asks Polly as they follow Xander out of the room.

'Yes, I think I will. Let's hope the rain keeps off.'

17

ESME

Forty-Two Years Ago

As soon as the contractions had started getting stronger, Stephen had thrown on his thick winter coat, pulled up the collar and shoved his big feet into his fur-lined boots. He'd turned his back on me then, headed out of the house, growling under his breath, muttering, muttering, muttering.

I'd watched from the window. Seen him drag on his gloves and hat as he strode out towards the lake, destroying the unblemished snow with his ugly footprints, an angry giant disappearing into the distance.

And I'm glad he's gone.

Crying out in pain, for him to show no emotion – no sympathy, no kindness – would have been intolerable.

I should have left him when I fell pregnant. I should leave him now. I should run and run and never stop running. And yet here I am. Here I stay. Too scared to leave, for fear he'll track me down and bring me back – and make my life an even darker hell than it is now.

Pain builds. Blocks of agony stacking higher and higher. And I feel so alone. So scared. I'm not due yet. *Go back to sleep, little ones, it's not time for you to come into the world.*

I stumble towards the bedroom window, pressing one hand against my lower back, the other against the icy glass, the cold biting into my flesh. The snow is deep out there, the lake frozen. Snowflakes tumble from the dusky sky, covering the countryside like a coat of brilliant-white emulsion. I imagine Stephen in the cabin, or maybe the bunker, sealed away with his morbid stash of Nazi memorabilia.

I cry out as another contraction hits like a demolition boulder slamming into me, reducing me to rubble.

I've called Perdita several times. She's eight months pregnant herself. Should be on maternity leave. But she insisted she would see my pregnancy through, and I'm glad of that. I just wish she was here. *She should be here.*

'The contractions are coming every five minutes,' I told her earlier down the phone. 'Stephen's not here. Should I call an ambulance?'

'The roads are treacherous, Esme.' I heard the concern in her voice. 'It will take far too long for the paramedics to arrive. I'm on my way.'

I watch from the window, waiting for her Mini Clubman to appear. But it doesn't. Outside there is nothing but a blanket of snow.

Where is she? Where is she? Where is she?

The pain is unbearable. Squeezing my insides.

'Stephen!' I yell, dropping to the floor. 'Help me, please.'

But apart from the imagined echo of my own voice, there's only a cold, frightening silence, and I know I'm going to give birth alone.

18

POLLY

Polly strolls down the path towards the lake, avoiding the shrinking puddles from heavy rain in the early hours, sun warm on her back.

Her blonde curls are bunched into a loose ponytail, and she's wearing a yellow floral ankle-length dress, and trainers.

Marsha is on the jetty, an e-cigarette dangling from her fingers, her sling bag across her body, animated as she talks to Janice who's dressed in a jazzy jumper and jeans. As Polly gets closer she picks up their conversation, something about tanks and manoeuvres and how much Marsha misses the armed forces. After her rather secretive start, the American woman seems to be getting involved, mingling more. Had she sent the note drawing Polly down to the basement? It doesn't seem likely. Marsha was at the reception desk when Polly returned, so couldn't have been the person lurking in the darkness, and she said it wasn't her handwriting on the note.

Harry stands at the end of the jetty, away from everyone, looking out over the water, binoculars pinned to his eyes. Beatrice, also alone, is looking at her phone. Janice turns from talking to Marsha, spots Polly and throws both arms in the air, hands rotating as though she's cleaning windows. 'Coo-ee!' she calls. 'A lovely day for a picnic, isn't it?'

Polly waves back. 'It is, yes.'

'Welcome.' Xander raises his arms like he's a preacher, as Polly steps onto the jetty. 'No sign of William, but we can't hang about. Let's climb aboard.' He picks up a large picnic basket and strides out towards the white motorboat moored at the end of the jetty. It's not a huge vessel but big enough for the guests.

Keys hang from the ignition, and he looks confident as he bounces on board, his trainers splashing in a pool of water. 'Shit!'

'I just want to give everyone a heads up,' Janice says, as Xander takes her hand, helping her onto the boat. 'I do get a bit seasick.'

Xander's skin pales as she sits down. 'Are you sure you want to come with us?'

'Oh yes indeed. I wouldn't miss this for the world.' She pulls a plastic bag for life from her bag. 'I've come prepared. No need for a fuss.'

'I'm not a fan,' Harry whispers into Polly's ear from behind.

She glances back to see his face paling too. 'Sorry?'

'Of people throwing up.'

'Show me anyone who is.' Polly attempts a laugh, but he doesn't smile.

'It makes me queasy. I'm of a delicate disposition. Always was as a child. Mother had to keep me off school on quite a few occasions.' He glares at Janice. 'I'll need to sit as far away from that woman and her carrier bag as possible.'

'The trip isn't compulsory, Janice. We have plenty more events on the itinerary,' Xander is saying. 'If you think—'

'I'll be just fine,' Janice says. 'It's a short journey, let's not get our knickers in a twist.'

'No life jackets, Xander?' Beatrice says, as he helps her on board. 'I can't swim.'

'It's not far, and I'm an excellent swimmer,' he says. 'You'll be just fine.'

Once everyone's on board, Xander takes the wheel, starts the engine.

'I'm going to take you across the lake,' he says, pulling the boat away from the jetty, the engine emitting a relaxing purr, the smell of diesel. 'To where there's a stunning picnic area. You can get a different perspective of Kendalmere from there and do some sketching if you'd like to.'

'Is this the only access to the picnic area?' Harry says, looking about him, flicking back his fringe. 'By boat?'

'You'd never see the enemy coming with those bangs, Harry,' Marsha says, peering at him over her sunglasses. 'Do you ever stop fiddling with them?'

Harry moves his gaze to Marsha, furrows his forehead.

'She's talking about your fringe,' Xander volunteers, keeping his eyes on the water in front of him. 'And in answer to your question, the area is accessible on foot if you walk around the lake. It's a stunning two-hour walk, though sadly the weather's made some of the paths rather boggy. It's over here that we are hoping to build two holiday cottages and another art studio. We also hope to extend the main house even further. All very exciting.'

Harry scowls, lifts his chin and, seemingly for Marsha's benefit, flicks back his fringe. 'And it's destroying natural habitats,' he says.

Xander glances over his shoulder, blinking, not meeting Harry's eye. 'We're planting trees to replace those we cut down, what more can we do?'

'Not do it at all. Protect the environment. Simple.'

For a moment Xander is silent, his cheeks flushed, though from embarrassment or anger, Polly can't be sure. He flashes a smile at the rest of the guests before returning his attention to the lake and clearing his throat. 'I had hoped we might be able to sit on the grass,' he says, the change of subject obvious, 'but the rain has put paid to that. We have benches though. The sun will have hopefully dried those. If not, I have some plastic sheets on the boat for you to sit on.'

The sun glistens on the water as the boat hums its way across the lake, leaving a stream of frothy bubbles in its wake. Polly glances back towards the jetty, where the rowing boat is moored against the grass bank, a feeling of tranquillity washing over her.

Her eyes drift back to the guests: Harry, now seemingly over his confrontation with Xander; Janice clasping her carrier bag; Beatrice twirling a strand of her hair round her finger, a look on her face Polly can't quite work out, her desire to confide in Polly seeming to have died a death. A lazy wasp buzzes around her. She swipes it away with the back of her hand.

'Leave it,' Harry cries. 'They're valuable pollinators.'

'Yes, and they fucking sting.' Beatrice rolls her eyes and turns to look out over the water. Harry doesn't respond.

'The weather's so unpredictable, isn't it?' Polly says, after a silence. 'Quite extreme,' she adds when nobody responds.

'At least you don't have tornadoes,' Marsha says after a few moments. 'We had five in one day in Maine a few years back.'

Polly feels scolded, as though she's making far too much of a few rain showers. But then they haven't been *just* rain showers. The downpours have been ferocious, and another storm is heading their way.

'I have friends who live in Maine, Marsha,' Janice says, looking a little yellow. 'Clive and Clare Carter, do you know them?'

'Maine's a big place, Janice,' Marsha says.

'Maryland,' Janice corrects herself. 'Not Maine.'

'Even less likely, then.' Marsha moves her eyes to the back of Xander as he rests one hand on the wheel. 'Have you ever been to the US, Xander?'

His body tenses. 'Yes. A long time ago.'

'And how did you find it?' There is something in the way Marsha maintains her stare. It's as though she's jibing him. And the way her fists are clenched in her lap makes Polly wonder if there's a motive to her questions.

'As I say, it was a long time ago,' Xander says, wiping beads of sweat from his forehead with the back of his hand.

'Are you enjoying your stay, Beatrice?' It's Janice. Perhaps she senses the tension too. It's hard to miss.

Beatrice snaps from her trance, leaving an outstretched finger pressing against her tattoo. She stares at Janice with a look of surprise. 'Sorry?'

'I asked if you're enjoying your stay.'

'I am, yes. My boyfriend has been calling and messaging three or four times a day. It's as though he's here with me, which is comforting.' Her voice is so soft, it's barely audible above the rhythmic whir of the engine.

'He sounds very protective,' Polly says. *Too protective.*

'He is. He hates that I'm away from him. But that's how it should be.'

Another silence descends, and they're almost across the lake when Marsha asks, 'Have any of you seen William lately?'

Harry takes off his sun tinted glasses, rubs the lenses with the corner of his cotton shirt, and slips them back on. 'Afraid not,' he says. 'Why?'

'I haven't seen him since yesterday, and I'm worried about him. He's not in his room, but his bag is still there. I don't buy that he's just taken off.'

'Is his car still here?' Harry asks, pulling out a bottle of suncream.

'He came by taxi,' Marsha says.

'He's left Lakeside,' Janice says, still clutching her plastic bag with tight fists. 'I heard a car pull up late last night. It woke me up, and I looked out. A taxi was idling on the drive, lights on, and William appeared, no bag that I noticed, and got into it.'

'Well, that's a relief.' Marsha presses a hand against her chest. 'I've gotta say I was quite worried about the man.'

'We're about to moor up,' Xander calls from the deck, steering the boat towards another, smaller jetty.

Once Xander has tied the ropes, they climb out and make their way to a pretty picnic area. The sun has dried the wooden benches, so they all find somewhere to sit, opening sketchpads and laying out pencils.

Polly loses herself in thought as she makes a mediocre effort to sketch the surrounding trees, so much so that Janice's nudge sometime later startles her.

The woman is standing next to her, a plate brimming with food in her hands. 'Xander's got out the picnic,' she says. 'We can help ourselves.'

'Oh. Thanks.' Polly rises and stretches her arms above her head, noticing dark clouds gathering once more. She approaches the trestle table laden with food. She's helping herself to flavoured sparkling water and an apricot and pistachio sausage roll when she notices something in the reeds by the water's edge. She puts down her paper cup and plate, and heads over. Crouching down, she pulls back the reeds and picks up a large bone.

'An animal, I should think.' It's Janice, right behind her, peering down at the bone.

'Could be, I suppose.' Polly turns it over in her hands, a slither of unease sliding down her spine. 'Though it seems rather big.'

'We get deer around these parts.' Xander snatches the bone from Polly, studies it, runs his finger along the length of it. 'Or wolf bones are sometimes found in the UK. There's even been sightings of big cats over the years.'

Polly doesn't know enough about animal skeletons to have any idea if he's right. Though, to her, the bone looks human.

The other guests have gathered behind them, muttering.

'We should take it back to the house,' Polly says.

'Whatever for?' Janice says.

Xander looks towards the water and, after a moment, hurls the bone. It splashes a fair distance into the lake, as a loud rumble of thunder crosses the sky, followed moments later by dazzling forked lightning.

'Why did you do that?' Polly asks. 'It could have been of archaeological importance. It looked human to me.'

Harry steps forward. 'I must agree with Polly. It looked like a human femur.'

'Seriously?' Xander says with a sarcastic tone, looking from Polly to Harry, finally turning his back so they can't say any more. 'Eat quickly, guys. Looks like more heavy rain's coming.'

Back at the picnic table, Polly pops a prawn sandwich and some posh crisps onto her plate and makes her way to where Janice is now sitting. She lowers herself down opposite her, recalling the person she saw throwing something into the water that morning. Was it connected? She stares at Janice, who's munching on a bite-size toad-in-the-hole, wanting desperately to confide in her, but can she really trust her? Can she trust anyone here?

'It's beautiful, isn't it?' Polly says, taking a bite of her sandwich and nodding at the lake.

Janice looks up, her gaze moving across the water. 'It is.' She picks up a pastry, hovers it in front of her thin lips. 'But I feel something here.'

'Feel something?'

'Mmm. I'm no psychic, but I sense things. Dark things.' She bites down into the pastry. Chews. Swallows, then leans forward, her eyes seeming too close to the lenses of her glasses. 'We should all leave before the storm comes.'

'It's spitting with rain.' Xander is filling the wicker basket with leftover food. 'Once we've eaten, we would be wise to head back.'

Polly narrows her eyes. She may have imagined it, but it's as though Xander overheard Janice talking. Wanted her to stop. And she couldn't help wondering why.

19

TARA

Tara locks Room Six and walks across the hallway to Beatrice Fuller's room, picking up a handful of clean towels from a trolley on the way.

A woman from Marplethorpe was meant to start this week but she's gone down with a virus, so it's down to Tara to clean the rooms. She doesn't mind. Likes learning more about the guests. It's amazing what they reveal about themselves by how they leave their rooms: Harry's room was spotless, not a thing out of place. Obsessive compulsive, she wonders. Strict parents perhaps. Marsha's bed was already made – you could bounce a coin on it – her clothes sharply folded, a photo of a much younger man with long hair and a full beard on her bedside unit.

In contrast, Beatrice's room looks as though she's been burgled, with clothes strewn everywhere: a kaftan dress slung across the back of a chair, a pair of jeans screwed up on the floor under the window and the quilt in a heap on the bed.

The aroma of a strong cloying perfume catches in Tara's throat, making her cough as she places towels on the end of the bed. She goes to pick up the jeans, her gaze drifting through the window, the fat raindrops hitting the glass. Fear of The Stranger fills her head. Could they be out there somewhere, in the grounds, stalking Lakeside? Are they the figure in black she's seen?

She shudders, puts the jeans on the chair and snatches the towels from the bed.

Beatrice has abused the stunning marble bathroom. Wet towels are everywhere, bottles open, sticky liquid spilling over surfaces. The toilet hasn't even been flushed.

It's then that Tara sees paint smeared in the sink. There's been some attempt to clean it away, but this woman is clearly lazier than a koala, and nowhere near as cute. Tara picks up a cloth and vigorously scrubs it away, then flushes the toilet, pours bleach in the pan.

Back in the bedroom, she straightens the quilt and plumps the pillows, her eyes moving towards the bedside unit. There's a Kindle plugged in to charge and a framed photo of a good-looking man. She picks it up, taking in his dark hair, his blue eyes. He must be Beatrice's boyfriend, or maybe her late husband, David. The man who died a year ago. She puts down the photo, noticing through the window Xander and the guests coming across the lake by boat, the rain getting heavier. She grabs the caddy and wet towels and leaves the room.

* * *

Tara stands at the window of her bedroom, watching as the guests run up the path towards the house, splashing in puddles. Xander is out in front where he always likes to be, wet, dark hair clinging to his skull, still managing to look good; Polly, a few paces behind, is balancing a green rain jacket over her head, Marsha striding out beside her. Janice, in a yellow mac to her ankles, looking like a lollipop lady, and Harry, in a red jacket, holding a blue Lakeside umbrella above his head, are trailing behind.

Tara fiddles with her emerald necklace. Xander bought it for her. Said it made her look as though she belonged at Lakeside. Belonged with him. He'd replaced her whole wardrobe when they first got married. She'd been thrilled at the time. But now she remembers how much she'd loved her faded jeans with the holes in the knees, her trusty Converse trainers, her baggy, cosy jumpers with frayed cuffs.

She moves her gaze from the approaching guests and stares down at the note in her hand. She found it on the doormat as she came down from cleaning the rooms. She knew before opening it that it was from The Stranger, recognised the capital letters scrawled across the envelope.

Leave Lakeside NOW

Three little words that send a chill down her spine.

She wants to show it to Xander but knows he'll dismiss it, as he always does. He'll say it's 'something and nothing'. That there's no point in calling the police, they can't do anything, and anyway, if word got out, it could put people off coming to the retreat.

Is whoever's been sending the letters the same person who added the corpse to Polly's painting? Her stomach tips at the thought. How far are they likely to go to get Xander to leave Lakeside? Are they dangerous? Should she warn the guests?

And where is William Doyle?

But Xander would never forgive her if she made a fuss. If word got out that Lakeside is a dangerous place, it would destroy all he's worked for. Ruin Lakeside Art Retreat. Ruin her, she supposes. After all, this place and her husband are all she has. But then what if someone does something awful? What if someone gets hurt? Would she ever forgive herself? She takes a diazepam. It will help.

The door slams. Xander's back. She screws up the letter, tosses it into the wicker basket by the bed. Taking a long deep breath, she makes her way into their private lounge, where her husband is towel-drying rainwater from his hair. He pauses, damp hair unruly, and looks across at her with piercing blue eyes. 'Everything OK, darling?' he says. 'You look as though you've seen a ghost.'

'Everything's fine,' she says, pinning a tight bright smile on her face. 'Totally fine. Why wouldn't it be?'

20

POLLY

Polly swerves round a sharp bend, taking yet another detour to avoid flooding in the narrow country lanes. Rain hammers against the windscreen, the slate grey sky low and ominous. She's been driving for over forty minutes and is beginning to think she's a complete fool for attempting to return to Marplethorpe to talk to Cathy Tipton.

'You have reached your destination,' the satnav finally announces as she enters the village fifteen minutes later. Dark clouds still hover, shards of sunshine squeezing through, making puddles glisten with rainbow colours.

The rain has stopped for now.

There's not a soul about. In fact, it's like a ghost village. She shudders, scaring herself by expecting the creepy Children from the *Midwich Cuckoos* to appear.

She pulls into a layby near the pond, kills the engine and pulls on the handbrake. A row of pretty stone cottages on the other side of the pond look out over a green, wildflowers edging a lush lawn. According to the pub landlord, Cathy Tipton lives in the one with the wooden porch.

Polly takes a deep breath. 'OK. Let's do this,' she mutters, opening the door and snatching up her damp rain jacket from the passenger seat.

She locks the car, slips on her jacket and strides out towards the cottages, pausing for a moment as she gets closer. It's been years since Cathy last saw Esme Frampton, or anyone has seen her for that matter. What does Polly really hope to gain? But then this woman must know about Esme's child. Whether it was a girl or boy. What the baby's name was. If it's possible that the Frampton child was Polly's mother.

She knocks on the door, a prickle tingling her neck. She turns to see the woman from the pub standing on the far side of the green, her hair loose, free of its ponytail, flying about her face like escaping snakes, tendrils clinging to her cheeks. She doesn't move. Just stares from a distance like an eerie waxwork, her black dress flapping her ankles.

The door swings open, and Polly turns her gaze to a woman in her sixties framed in the doorway. Lycra shorts encase wide thighs, and she's wearing flip-flops – her toenails painted black – and a long black T-shirt with 'AC/DC' on the front. Her black hair is buzzed short, and there's a studded earring in her nose and several in her earlobes. 'Yep!'

'Cathy Tipton?'

'Yep!' The woman sniffs, runs a hand under her nose. 'Who wants to know?'

'Hi.' Polly raises a hand in a quaint wave, aware of heavy metal music coming from inside the cottage. 'My name is Polly Ashton—'

'And?' Cathy places a tattooed arm across the doorframe like a barricade.

'I understand you knew Esme Frampton.'

Her rigid face softens. 'Yep, I knew Esme. We were close at one point – a long time ago. And…? What's this about?'

'I'm staying at Lakeside and wondered if I could pick your brain about the Framptons.' Polly's sure this woman won't know what happened to the couple – it seems nobody does – but she has to ask. 'I was wondering what happened to Esme, if you—'

'How the hell would I know?' It's the answer she expected. 'You a journalist or *someink*?' The woman goes to close the door.

'No. No…' She can see she's losing her. 'I wanted to find out more about her.' She takes a deep breath and pulls out the framed photo from her canvas bag. 'It's just I was given this picture.'

Cathy nods, takes a deep breath and looks out over the green towards the pond. She returns her eyes to Polly, stares for some moments before saying, 'OK, you had better come in.' She lowers her arm and moves out of Polly's path so she can enter the house. Before stepping in, Polly glances back at the green. The woman has gone.

* * *

'I was friendly with Esme for quite a while,' Cathy says, handing Polly an oversized mug of steaming, super-strong tea. She's turned off the music. Slipped the black vinyl back into its cardboard sleeve and put it with the rest of her collection propped up along the wall. Polly's taken off her wet rain jacket and is now sitting on a battered black sofa that's flaking in places, the lighter fabric showing through the leather like cracks in dry earth. It's hot in the house, despite the rain that's teeming from the sky once more, pounding against the grubby window. The room is small, the beamed ceiling low. There's a pungent, spicy scent of marijuana mingling with the smell of wet dog – though there doesn't seem to be a dog.

'First time I met Esme was at the school gate many years ago,' Cathy says, perching on the arm of the chair, cradling her mug with both hands. 'I went over and spoke to her. Felt a bit sorry for her, I s'pose.' She takes a swig of her tea before putting it down on a cluttered side table. 'She would stand away from the other parents, you know,' she continues. 'Always looked a bit lost and vulnerable. Not a small woman, but the way she held herself – hunched up, like – made her look small, invisible, if you catch my drift.'

'When was this?'

'Our kids were about six, I s'pose.'

'Was her child a boy or girl?' Polly's trying to keep her tone calm. *Could it have been my mother?*

Cathy stares at her for some moments before saying, 'A little girl.'

Polly's heartbeat quickens as she fumbles in her bag for the photo once more. 'Was this her?'

Cathy takes the photo. 'Yep, that's Lila. Nervy little thing, but a nice kid.'

Polly reels in her emotions, the excitement that she finally knows her mother's name, that Esme and Stephen were her grandparents, making her wobbly.

Cathy hands back the photo. If she's curious why Polly has the picture, she doesn't say. 'My daughter was friendly with Lila for a while, so that's when I reached out to Esme.'

'So, she had a daughter. A girl. A girl called Lila.' *My mother.*

'Yep, that's what I said.' Cathy furrows her forehead, stares at Polly for a long moment. 'The girl took off when she was sixteen. Left a note for Esme saying she was leaving, that once she got settled she'd be in touch, but she never did – as far as I know. And then the Framptons took their own lives. Supposedly.'

'You don't think they did?'

'Truth is, I could believe Esme might – she was volatile, low, in a right ol' state after Lila took off. But a suicide pact with Stephen doesn't ring true. I know it sounds odd, but they weren't close enough to go together, if you catch my drift. I'm convinced there was more to it. Wouldn't be surprised if he bumped her off. Stephen was a nasty piece of work.' She picks up her tea, takes a long gulp and wipes the back of her hand across her mouth. 'A *really* nasty piece of work.'

'But you liked Esme?'

'I liked her all right, but in equal measure I wanted to shake the bloody woman. She overprotected Lila to the point of... well I suppose it was obsession really – possessive, like. I used to say, "Esme, let the girl live her life. Give her some space." But she didn't like that, got a bit funny with me. Said she had to protect the girl from her father, so I gave up trying in the end. And, as I say, Lila just took off. Bravely claiming her freedom from that domineering father of hers, I shouldn't wonder.' She shrugs. 'Esme was distraught when Lila left, of course, and I felt for her, wanted to help – she was pregnant again at the time, so—'

'Esme was pregnant when Lila disappeared?'

'Uh-huh.' But once Lila took off, Esme changed, wouldn't take my calls, pretty much cut herself off, so our friendship kind of dissolved.' She puts her mug down. 'She never came into Marplethorpe again after that. I went up there a couple of times, you know, to Lakeside House. But she never answered the door.'

'What happened to the baby?'

'No idea. Never once saw it. Perhaps the wee mite never made it into the world. Or maybe Esme put the child up for adoption. Who knows?'

'And you never saw Lila again?'

She shakes her head, rubs a thumb across her palm. 'She never returned, well not that I'm aware of. I'm guessing the police would have tracked her down to tell her about her parents' disappearance.'

They wouldn't have found her. Lila was dead by then.

'And you said your daughter was friends with Lila when they were children?' Polly takes a sip of tea, trying not to wince at the strength of it – attempting to sound natural despite her racing heart.

'Not for long – kids of that age can be fickle with friends – but Esme and my friendship... well, that lasted pretty much right up to... well, as I say, Lila leaving. Despite Stephen not allowing Esme to have friends, we would get together over the years without his knowledge. She used to say I was a great support to her.' She pauses for a moment, her eyes glazing over, which seems at odds with her brusque persona. 'I offered to put her up on several occasions, help get her away from him, but something made her stay. Fear, probably. Who knows?' She rubs a hand across her mouth. 'Of course, Stephen had his creepy mate, Giles Alderman.'

'Do you remember him?'

She screws up her nose. 'Vaguely. He lived in Windermere, I think. A doctor or consultant, something like that. Esme said Giles would often come to the house. She didn't like him, told me that much.'

'So, Lila was a nice girl?'

'Yes, she was, though, as I say, a bit of a nervy, sickly child when she was younger – off school a lot with this and that wrong with her.' Her eyes seem far away, as though recalling. She expels a puff of air, rubs a hand across the back of her head. 'Later she would come into the village sometimes, got friendly with the lads and lasses from the fair – seemed to be rebelling a bit. I'd often see her sitting on the green, smoking dope, laughing and messing about with the other teens. She got on well with one of the fairground lads, Elijah Lovell, a lovely-looking boy – a free spirit, you know. He would strut around the village in one of those long military coats with his collar up, thought he was the bee's knees.' She smiles. Shakes her head. 'Always wore the thing, never took it off even in summer – it probably ponged a bit, truth be told.' She laughs. 'I remember there was a yellow smiley face badge sewn on one of the arms. Though God knows why, it looked ridiculous on an army coat.' She wipes a hand across her mouth. 'He disappeared around the same time as the Framptons.'

'Elijah?'

'Yep. Ran away, they reckon.'

'So, this was after Lila took off?'

'Oh yes, about a week later, I'd say. Perhaps he went after her – they did seem close.' She pauses for a moment. 'Lila certainly seemed at her happiest when she was with him. I remember how Esme came into Marplethorpe looking for her. She'd drag her back to Lakeside. Always worried Stephen would catch the girl with the fairground crew. In Esme's favour, they were a mischievous lot, though harmless for the main part. But Stephen and Giles were total bigots.' She glances up at the clock on the wall – it's quarter past four.

Polly senses it's time she made a move and rises. 'Sorry, I didn't mean to keep you talking for so long.'

Cathy gets to her feet, rests her hand on Polly's arm. 'You have her eyes, by the way,' she says. 'You have Lila's eyes.'

Tears sting, and Polly covers her mouth. 'You knew?'

'When you showed me the photo the second time, yes, I knew.'

Polly breaks down in tears, and Cathy – a stranger – wraps her in her arms and hugs her close.

'There, there,' she says, patting Polly's back. 'Come and sit back down, love. I'll make you another cup of tea.'

* * *

'Thanks so much for talking to me,' Polly says as she steps out of the front door into the pouring rain fifteen minutes later. 'I appreciate it.'

'No problem. It's good news that you've found out who your mum was, though sad she's passed on – as I say, she was a nice girl. I don't think we'll ever get to the truth about what happened to your grandparents. And to be fair, you wouldn't want to find your grandfather – he was an absolute a-hole.'

Polly smiles. 'Can I leave you my phone number?' she asks. 'Just in case you remember anything else.'

'Sure.' Cathy takes out her phone and adds Polly's number, sends her a text.

'Thanks.' Polly pulls up the hood of her rain jacket, glances towards the dark sky. 'You said the fair came a lot.'

'Used to, a long time ago, every six months or so. Stopped coming when Elijah vanished.'

'Was it held on the green?'

Cathy shakes her head. 'No, on the field behind the pub. You take care, yeah.'

'Thanks,' Polly says, as Cathy closes the door.

21

POLLY

Polly sits in her parked car, grips the steering wheel and rests her forehead against her hands. Rain bombards the roof and windscreen like marbles, a feeling of being trapped washing over her. Should she go home to Oxford? Stop off in Blackpool to see Nicky? Plan her future instead of delving into the past? She has the answers she came for. She knows her mother was Lila Frampton, the daughter of strange, overprotective Esme and cruel Stephen. She knows Lila, apart from her time with the fairground youngsters, had a short unhappy life, the depressing fact making her stomach twist.

She struggles to lift her heavy head, weighed down by everything that's happened since she arrived at Lakeside. The questions spin off in every direction, multiplying like invasive weeds:

Who painted the hanged man on her painting? Who is The Stranger? Who was Xander threatening to evict from Lakeside? Was the bone found by the lake really from an animal? And who is the figure in black? She needs to leave. She needs to leave now.

But, like a magnet, Lakeside is drawing her back. There are dangers there, that much is clear, but she still needs to know what happened to her grandparents. Had they really taken their own lives? And where is the baby Esme was carrying when Lila disappeared? And where is Elijah Lovell? Could he be her father?

No, she can't go home. Not yet. Anyway, home isn't home any more – a stalker chased her from her safe place. And although living with her brother and his wife is OK, it's not where she wants to be right now.

She takes a deep breath. She'll stay a while longer, then go to Blackpool to see Nicky. Then... who knows? Further ahead than that looks blurry, uncertain. She feels adrift, and there's nobody to pull her to safety.

The rain eases, and Polly climbs from the car, looks up at the low dark sky. There'll be more rain soon, but now she decides to explore Marplethorpe, get a feel for where Lila spent her time when she briefly escaped her stifling existence.

She takes off towards a row of shops: a grocer's, a bakery, a nail bar that was once a post office going by the concrete sign above it, and Marplethorpe Emporium, the company that cleared Lakeside and, according to Pete Chester, is now owned by the son of Giles Alderman – Stephen Frampton's friend.

She pushes open the emporium door, the musky smell of antiques and once-loved items hitting her as she steps inside. Her eyes dart around the shop taking in a bookshelf full of hardback books on the Lake District with battered jackets; a crate of cuddly toys; a rail crammed with a jumble of clothes. A woman in her fifties with frizzy grey hair and rosy cheeks sits at a table near the entrance. She looks up from tapping on her phone and smiles. 'Awful weather we're having,' she says. 'Traffic's almost at a stand-still for about five miles, apparently.'

Polly nods, pushing the thought that she could be stranded here to the back of her mind. 'Is it OK to look around?'

'Of course. Give me a shout if you need any help.' She looks back at her phone.

Polly's about to head down the shop when she has a change of heart and makes her way back to the desk. 'Actually, I was wondering if there's anything left from the clearance up at Lakeside.'

The woman puts down her phone with a clunk. 'I wouldn't know, I'm afraid. It was a while ago now, and we've had several clearances since then. House clearances tend to get jumbled together in categories, you see.' She tilts her head. 'Why do you ask?'

The woman has a round, pleasant face and a warm smile, and before she can think it through Polly blurts, 'The Framptons were my grandparents,' the words feeling all kinds of wrong on her tongue. Her grandparents are Grandma and Grandad Ashton who live on a farm in Wales, and Grandpa Jack who is training for the next London Marathon. Esme and Stephen Frampton were never her grandparents – you have to earn that status.

The woman widens her eyes. 'We were told there were no living relatives, that the Framptons were declared dead after seven years, and the house went to—'

'It's not a problem,' Polly cuts in, her stomach churning as she leans forward and rests one hand on the table. This suddenly feels too much.

The woman widens her eyes further. 'Is everything OK? You look a little pale.'

'I'm fine.' Polly straightens. 'I just hoped I might find some of my grandparents' belongings, is all.'

'Well, as I say, items get mixed up into categories. Do you know what you're looking for exactly?'

Polly shakes her head. She hasn't a clue. 'He... Stephen... he collected Nazi memorabilia.'

'Ah, yes, I remember the owner of this place found a photo of it when we were clearing. He was desperate to discover it but had no luck. You won't find any of it here, I'm afraid. But do have a look around.'

'Thanks.' Polly moves away from the woman once more and makes her way down the shop, darting her eyes across glass cabinets full of ornaments, a feeling of sadness washing over her that everything behind the glass was once loved by someone.

She looks through the dresses, jackets, cardigans, all giving off a musty smell. She's wasting her time here. Anything could have been theirs. The sound of footsteps approaching makes her swing round.

'I've just had a thought.' It's the woman she just spoke to. 'There are some boxes out back. I think one of them was from Lakeside. If you keep an eye on the shop, I'll nip and get it.'

'Thank you,' Polly says, as the woman bangs through swinging double doors and disappears.

Five minutes later she reappears, lugging a box, making grunting noises as she manoeuvres it through the doors. Polly dashes over, gives her a hand, and together they dump it in the corner.

'Go wild,' the woman says with a laugh, wiping her forehead. 'I'll be up the front of the shop if you need me.'

The wooden box has 'Lakeside' written on the side in large, capital letters. Polly kneels down on the grubby floor and, her heart pounding at the thought of finding something of her mother's, begins to rummage.

She lifts out a pile of heavy books: two on Hitler, a couple about antiques and a pile of romance novels. There's a casserole dish, several cups and plates – which could have belonged to anyone – and her excitement wanes. Finally, there are clothes: a man's jacket, a faded floral apron. And then she sees it, right at the bottom: an army coat with a yellow badge sewn on the upper arm.

She pulls it out of the box, presses it against her cheek. *He always wore it, never took it off even in summer,* Cathy Tipton had said. Then why is Elijah Lovell's coat in with the things that were cleared from Lakeside?

Polly puts everything back in the box and takes the coat to the counter.

The woman looks up and smiles. 'It's a lovely coat.' She runs her hand over the fabric. 'They don't make them like this any more.'

'It is, yes.' Polly has no idea why she wants the coat. But something inside her tells her to buy it. That she needs it. She needs this link to the young lad her mother liked spending time with.

It's as the woman takes her money that Polly spots a photograph of a group of people, pegged on the wall behind the table.

The woman follows Polly's gaze. 'Ah, that's the team,' she says. She points at herself on the end. 'That's me,' she says with a laugh. 'Quite chubby there. It was taken before the latest diet.'

Polly peers closer. She knows the man in the middle. 'Who's that?' she asks, but in truth she already knows exactly who he is.

22

POLLY

'That's the boss. Will Alderman.' The woman hands over Polly's change and pushes the coat into a carrier bag. 'There you go, love.'

Heat creeps up Polly's neck. 'Can I speak to him?'

'Will? Why?'

'It's just... if he cleared Lakeside, he may recall—'

'Well, I'm afraid he's away at the moment.' She shuffles forward in her seat. 'To be honest, it's a relief to see the back of him for a while.' She looks up at the CCTV camera. 'I hope he can't read lips.'

'You don't like him?'

'I don't *dis*like him – he's just a bit of a money-grabber, is all – runs in the family. His father was the same. There's been a few times I've been tempted to walk out after seeing him diddle old ladies out of their valuables, but jobs are hard to come by around these parts, and I'm not going back to cleaning the pub toilets – the state of them, you wouldn't believe.'

'Do you know where he's gone?'

'No. Doesn't tend to tell us mere mortals anything.' She looks again at the photo.

'Well, thanks anyway,' Polly says, dashing from the shop.

Outside on the pavement she takes a breath, clutching the bag with the coat inside to her chest. 'Jesus,' she mutters, struggling to compute what she's just learnt. Why the hell was William Alderman, Giles Alderman's son, masquerading as William Doyle at the retreat? And where is he now?

Though the rain has eased, Marplethorpe is gloomy, the sky dusk-like despite it only being five o'clock. Polly needs to head back to Lakeside before the roads are entirely blocked by floods. She hurries towards her car, climbs in, and throws the carrier bag onto the passenger seat. Flicking on her headlights, she keys Lakeside into the satnav.

She's been on the road fifteen minutes when a car starts tailgating – its headlights on full beam too bright, like invading eyes.

'Keep back,' she whispers under her breath, braking to a crawl, water splashing the doors as she drives through another build-up of water, but the car behind is so close – too close – making her uncomfortable.

Polly continues, picking up speed, heart thudding as the car behind does the same.

'For Christ's sake,' she cries, her fear taking her back to the day she and Nicky spotted the cameras in their apartment. The day they'd called the police. The day Polly's brother suggested she moved in with him immediately, fearing for her safety.

'Get back, you idiot.' She's so close to tears but she can't let herself cry – it's hard enough driving without blurred vision. She's angry, too, that once again she's afraid. She hates it that someone she doesn't even know can make her feel so helpless.

Her hands tremble on the steering wheel, the narrow road and canopy of trees making her feel trapped. She still has at least another forty minutes to go before she reaches Lakeside. What if the driver is a crazy person? What if they ram her car? She presses her foot down on the throttle as she swings round a bend, tyres skidding. She has to lose whoever it is. But the faster she drives, the faster the other car goes – and the greater the chance of her skidding off the road.

'Oh God.' She flashes her eyes to her rear-view mirror. She can't see the driver, just the bright beam of the headlights blurring her vision. But she hears the sound of their horn. And as the road widens, whoever's behind the wheel speeds up, attempting to overtake.

'What the f—'

Suddenly the car is beside her, squeezing her against the hedgerow. An old Mini Clubman. In the driving seat is the woman Polly saw standing near the duckpond in Marplethorpe, and sitting in the pub. The woman with the long black dress and intense stare is now looking through her side window at Polly, hands gripping the steering wheel.

Polly swerves into a layby and screeches to a stop. The other car continues down the road, braking some distance further on. A speedy three-point turn, and Polly roars away in the opposite direction, heart thudding, eyes on her rear-view mirror. There's no sign of the Mini so she turns into the entrance to a farm, pulling her car out of sight behind some trees. Whatever the woman wants, she's not prepared to find out. Not here. Not now.

A few minutes later a car speeds down the road. Polly can see through the branches that it's the Mini Clubman, but the woman doesn't seem to see her – and before long the car is out of sight, the noise of its engine fading into the distance.

* * *

Polly almost falls into the lobby at Lakeside and stands for some moments, clutching the carrier bag with Elijah's coat inside, a strange buzzing in her ears, panic twisting her stomach.

Marsha is leaning against the counter talking to Tara, who sits on the stool behind her laptop.

Polly takes three deep breaths, dropping onto the sofa in the bay window, trying to stop trembling. Slowly the buzzing fades and she hears Tara's voice.

'He painted it when he was in his early twenties, when he lived in the US.'

'Really? Well, it's totally awesome,' Marsha says. 'I'm not surprised it sold for millions. It's a shame he hasn't done anything as good since.'

'I guess that's subjective.' Tara's voice is defensive. 'If I'm honest, I prefer his later stuff.'

'You do?' Marsha leans back from the counter, her eyes wide. 'Well, I have to disagree. *New York in Spring* is a masterpiece.'

'Are you OK?' It's Tara, her eyes now on Polly.

Polly rises, makes her way towards them, a slight stagger in her step, her head swimming. Should she tell them about the woman chasing her? No. One thing at a time. And there's nothing anyone can do. The woman has gone. 'I wondered if I could have a word with you alone, Tara?'

Marsha seems to get the message and smiles. 'Well, I'll leave you to it,' she says, turning and ascending the stairs.

Once Marsha has disappeared, Polly begins. 'I've been into Marplethorpe—'

'Gosh, that was daring – according to the news, the roads are pretty dangerous at the moment. No wonder you look so awful.'

'Thanks.'

'Oh, no. Sorry, I didn't mean—'

'It's fine.' Polly raises her palm. 'I just wanted to say that I went into the emporium.' She takes a breath. 'The thing is, William Doyle isn't who he says he is.'

'I don't understand.'

'William Doyle is William Alderman, the owner of the company who cleared Lakeside when Xander bought the place.'

Tara covers her mouth with her hand. 'What? Why would he lie?'

Polly shrugs. 'I have no idea. According to the woman in the shop, he's away on holiday, so clearly he hasn't returned to the village yet. I think you need to let Xander know, as the man obviously had other motives for being here. And maybe call the emporium and bring them up to date. They may have another number for him.' Polly pauses for a moment. She's so tired, emotionally exhausted and almost dropping on her feet. 'The thing is, he had that picture of the Nazi memorabilia in his room upstairs. Could he have been looking for it? It must be worth a fair bit. The woman in the emporium said he was desperate to find it when he did the clearance.'

'Was he? I hadn't realised. Not that I met him at the time. We did all our chatting over the phone and via messages. I'll talk to Xander. He'll know what to do.'

'Great, thank you.' She stares at Tara, wondering if there's something else behind her pretty exterior. Who can she really trust? Will Tara even tell Xander? And, if she does, will Xander do anything? If he's as proactive as he was with the CCTV, probably not.

Unable to face dinner, she heads to her room, the stairs seeming to go on forever, relieved to get inside and close her door behind her.

She's cleaning her teeth when she realises the necklace Nicky gave her is not on the windowsill where she's sure she left it. She rinses her mouth before heading through to the bedroom, noticing her case is open, her clothes messy. She's sure she didn't leave them like this. Had someone taken her key? Let themselves in? But overwhelming tiredness takes over. Perhaps she did leave her case open, and maybe she's lost her necklace – the catch was always awkward. She'll ask Tara in the morning if anyone's handed it in.

She drops onto her bed, her eyelids closing like shutters. She's asleep by seven.

* * *

The door creaks open. The full moon shines through the window, glinting off a silver blade. A figure in black moves fast, with long strides, as though they're flying. A sudden weight against her chest, a knife to her throat.

She jolts awake, disturbed by the recurring nightmare, a glance at the clock telling her it's 11.05 p.m. She pulls herself up, hearing a sound in the room. It's the tinkling music she heard outside her door on the first day. 'Polly Put the Kettle On'.

The curtains are still open. A full moon, blurry through clouds, is visible from the bed. She flicks on the bedside lamp just as the music stops. The door to her room stands open.

She leaps from the bed, checks there's nobody hiding in the bathroom or the wardrobe, before slamming the bedroom door. She rests her body against it – heart pounding. Someone *has* been in her room.

After several deep breaths she moves towards the window, when she spots a figure dressed in black near the lake. She steps closer to the glass, certain it's the same person she's seen before. Seeming to sense Polly's stare, the figure starts walking towards the building. As they get closer, Polly knows exactly who it is.

Deal with it! her inner voice cries. *Go down and deal with it.*

Polly pulls on her trainers and robe and grabs the key to her room. This has to stop. Now.

When she gets down to the lounge, the figure is standing on the lit veranda, staring in, dark eyes haunting. It's clear she can see Polly as she raises a hand, not in a wave exactly but a greeting of sorts.

What if she's here to kill me? Is this the person who threatened Tara and Xander? 'The Stranger'?

Polly, annoyed by her fear, dashes back into reception and takes an umbrella from the porch before returning to the lounge.

The woman is close to the window now. Skin sallow, eyes dark, her black dress shrouding her small frame as she tap, tap, taps on the glass with her nails. Polly sees her lips move. She's mouthing something as she taps and stares, stares and taps.

'Lila?' she's saying. 'Lila, is that you?'

23

POLLY

You have to confront this, Polly, she tells herself, taking deep breaths as she approaches the French door, a finger of fear travelling down her spine. She reaches for the handle, throws the door open.

'Who are you?' The woman grabs Polly's arm, grubby nails pushing into her soft white robe. 'Your eyes... they are so like Lila's.'

Polly lets out a gasp. Tugs away from her, finding strength from the knowledge this woman is small, thin, fragile. She could overpower her in a moment.

The woman moves backwards. 'But you can't be Lila. She would be in her forties by now.' Her voice sounds far away. 'You can only be in your twenties.' She reaches out a hand then lowers it back down to her side. She's unkempt, her teeth in poor shape, hair greasy. Polly steps out of the lounge onto the patio, her confidence growing. There's no danger here.

The woman tilts her head. 'Do you know where Elijah is?'

'Elijah?' *Lila's friend.*

'My boy. Do you know where he is?'

There is something desperately sad about this woman. Deep

pain etched into the lines on her face. She hands Polly a photo. It's old, creased in several places, as though handled many times, and it's difficult to see the young lad's face clearly. He's standing up straight, confident, his hair falling to his shoulders in dark waves. He's wearing a military coat, collar up.

The woman snatches the photo back. 'He disappeared,' she says. 'They said he ran away. But he's been gone so long. He would have contacted me by now. But nobody listens. Nobody.' She shakes her head.

'I'm so sorry.'

The woman looks up at the house. 'I've always wondered if he came here looking for Lila. They were so in love, daft things. And he was so determined her father wouldn't keep them apart. What if Stephen Frampton hurt my boy?'

Polly thinks about the coat she found at the emporium but stays quiet, unsure how the woman would react if she knew it was found here at Lakeside.

'I came here looking for him when he vanished, but the place was deserted. Locked up. The note pinned to the door.'

'You found the suicide note?'

She doesn't reply, her eyes trancelike as she steps away from the door. 'I just want to know if he's OK,' she says. 'I don't care about anything else. Just that he's OK.'

Polly walks towards her. 'You were with the fair back then?'

'Yes. I was a midwife before that, before I met Elijah's father.' She's talking, her voice low, but it's as though she's far away. 'I loved being part of the fair.' She swallows, runs a thin finger across the photograph, her eyes dull, lifeless. 'We would come to Marplethorpe regularly. Right up to Elijah's disappearance. He was restless. Even got a tattoo on his arm of a carousel horse breaking free. He said it represented his love for the fair fading, that he wanted more from life.'

'But you don't think he left by choice?'

She shakes her head. 'He wanted to leave, yes. Wanted to be with Lila, work on his art. A talented boy, much like his father.' Her voice cracks. 'But he wouldn't have gone without saying good-bye.' She slips the photo into her pocket. 'He used to man the bumper cars. I worked on the ghost train. His dad the Ferris wheel.' Her eyes shimmer with tears.

'And his father? Where is he?'

'I settled in Marplethorpe when my boy vanished. His father stayed for a while, but he couldn't cope. It was too much.' She pauses for a moment. 'Grief affects us all differently. His go-to was anger. Never at me. Always at the world. He took off in the end. I have no idea where he is now.' She nibbles loose skin on the side of her thumbnail. It looks sore, oozing, infected. 'I wait and wait for Elijah's return, and I come up here often, just in case.' She looks up. Gazes at Polly. 'Who are you, if you're not Lila Frampton?'

Polly swallows through a lump in her throat. Should she tell this woman who she is?

She takes a breath. 'My name is Polly,' she says running a hand across the back of her neck. 'Lila was my mother.'

The woman places a soft hand on Polly's cheek, and stares, searching her face. 'You're Lila's daughter?'

'Yes.' Tears sting behind her eyes.

'Well, I'm Perdita,' the woman says. 'My name is Perdita.'

'You OK out there?' Polly swings round to see Janice standing in the doorway in a pink robe and PJs.

'Yes,' she calls. 'I'm just talking to...' But, as she looks back, Perdita is running down the path towards the woods, darkness shrouding her small frame.

'Who was that?' Janice asks, her forehead crinkling as Polly steps back into the lounge.

'Her name's Perdita. Her son disappeared years ago. I should probably tell Xander tomorrow that she was here on the grounds.'

Janice glances back over her shoulder as they make their way across the lounge, narrowing her eyes and giving a little shudder. 'Well, she certainly looked like a strange one,' she says. 'I would keep away from her if I were you.'

24

POLLY

A dark figure defies gravity as it ascends the bedroom wall, each hand and foot adhering to the surface, its silhouette illuminated by moonlight creeping through a gap in the curtains, straggly hair falling about its face. Polly lies in her bed, helpless, paralysed, as the figure stares down at her with haunting eyes.

Polly wakes with a start, heart thudding, and drags herself up, resting her head against the cushioned headboard. It's been a humid night, filled with strange and confusing nightmares. She flicks on her bedside light as a crack of thunder, so loud it makes the window vibrate, rumbles across the sky. Her body prickles, the happenings of the last few days messing with her mind.

She glances at the clock. It's just after six in the morning. She won't get back to sleep now.

Elijah's coat spills from the carrier bag on the chair, where she'd put it the night before. Should she have told his mother she's found his coat? Would it have helped Perdita come to terms with her son's disappearance, or make things worse? Discovering it wouldn't have told the woman where he is now, just that he got as far as Lakeside the day he went missing.

'Where are you, Elijah?' Polly whispers, as though the coat holds the answers. 'Why were you here all those years ago? Were you searching for Lila?'

She climbs out of bed and makes her way across the room, pressing the remote for the floor-to-ceiling curtains. They glide back with a low whir, revealing the stunning view across the lake, the sun rising in the distance shimmering on still water. The rain has stopped, and another rumble of thunder sounds in the distance, moving further north.

She pulls on a baggy T-shirt, a hoodie and butterfly-print leggings. An early morning jog may calm her thoughts, her anxiety.

Trainers on, she slips her door key and phone into her pocket and makes her way downstairs.

'Morning, Polly,' Ralph says, appearing from the lounge, a skip in his step, his smile bright. 'You're an early bird this morning. How are you enjoying your stay?'

Creepy, sinister, unsettling. 'Fine, thank you,' she says. 'You're early yourself.'

'Ah, yes, always have been an early riser. The walk from the cabin is beautiful this time of the day.'

They both turn at the sound of footsteps on the stairs behind them. Beatrice, a rolled-up towel under her arm, smiles. 'Morning,' she says, raising her hand in a wave as she passes.

'Off for a morning swim?' Ralph asks.

'That's right.'

'Well, enjoy.' Ralph adds as the woman continues across reception and descends the stairs towards the pool. 'Now, what was I saying?'

'The cabin?'

'Ah yes, it's on the other side of the lake. It's my home. It's so quiet out there, I don't even need to lock the door. I came across it when I first arrived here, when the Caldwells were renovating the place. It was run down, but I offered to do it up. It's my sanctuary – where I find peace. Meditate.' He takes a breath. 'I'm dreading it being torn down.'

'It's being demolished?'

He nods. 'When the plans go ahead for the new cottages and art studio, there'll be no room for the cabin.'

'I'm sorry to hear that. What will you do?'

He shrugs. 'Tara insists there'll be alternative accommodation. I hope so. I love living here surrounded by nature, away from the cruel world. A free spirit, I suppose.'

Polly takes a deep breath. She's got him talking. 'I know you said you're not supposed to talk about the Framptons...'

He furrows his forehead, looks about him.

'It's just, if you can tell me anything at all about them, I'd be grateful.'

If he wonders why she wants to know, he doesn't ask. 'All I remember is Stephen drank in the pub in Marplethorpe years ago. He would get a bit loud, controversial. Had a real problem with ethnic minorities – well, anyone who didn't quite meet his ideologies. I kept right away from him.'

'And Esme?'

'Never met her. But I know she often came into the village searching for her teenage daughter. Always a bit manic, apparently. Saying her girl needed to come home before Stephen realised she'd gone. Life must have been awful for the poor kid.' He shakes his head. 'That's all I know, I'm afraid.' He looks at his watch. 'If that's all, I'd better get on.'

* * *

Outside on the patio, Polly takes several long deep breaths and slips on her sunglasses. Setting off at a slow jog, avoiding puddles, she's comforted by the songs of waking birds. Closer to the jetty, she picks up pace, her trainers slapping the damp ground. The sky is a watery blue with tufts of grey, the lake still. A beautiful place, spoiled by someone – someone with a desire to ruin things for Xander and the guests. Someone hiding in plain sight?

A glance back at the house tells Polly most of the residents are still asleep. Curtains are closed at all but two of the bedroom windows, and the blinds are down on most of the French doors in the lounge and dining room. She squints. Someone is standing at one of the bedroom windows, waving. It's Janice.

She returns the wave and continues on her way.

At the jetty she looks about her. The grass area heading towards the kitchen garden is sodden, but a drier path leads into a wooded area. She runs on until the trees block out the sunlight, the sound of birdsong louder here. It feels so good to be away from the house.

She's been running for another five minutes when she comes to a large pool of rainwater blocking her path. There's no way forward. She needs to go back.

As she goes to turn, there's a rustle nearby, breaking the quiet. Her eyes skitter across the trees. A red squirrel races up the trunk of an oak. She presses a hand against her chest. It's lonely out here amongst the towering trees.

'Stupid,' she mutters. Why has she come out alone so early, with everything else that's happened? But she couldn't have stayed in her room – she had to do something to relieve her tension.

A breaking of twigs. Oh God, there *is* someone here. She catches sight of a figure dashing through the trees. *Perdita?*

She turns, blood thumping in her ears, and runs back to the jetty at speed, not wanting to stick around. Once out in the open she pauses for a moment, hands on her thighs, bending over, catching her breath. It must have been Perdita still hanging about.

She looks back over her shoulder at the dense wooded area she has just emerged from. And that's when she spots it. Hanging from the ancient oak tree that she'd painted in her landscape. A doll swings by its neck from one of the branches, swaying as a rogue gust of wind cuts across the area. Nausea rises. The doll has blonde curls and – Polly covers her mouth – it's wearing a pale blue dress with tiny white daisies, made of the same material as her dress: the one that went missing from her apartment. The stalker is here at the retreat, watching her.

She spins on the spot, everything seeming to zoom forward: the house, the lake, the wood. And then she runs.

* * *

'Let's head out there now, shall we?' Xander says, once Polly has explained about the hanging doll.

She'd spent the last hour in her room with the chest of drawers rammed up against the door, curled in a ball under the duvet. She considered calling Nicky, her mum and dad in France, her brother, even the police, but finally, at just after nine, she'd headed down to the lobby, deciding the Caldwells should be the first to know. This is their house, their grounds; they must deal with it.

And now she's following Xander as he strides across the lounge and out through the French doors.

'It could be we have a trespasser,' he says, keeping his tone light.

You have. Perdita, Polly almost says, but decides to keep quiet for now – this wasn't Perdita's doing.

'We have plans for a high perimeter fence around the grounds.' He draws a semicircle across the sky with his finger. 'The one we have now is too low, doesn't take an athlete to vault it.' His obvious attempt to sound breezy grinds on Polly, though he's struggling to hide the tension in his jaw. Surely he must see the connection to the addition to her painting? Real life mimicking art.

They continue down the path towards the tree, the sun now hiding behind gathered dark clouds, rain imminent once more.

'Which tree was it?' he says, as they pass the pods.

She takes over the lead and, reaching the tree, stares up at it, her heart sinking. 'I don't understand. It was here an hour ago.' She turns to look at Xander, who's folding his arms, looking up. 'You must believe me. It was here. Hanging from that branch.'

'You're sure?' He unfolds his arms, rubs a finger across his eyelid.

'Of course I'm sure. It's not the kind of thing I would imagine.'

His hands drop to his side. 'Well, it's not here now.'

Sudden torrential rain breaks through the trees. They'll be soaked within moments.

'We need to get back,' he says, leaving her standing alone and heading off towards the house.

Polly stares up at the branch. A small piece of blue material flaps in the wind. She hadn't imagined it. 'Xander!' she calls, but he doesn't look back.

Her mind whirs. The stalker must have followed her here, is trying to scare her. Had they been in her room? Were they responsible for the music? The bone by the lake? Is it possible they sent the notes to the Caldwells? Whatever the truth is, there's no doubting she's afraid. She drags her phone from her pocket. She needs a photo of the flapping piece of cloth to prove she's not going crazy. But before she can focus the camera, a gust of wind snatches the snagged material, whipping it away and out of sight.

She hurries after Xander, desperate for him to take her seriously.

'Mr Caldwell, Xander,' she says, catching him up on the patio, her curls plastered to her head. 'I know about the notes.'

He swings round. 'Notes?'

'The notes you've received from The Stranger – and I'm wondering if it's connected.'

He runs a hand over his chin, his polo shirt soaked. 'I don't know what you're talking about.'

She narrows her eyes, fat raindrops on her lashes, the end of her nose. 'I happened to overhear you and Tara—'

'You happened to overhear?' He clenches his fists, turns and storms into the lounge.

Polly follows. 'Xander,' she says. 'The notes, the sinister addition to my painting—'

'Let's not be dramatic, it was hardly sinister—'

'And William's disappeared, and he's not even who he said he was.'

'Yes, Tara said, but I can't see—'

'And now a doll hanging from a tree.' She's talking fast, gasping from the run back to the house. 'You can't ignore the things that are happening. They won't go away. Whoever sent you those weird notes could be here at Lakeside. Whoever they are, they could be dangerous.'

'You're overreacting, let's get things in perspective. Nobody's been hurt.'

'You don't know that. What about William? And someone lured me into the basement.'

'Did they? When was this?'

'Yesterday, and if Lorcan hadn't turned up, I've no idea what would have happened. And—'

'Yes, OK, you're right.' He raises his hands in defeat. 'If I'm honest, we've been receiving the notes since we moved in.' He shakes his head. 'I thought it was those bloody protesters, but it's clear things are getting out of hand.'

'You need to tell the other guests. They have a right to know, Xander, so they can decide whether to stay. I, for one, will be leaving today. And *you* must call the police.'

Xander collapses onto a leather sofa, drops his head into his hands and runs his fingers through his wet hair. He sucks in a breath, clears his throat. 'It could be Marsha.'

'Marsha?'

He nods. 'She could be doing all of this for revenge.' He glances towards the French door they just came through. Rain clatters against the glass. 'She suspects me of something...'

'But it's me who's being targeted the most, Xander, and I think—'

'I suspect it's simply because you're a guest here.'

She thinks of the doll. The piece of material. It has to be connected to the stalker. 'It's just—'

'I'll get the guests together – update them about everything – and I'll call the police.' He rises to his feet. 'I promise.'

'Good. And make it sooner rather than later. Before something terrible happens.'

As he walks away, Polly can't help wondering why he immediately thought Marsha could be The Stranger. Had Marsha been the guest he was threatening to evict?

25

POLLY

Janice turns from staring up at Xander's painting, *New York in Spring*, in reception, a large bottle of water under her arm. 'Gorgeous painting, isn't it?' she says, pinning on a smile for Polly, and if she notices she's soaked through, she doesn't mention it.

'It is, yes.'

Janice returns her eyes to the painting. 'I can't get over Xander's flamboyant signature – quite large and swirly, isn't it?'

Polly stares up at it – it's true that the *X* is especially ostentatious.

'I didn't see you at breakfast,' Janice says, still admiring the painting.

'I have no appetite this morning,' Polly says. *And I'm in no mood to talk right now.* She goes to walk away, but Janice steps out in front of her, blocking her path. 'Are you OK after last night? That woman was a strange fish, wasn't she?'

'I guess so.' Polly doesn't want to discuss Perdita, her mind too full of the hanging doll and her recent discussion with Xander.

'Are you going to tell the Caldwells she was on the grounds in the night? I mean, she's gone now; I guess there's little point.'

'I'm not sure what to do.' Polly feels shaken. Rain drips from her hair onto the marble tiles at her feet. She can't help thinking Perdita has nothing to do with the weird goings-on at Lakeside. 'I can't think straight right now,' she says, needing Janice to move out of her path.

Janice shrugs. 'Well, whatever you think is best, dear.' A beat. 'Are you coming to the pottery session at ten?'

Will there be one? Surely things can't go on as normal. Please get out of my way.

'I really don't know.' Polly pushes past Janice, makes her way towards the stairs. Pottery is the last thing on her mind.

But Janice is still on her tail, scurrying for the staircase right behind her like a shadow, when suddenly the front door is flung open.

'That's Lorcan, the chef,' Janice whispers, as he steps into the porch.

'Yes, yes I know.' She sounds blunt, irritated, but Janice doesn't seem to notice. Lorcan looks different this morning out of his chef whites, in jeans and a T-shirt, a glimpse of a tattoo on his upper arm. 'Good day to you both,' he says, pausing for a moment and looking at them with a wide smile, shoving his fingers into the pockets of his jeans as though giving his hands a rest. 'How are you two beautiful ladies this rainy morning?'

'Good,' Polly says, though she feels far from it. 'You?'

'I'm well, thanks for asking.'

'Doesn't seem to get any cooler though, does it?' Janice tugs at the neck of her jumper and blows down it. 'Must be hard for you in the kitchen.'

'Not too bad, to tell the truth,' he says. 'The air-con helps no end. Are you off to do some pottery?'

'Not quite yet,' Janice says looking at her watch.

'Well, I won't keep you.' He steps away, striding towards the kitchen, raising his hand in a friendly wave as he goes.

* * *

Polly finally escapes Janice at the top of the stairs, and once she's locked in her bedroom, the chest of drawers again in front of the door, she drops down onto the chair near the window. Closing her eyes, she tries to calm her frazzled nerves, attempts to make sense of everything, when her phone rings. It's Cathy Tipton.

'I know this is going to sound a bit random,' Cathy says down the phone when Polly answers, 'but you said if there was anything else I could recall about Esme, you would want to know.'

Polly pulls herself up straight, trying to get enthused. Despite the reason she came here to Lakeside slowly slipping out of view, replaced by the weird doll and thoughts of the stalker, she still wants to know what Cathy has to say. 'Yes, go on.'

'Well, I don't suppose it's relevant at all to the Framptons' disappearance, and I debated whether to call you, but the thing is…' She hesitates and Polly holds her breath. 'Lila—your mother… she was a twin.'

'A twin?' Her neck prickles.

'Yes. It was an awful winter that year, when Esme was expecting,' Cathy goes on, and Polly moves to the edge of the chair, her interest snared. 'The roads were treacherous, deep with snow. Perdita—'

'Perdita?'

'Yes. Perdita Lovell. Perdita Brook, she was back then – she didn't get married until after her boy was born. Anyway, she was Esme's midwife.'

Polly's head spins. *Perdita was my grandmother's midwife.*

'Well, she couldn't get to Esme quick enough the night she

went into labour,' Cathy continues. 'And Stephen had taken himself off. Abandoned her. Esme blamed them both for the loss of Lila's twin brother, Edward.'

'He died?' The words catch in Polly's throat. 'My mother's twin died?'

'Yes, I'm so sorry. I should have said that at the beginning.' She pauses for a moment as though waiting for Polly to speak. But Polly has no words, and the silence down the phone hangs for some time. 'Polly? Are you still there?'

'Yes.' But she didn't feel as though she was there, her mind trying to comprehend Cathy's words.

'And too right she should have blamed Stephen,' Cathy says. 'That man was evil. But Perdita wasn't at fault, she tried to get to Esme. She tried her best.'

'That's heartbreaking,' Polly whispers, the tragedy of so long ago seeping into her bones, tears pushing against her eyes. 'I can't imagine how Esme must have felt. That poor woman.' But it was more than that. This baby – the little scrap that didn't survive – would have been her uncle. Polly pushes the thought down. She didn't even know her birth mother. Her grandmother. Why is she letting this get to her? But she knows why. It's the sheer tragedy of it all. If Esme hadn't stayed with *that* man, her mother and uncle would be here now – maybe Esme would be here now.

'I'm not sure Esme fully got over the loss of her baby, and it goes a long way to explain her fierce protection of Lila,' Cathy goes on. 'She feared she would lose her too. Perhaps that's why she got pregnant again all those years later.'

Polly dashes a tear from her cheek. 'And I guess we'll never know what happened to that child. Whether Esme took her own life.'

'When Lila left,' Cathy continues after a few moments. 'Esme must have felt that tremendous feeling of loss all over again. Who knows where her mind was. I just wish she'd let me in. Let me help her, you know. Maybe I should have done more. I go over and over what I could have done – should have done.'

'But you said she cut herself off from you, from everyone.'

'She did. Yes. Locked herself in with that brute of a husband. As I said before, she wouldn't answer the door when I went up there. Ignored my calls.'

After a pause, Polly says, 'What was she like – in appearance, I mean?'

'Esme? Well, I tend to only see what's inside a person – looks are superficial to me – but I guess she was ordinary looking. Mousey-coloured hair that she mainly wore in a stubby ponytail. Plump, if you catch my drift – not fat.' There's another long pause. 'Yes, ordinary, you know. The kind of woman you couldn't pick out in a line-up.' She pauses, and Polly hears her take a deep breath. 'Listen, there's one more thing you should know.'

Polly braces herself. Nothing can shock her any more. 'Go ahead.'

'It was years after Esme lost Lila's twin, Edward.' A beat. 'Esme got it into her head that Perdita's son, Elijah, was her son – the baby she lost. She told me she thought Perdita had taken him the day he was born.'

'What? That can't be true.'

'It isn't. Perdita arrived too late to save the little boy, but because a week later Perdita gave birth to a son herself, Esme concocted a bizarre notion in her head that she had swapped the babies, if you catch my drift. That when Perdita arrived that dreadful winter's day, she already knew her baby would be still-born, and took Esme's child.'

'But there would be records at the hospital.'

'No, there were no records. Perdita gave birth at home, alone – which made Esme even more certain her crazy theory was true.

But I promise you it wasn't. And I told her she was being ridiculous. I said, "Esme, Elijah is a ringer for his father and has Perdita's eyes." The boy was Perdita's son, all right. Eventually, I convinced Esme she was wrong – and she seemed to accept it. And then she got pregnant again. And then, of course, Lila left.' She's silent for a moment. 'I'm not sure if this is the kind of thing you wanted to know, Polly, but you said if I could remember anything.'

'I'm grateful. Thanks. It's good to know as much as I can about my mother's past. I appreciate you calling. And there's something else I wanted to mention to you, if that's OK?'

'Of course, fire away.'

Polly rises, starts pacing. 'The thing is, it's about Perdita. She came to Lakeside last night.'

'She did? Why?'

'She said she comes here a lot, searching for Elijah.'

'Poor woman.'

'She said she always suspected Elijah came to Lakeside the day he disappeared, and I feel I should talk to her again. Do you know where she lives?'

'In a caravan up in Marplethorpe Wood. It's a bit of a wreck. Like her life. I think it's the not knowing what's happened to Elijah that's killing her. There's no closure, no end point.'

'Heartbreaking.'

'I've tried talking to her over the years. Suggested she see a doctor or a therapist, you know. But it's no good. I can't get through. She just walks about the village on her never-ending road, asking people over and over if they've seen Elijah.'

'How awful.'

'Tragic is what it is.' There's a crack in Cathy's voice. 'I remember her years ago when she was in her early twenties, when she fell for the bloke from the fair – can't recall his name off the top of my head. Even *I* noticed he was a looker, and she was happy, you know.' She sighs. 'Hard to believe it's the same person when I look at her now. That she was once so happy and confident, so vibrant. Life can chew you up and spit you out at times.'

'Was there a police investigation when Elijah left?'

'Of sorts, I suppose. They didn't do a lot. He'd travelled everywhere with the fair, and he'd been in trouble with the police over the years. He'd even told Perdita and several others that he'd had enough of fairground life, so the cops concluded he ran away. All a bit odd, as it was around the time the Framptons went missing, yet nobody seemed to connect the dots.'

'Do you think the disappearances are connected?'

'I don't know about that, but if I was the police, I would have at least looked into it. Perdita tried to connect it at one point, but nobody listened. You have to keep in mind she's desperate, and often knocks on doors in the village, asking residents if they are hiding Elijah inside their houses, that kind of thing.'

Polly looks over at Elijah's coat, wondering whether to mention it, but decides against it – for now at least. 'Well, thanks again for calling, Cathy,' she says. 'I appreciate it.'

'No worries,' Cathy says. 'I hope one day we'll find out what happened to Esme and Elijah.'

'Me too,' Polly says, and ends the call.

26

ESME

Twenty-Six Years Ago

'Where is she?' Stephen yells, gripping my shoulders so hard there will be bruises by morning – there always are.

'I don't know.' But I do. I saw my daughter disappear down the basement steps. She's using the tunnel to go into Marplethorpe.

Stephen has banned her from going into the village. He locks her in her room for hours, attempting to control her. But Lila has fight. The kind of fight I've never had. But what's the point of fighting when your opponent is far stronger? How will she ever win?

Sometimes I wonder if Lila has deliberately befriended the fairground crew in an act of rebellion against her father. She's not daft. She knows they're the kind of people he despises, and part of me thinks *good for her*. But then I worry for her too. I've been into Marplethorpe a few times to bring her home, fearing Stephen would beat her if he knew. She says she's going to run away from this place, and I wish I had the courage to go with her. Make her safe, somewhere new, miles from here. But I'm a coward. Fearing he will find us. And what would our life be like then?

'You *must* know!' he yells now, smashing his hand twice across my face. I've had a migraine most of the day, yet it seems to vanish as he beats me, replaced by a different kind of pain. 'Is she in Marplethorpe? If she's with those scummy losers, I'll kill her, and I'll kill them.' With that he shoves me into the cupboard under the stairs, bolts the door. 'I will find her, Esme! And God help her when I do!'

The front door slams. He's gone. He's gone to track her down. And I can't do anything. I'm helpless.

I sit in the corner of the claustrophobic cupboard, my arms cradling my knees, listening, crying. Trying to find some strength inside me to protect my daughter. But I'm ground down. Too afraid.

Hours later, the front door opens once more, and I hear the sound of Lila sobbing, and my heart breaks for her.

'Lila,' I cry from inside the cupboard. 'Lila, are you OK?' *Of course, she isn't.*

'Help me, Mum,' she cries. 'Please!'

I hear the slap of Stephen's hand across her young cheek, I hear him drag her upstairs and throw her into her room. I hear her stumble across the floorboards. I hear him lock her inside. 'I'm going to brick up that bloody tunnel,' he yells. 'You'll never go to Marplethorpe again.'

The stomp of his feet as he descends the stairs sends a chill down my spine. The sound of the bolt flying across the cupboard door makes my stomach lurch. I shuffle close to the wall, my heart thumping.

He opens the door, his large body looming.

He's a monster. I'm his prey.

27

POLLY

When Polly ends the call with Cathy, she spots a couple of new WhatsApp messages. One from her mum: a generic *How are you?* The other from Nicky demanding photographs of Lakeside.

Polly replies to her mum first, saying she's fine despite feeling far from it. The last thing she wants to do is worry her, especially as there's nothing her parents can do from France – and they have no idea she's here.

She then heads for the window, desperate to call Nicky. Mention the doll, the dress – *her* dress. But would it be fair to explain it all in a call or message? No, Polly will pack her bags today and head to Blackpool to see her friend, explain everything when she gets there.

Below her all the guests are out on the veranda, making the most of a spell of sunshine, a break from the spasmodic downpours, though the patio is strewn with deep puddles. A rainbow stretches across the sky.

Marsha and Janice are deep in conversation; Harry, at the same table, is reading from an iPad, mugs of half-drunk coffee in front of them. Ralph is brushing the water from the veranda with a broom.

It all looks so normal down there, so civilised. As though nothing bizarre is happening at the retreat at all.

Polly opens the window and looks out. Tara is leaning against the low wall that separates the retreat from her and Xander's apartment. She's in deep conversation with Beatrice – and Polly wonders if Tara's become the woman's new go-to. Though it's Tara who looks a bit upset. She's smoking. Closing her eyes as she takes in a lungful of nicotine, puffing it out through her nose like a dragon. Polly snaps a photo of them both, then slides her phone towards Ralph and takes another; finally, she takes a picture of the other guests and sends them all to Nicky.

> This is the motley crew I'm with.

She adds a kiss and a smiley face. Presses Send. Keeps up the pretence that all is OK, until she arrives in Blackpool later today.

She shoves her phone into her pocket, closes the window, and drops down onto the edge of the chair. Despite talking to Cathy and desperately wanting to know about Perdita and Elijah, Esme and Stephen, and her mother's life at Lakeside, she knows she has to leave. Now. If she stays, she'll be no better than those stupid girls in slasher movies who she yells at from the comfort of her armchair when they go outside into the darkness, notice an elongated shadow brandishing a knife, and step out towards it. People don't behave like that in real life, and she's not about to start a trend. She drags her fingers through her hair, presses down on her skull, attempting to ward off a looming headache.

She rises, picks up her case, slings it onto the bed, and as she unzips it a crash of thunder clatters across the sky and rain, intense as a waterfall, crashes against the window.

* * *

Tara

'Xander?' Tara calls.

Polly swings round. She's pulling her suitcase across reception, a carrier bag in her other hand, the hood of her green rain jacket pulled up, clearly about to tackle the ferocious weather.

'Oh, sorry,' Tara says, placing a hand to her mouth. 'I thought you were Xander for a minute there. You have the same jacket.'

'I'm leaving,' Polly says, dropping her key on the counter before heading for the front door and throwing it open. 'I'd have to be a loop short of a fruit if I stayed.'

Polly dashes from the building without another word, and Tara moves from behind the counter. 'Excuse me!' she calls after her. 'You need to pay for the loss of your key.' But the door has slammed, and there's no way she's heading out into the storm.

Tara makes her way towards the bay window, watches as Polly is swept across the drive by the wind, seeing her throwing her case into the car boot, the carrier bag onto the passenger seat, before clambering in. And as she pulls away, wipers thrashing the car windscreen, tyres splashing through puddles, driving towards the opening onto the road, Tara knows from looking at the forecast that she won't get far. That she'll be back.

28

TARA

Tara sits in the lounge of her apartment, sketching, refusing to give up on her own art despite Xander insisting her talent is waning, that her drawings are no more than mediocre.

'Are you ready?' Xander says, looking at his watch.

She puts down her pad and pencils on the table in front of her, rises and silently follows him to the art studio.

Beatrice, Marsha, Janice and Harry, all looking serious, wax-like, shoulders drooped as though they're not quite sure what they're doing here any more, stand at benches, pottery wheels beside them, aprons on.

Tara moves up behind her husband, leans in close to his ear and whispers, 'Polly's gone.'

He lets out a relieved sigh, nods and turns to the guests. 'Don't look so worried, it may never happen,' he says with a laugh.

'What if it already has?' Marsha says, narrowing her eyes.

Xander ignores her. 'On your benches you'll find all you need to create an ornamental vase,' he begins. 'Try to be imaginative, to create something that reflects your personality, if you can. Tara and I will take it in turns to be here throughout the process, offering you tips on throwing your vases, working the clay and hand building. Once you feel your creations are ready, they can go into the drying room.' He's speeding up, talking faster, as though he's desperate to get his words out. 'And once your work is completely dry, Tara will take them to the kiln, where over a thousand degrees of heat will fire your pieces.' He nods through the window towards the large brick-built kiln he insisted they had installed, costing a small fortune. 'This will harden the clay ready for decoration tomorrow,' he goes on, 'when we'll supply you with glazes.'

He pauses for a moment, eyes moving across the guests one by one. 'Any questions?'

The guests are silent.

'I think you've pretty much covered everything,' Tara says, forcing a smile.

'Great,' he says. 'You may begin. Tara will be here for the first hour.'

Tara watches him leave and looks over at Janice, who's rummaging through her bag, looking a little frantic. 'I've forgotten my glasses,' she says. 'I'll need to go back for them.'

Tara wants to scream. This woman is the stupidest woman she's ever met. 'They're on your head, Janice,' she says.

'Oh, how silly of me.' Janice removes them from her head and puts them on.

* * *

Polly

As she drives through deep puddles, barely able to see the road in front of her for torrential rain, Polly snatches a glance at the carrier bag on the passenger seat next to her, the musty smell of

Elijah's coat filling the car. She intended to take it into Marplethorpe on her way to Blackpool, attempt to find Perdita's caravan and give it to her, let her know where it was found. And she'd planned to go to the emporium too, all set to tell them how William had been at Lakeside, how he'd left in a taxi without taking his bag or leaving his key. But truth is, she's been on the road for almost an hour and she can't get anywhere near the village for flooding. In fact, she's barely made it a mile from Lakeside.

The storm intensifies, the rain torrential. Thunder and lightning ravage the sky. Wind tears through the towering trees flanking the narrow country road. She pulls into a layby. Leaning back against the headrest, she closes her eyes for a moment. She has no choice. She has to return to Lakeside.

After some moments she starts her car once more, does a three-point turn in the narrow road, praying another car doesn't race around the corner, and drives back the way she came.

Once there, she'll tell the other guests everything she's experienced at the art retreat. They all need to know, because whatever way you look at it, there's somebody dangerous at Lakeside. They may be targeting her, but surely nobody is safe.

* * *

Tara

'Am I wrong to still be concerned about William?' Marsha says as she turns her potter's wheel, and Tara cringes with the knowledge he wasn't who he said he was.

Beatrice blows escaped tendrils of red hair from her face. 'Do you think something bad has happened to him, Marsha?'

'Well, I don't know. I just—'

'I told you I saw him leave,' Janice says, rubbing her face, depositing lumps of clay on her cheeks. 'The man wasn't getting into the taxi against his will. He probably had some urgent business to attend to – family business perhaps – and intended to return but can't get back to Lakeside because of the floods. Please try not to worry.'

'Yes, you're right, Janice. I'm being foolish. It's not like me at all.'

Tara bites down on her lip. Should she tell them what Polly told her, that William isn't who he said he was? Will they fly into a panic if she tells them? Grab their belongings and leave?

And is Marsha right to worry about William? Maybe she should call the emporium. Check up on him. She really should, and she will. *She will.*

The windows rattle in the wind, as though someone's demanding entry. A crack of thunder so loud, like giants stomping across the roof, makes everyone freeze for a moment.

Marsha moves her eyes across the other guests and places her hand against her throat. 'I must admit, I'm considering leaving today. Something's amiss here. And what with William and Polly already gone... Perhaps it's time for us all to call it a day.'

Harry looks at Marsha, the hum of Janice's wheel whirring the only sound breaking the silence.

'What?' Marsha glares at him. 'I just feel we should leave before something terrible happens.' She turns back to her clay and mumbles, 'If it hasn't already.'

'If you must know, I think you are right,' says Harry. 'This place is strange. I've thought it from the moment I walked through the doors. Can't you all feel it?' He looks at Tara, who lowers her head, looks at her fingers. She can hardly say he's wrong. 'We need to—'

He's cut off by the sound of fast footsteps in the hallway, and suddenly Polly appears, still wearing her rain jacket.

'You're back!' Tara moves towards the door. 'I knew you would be. It's treacherous out there.'

'The roads are blocked,' Polly says. 'None of us will be leaving here for a while, and the thing is—' Her eyes drift to the paintings propped on the floor near the window. 'Oh my God!' she cries, racing towards them.

'The thing is what, Polly?' Beatrice says. 'Polly?'

But Polly's picking up her painting, and Tara is right behind her, her breath catching in her throat. Someone has defiled Polly's landscape again, painted a body floating face down in the lake – blonde-haired, wearing a blue dress with tiny white daisies on it.

'Is it meant to be a dead body?' Marsha says, appearing behind Polly and Tara. 'Who would add a floating cadaver to your painting? Gee, in all my years in the forces, I've never witnessed anything so crazy. And why target *your* painting, Polly?' She takes a breath as something registers in her mind. 'And this isn't the first time, is it?'

* * *

Polly

'It's meant to be me.' Polly's eyes fill with tears as Beatrice puts her arm around her. 'Who did this?' she cries, but she knows it can only be one person – the person who took her daisy-print dress from the apartment in Oxford. *The stalker.*

'I'll get Xander,' Tara says, rushing from the room, leaving a trail of floral perfume behind her.

'Damn right you will,' Marsha calls after her, resting a hand on Polly's arm. 'This is the second time this has happened – that's what the letter dragging you to the basement was about, isn't it?'

'What letter?' Janice asks, but Polly's silent, her eyes glued to the painting. She needs to tell everyone that she thinks the stalker may have followed her to Lakeside. But what if, like William, another of the guests is not who they say they are? What if one of them did this? Her heart thumps. Her legs feel weak. She falls to the floor. The fear is real.

Tara's back in two minutes with Xander, and everyone starts talking at once. There's panic in the art studio. Nobody feels safe.

'Calm down.' He flaps his hands as though scaring away flies and moves slowly forward to look at the picture, crouching down beside Polly.

'I thought the art studio was going to be locked after what happened last time,' Polly says, staring at him side on. 'You said we would need to get the key from reception. How did someone get in to do this?'

'It's my fault.' Tara raises her hand like a child in a schoolroom. 'The studio has been open since eight this morning, as I've been in and out setting things up for the pottery session. In fact, I left it open for a long stretch when I cleaned the bedrooms. Anyone could have come in here. I'm so sorry, Polly.'

'Let me get this straight,' Harry says. 'This has happened before, and you never said anything?'

'I think, in view of this incident, we need to postpone the completion of your vases,' Xander says.

'Too right, we do,' Marsha says. 'And I think we are all owed an explanation.'

'Yes, yes, of course. Could you all meet me in the lounge at two o'clock? There are things you need to be aware of going forward.'

'What things?' Marsha says, still eyeing the painting. 'Xander, please just tell us, stop being so cryptic.'

'It's obvious there are dangers here at Lakeside, Marsha,' Harry says. 'We need to pack our bags and leave this place. Now!'

'But I've just been out, the roads are hazardous,' Polly says, her voice small. 'Nobody can leave. We're stranded.'

'I'll inform you about everything at two o'clock,' Xander says. 'When we can decide what to do.' With that he turns and hurries for the door, raising his hand, halting any more conversation. 'In the meantime, I'll check the CCTV to see who did this to Polly's painting.'

'What do we need to be aware of?' Marsha races after him, her voice firm and loud. 'What things, Xander? Should we be worried?'

'Going forward, we all need to be on our guard.' A beat. 'Two o'clock, in the lounge. I'll explain everything then.' With that he strides from the room.

Tara follows close behind, turning just once, her eyes scanning the gathered guests. 'Please be careful, and keep your doors locked,' she says before disappearing.

29

POLLY

Polly races to her room, locks the door, and pushes the chest of drawers in front of it once more, deciding she won't step outside again until Xander's meeting at two o'clock. Why the hell he needed to wait until then is beyond her. She'd chased him out of the art studio, wanting him to make the meeting sooner, but he'd disappeared.

There's no denying she's scared. Scared of the stalker and unnerved that she's stranded at Lakeside – the house where her mother was born and raised by an evil man and a timid woman, the house where a baby died, the house where her grandparents may have taken their own lives. There's so much sadness and despair buried under all this luxury, deep within its walls. She can feel it.

Mouth dry, she pours a glass of water, knocks it back in one as she approaches the window. It looks so different out there than the day she arrived. Deep shades of grey fight for dominance in a heavy sky, fat raindrops cling to the window and a howling wind slams into the trees, bashing them, taking control.

Is the stalker really here? Could they have followed her, or overheard where she was heading on the cameras they installed? Do surveillance cameras even have microphones? Whoever it was had watched the friends before they even spotted the cameras, and Polly had talked freely about her pending trip to the Lake District. But why follow her here? It was Nicky they were obsessed with, not her.

She wonders now if the doll's dress really was like the one of hers that was taken from the apartment. She only saw it fleetingly, after all. Maybe this has nothing to do with her, and it's all about Xander and Tara opening the art retreat. The Stranger. Whoever they are they were sending notes long before Polly and the other guests arrived. And then there's William's disappearance, the fact he isn't William Doyle at all. So much is wrong here. *Someone wrote the notes to the Caldwells. Someone added dead bodies to my paintings. Someone hung the doll in the tree.* The events bounce around her head like balls in a pinball machine.

Eyes closed, Polly goes through the guests one by one like an amateur sleuth.

Marsha came over from the US. She mentioned her jetlag, that she'd only recently arrived at Heathrow. She couldn't have been sending the notes to the Caldwells if she wasn't in the UK.

What about Harry? Would his desire to protect the environment drive him to ruin Lakeside's reputation?

And then there's volatile Beatrice. Has she got some connection to the Caldwells nobody knows about?

And why was William Alderman masquerading as William Doyle? Does it have something to do with the lost Nazi memorabilia? Could he be hiding somewhere? Could he be The Stranger?

Janice enters Polly's head, appearing in a fluffy pink sweater in her mind's eye, ditzy, unthreatening. The ex-schoolteacher who paints dogs in jumpers and collects biros. In mystery novels it's always the person you least expect that turns out to be guilty.

'Argh!' Polly cries, springing open her eyes. Who does she think she is? Sherlock? This is not a mystery novel, this is real life, and the truth is Polly doesn't trust anyone here at the retreat.

* * *

Tara

'Where are you going?'

'For Christ's sake, Tara,' Xander says, stepping out onto the puddled patio and pulling up the hood of his green jacket. 'I just need some air. Some space to think.'

'But the weather is awful. And you said yourself we should be on our guard. Don't go out on your own, please.'

'I'm only going as far as the lake. Seriously, just leave me alone, for fuck's sake. Most of this is your fault, Tara. If you hadn't kept harping on about those stupid notes, that Polly woman wouldn't have heard and now be out to ruin us. I wouldn't be surprised if she's some kind of spy and painted those things on her own bloody pictures.'

Before Tara can reply, he's gone, shooting up an umbrella that she knows won't last five minutes in this wind, and striding down the path towards the lake.

Tara flops down on the sofa. He'd better be back for the meeting. And he needs to accept that, if he wants the retreat to have a future, he must deal with everything that's happened.

* * *

Tara feels as though she's been pacing the lounge for hours, though it's only been fifteen minutes since Xander took off. The man's surely too precious to get too wet. She goes to the window, squints through the raindrops, but he's nowhere in sight.

Grabbing her raincoat, she slips it on and steps outside. The wind's so strong, pushing her across the patio.

'Xander!' she cries, as the rain splatters her face, stinging her flesh. 'Xander, where are you?'

Suddenly, staggering across the grass, a figure appears. A man with a rucksack strapped to his back stumbles towards her. She doesn't run; she doesn't even move. This man with dark hair plastered to his skull is weak, pale, and there's something familiar about him. It's his eyes she recognises – a bright blue. She feels sure this handsome man holds no threat.

'I'm so sorry.' He sinks to his knees and bows his head, breathless. 'I didn't mean to trespass, it's just... I had to abandon my car back—'

'It's fine,' she says, reaching out her hand, all thoughts of Xander moved to the back of her mind. 'Let's get you inside and dried off. And then I'll let her know you're here.'

30

TARA

As the man gets unsteadily to his feet, leaning a hand against a patio table, Tara sees blood in his hair.

'Oh God,' she says, looping his free arm around her shoulder. She's tall and strong but still struggles to take his weight, her body buckling. 'What happened?'

'I fell,' he says, his voice fading as he closes his eyes. 'The ground...' His knees sag, and Tara almost drops him.

'Steady,' she says, hauling him into the apartment, where he slumps onto the sofa, blood and mud covering the fabric and cushions. *Xander's going to go ballistic.*

'I'll get you some water,' she says, dashing to the kitchen, her heart racing as she fills a glass, but when she returns, he's passed out. She kneels down next to him, placing the glass on the coffee table. With a shaking hand, she takes hold of his wrist. 'Thank God,' she mutters, feeling a pulse. She jumps to her feet, trying to calm her heartbeat. He's alive, but she needs to get help, and it's clear Xander isn't coming back any time soon.

She dashes through the door into reception. Nobody's about.

In fact the silence and semi-darkness, due to the grey day, feel almost creepy. She shudders, flicks on the light and dashes up the staircase, knocks on Beatrice's door.

'Beatrice, are you in there?' She waits, looking about her at the closed doors along the landing. Where is everybody? She hammers louder against the door. 'Beatrice, please, open up, it's Tara.'

Finally, the door opens. Beatrice, wrapped in a robe, a towel around her head, raises dark eyebrows. 'What is it? What's wrong? You look as though you've seen a ghost.'

'You need to come with me.'

'Why? What for?'

'It's your boyfriend.'

'My boyfriend?' Her eyes widen. 'What about him?'

'He's here.'

'*Here?*'

'Yes. At Lakeside. In my apartment. He's here to see you.'

'Oh my God. Why would he come here?'

'I've no idea, Beatrice.' Tara's getting agitated, her voice rising. 'You said he was protective—'

'That's right. He is, but it's a bit odd—'

'For God's sake, please just listen to me. He's hurt! You need to come. Now!'

Beatrice presses her fingertips into her temples, freezing for a moment before saying, 'I'll get dressed and meet you downstairs in five.'

* * *

Polly

At ten to two, Polly hurries down the stairs towards the lounge, a strange fear that someone could creep up behind her and push, that she could go tumbling to her death, making her glance over her shoulder. Nobody's there, and she sighs with relief as she reaches reception and hurries into the lounge.

Janice, Harry and Marsha are already there, sitting on separate sofas. There doesn't seem to be much chatting going on. In fact, the atmosphere is oppressive, as though they are all waiting on death row for the electric chair.

There's no sign of Xander, the handsome, rich man with a hint of an American accent, who had such high hopes for his precious art retreat. The man who invested so much time and money into this place, only to have it seemingly fall about his ears. Is that what all this was about? Did someone want him to fail? But that doesn't explain the doll in the tree or the additions to Polly's painting.

'Hey,' Polly says, approaching the group and sitting down on a free leather armchair.

Harry glances up from the hardback book he's reading and nods, and Marsha and Janice smile wanly.

Outside, trees contort in the wind and rain pours down from a dark sky. It's the kind of weather you'd expect in a haunted house movie set at Halloween, not at an art retreat in late summer.

Polly looks at each guest in turn, wondering how they will feel when everything is revealed. How they will all cope stranded here together until the floods disperse and they can leave.

'Rain has eased a wee bit,' Janice says, glancing out through the window beside her. It hasn't. It's worse, if anything. But nobody corrects her. Perhaps wanting to believe her.

Polly looks towards the double doors, no doubt that if Xander and Tara don't turn up soon, she'll tell the other guests everything she knows. She hopes Xander kept his promise and called the police, though there's no sign of them, no shriek of a siren. She needs to call them herself.

She shuffles her phone from her pocket and looks at the screen. Holds it in the air in the hope of getting some bars.

'No signal?' Harry asks, and Polly shakes her head.

'Me neither,' says Marsha, and Janice shakes her head. 'Must be the weather.'

Polly looks at her watch. 'It's gone two o'clock already.' But just as she's finding the courage to get to her feet and reveal everything, Tara appears. She hurries towards the gathered guests, her eyes wide.

'I don't know where Xander is,' she says, gripping hold of the back of a chair. 'He went out about an hour ago—'

'In this weather?' Janice says.

'Yes. He said he needed some air, but he hasn't returned. And there's something else. Beatrice's boyfriend has turned up.'

'At Lakeside?' Polly says.

'Yes, he just appeared out of nowhere. I recognised him from the picture on Beatrice's bedside table. She's with him now, in my apartment. He's hurt, had a fall.' She bursts into tears. 'This is too much,' she cries, covering her face with her hands. 'What are we going to do?'

Polly guides her to a chair, and as Tara sits, Marsha rises. 'We'll keep calm and carry on, as they say on all the best mugs. I did a medical course in the army.' She rubs her hands together and strides towards the door to reception. 'Show me the patient.'

'OK, yes.' Tara's voice is trembling as she gets to her feet. 'Thank you, Marsha.'

'And the rest of us will go out and look for Xander,' Polly says, jumping to her feet, wanting to be useful.

Janice and Harry get up too. 'I think I'll be much more use to Tara and Marsha,' Janice says, following them.

'Harry?' Polly says, pulling on her jacket.

'OK, yes, if I must.' Harry picks up his red rain jacket from the sofa beside him and shuffles into it.

Outside the ground is slippery, rain and surging mud from the previously neat borders coat the path leading to the artists' pods and lake.

'I wish I hadn't come here,' Polly says, attacking the awkward silence between her and Harry.

'Me too, it's been a total disaster.' His fringe is wet, drooping over one eye, and for the first time she wishes he would flick it back. 'And to be honest,' he goes on, 'after all the promises on the Caldwells' website about how much we'll learn at the retreat, I've barely learnt a thing. If it wasn't for his breakthrough painting, Xander Caldwell would be a nobody. And between you and me, I don't believe he even painted *New York in Spring*.'

She trots to keep up with him. 'And you're basing that on what?'

He shakes his head. 'Haven't you noticed how the style of his so-called masterpiece is so different to his later projects? He's never been able to paint another like it. Suspicious, if you ask me.'

'Maybe the pressure of coming up with something equally brilliant was too much for him.'

Harry finally pushes back his wet fringe and turns to look at Polly. 'So, why are you here?' he says. 'I sense you've more than art on your mind.' He stops, grips her arm, and with a playful playground chant says, 'I'll tell you my secrets, if you tell me yours.'

She shakes her arm free. 'I'm here to learn, is all.'

'Oh, come on, I saw you asking the pub landlord questions about the Framptons. You're hiding something.'

'OK, fine.' She knows she's given in far too quickly, but she knows, too, that everything will come out soon anyway.

The rain is torrential, yet neither of them moves. 'If you must know,' she says, 'the Framptons were my grandparents.'

'Christ on a bike! I didn't see that coming.' He smiles, continues to walk, splashing through puddles, and she follows. 'So, do you know what really happened to them?'

She shakes her head. 'No idea. I'm just here because I wanted to know who my birth mother was, and it turns out she was their daughter.'

'Is she alive? Your biological mother?'

Polly shakes her head. 'She died giving birth to me. There's a photo of her standing outside Lakeside House – my only link to who she was.'

'And you found out she was the Framptons' daughter since you've been here?'

'Yes.'

'And knowing that has helped you, how? Do you feel complete? Fulfilled?'

She doesn't reply. Truth is, it hasn't helped her at all, and Harry knows it. If anything, she was far happier not knowing.

'Now you tell me your secret,' she says.

'I haven't got one.'

'Traitor! You implied you did. You must have something—'

'I'm not that interesting, purely here for the art...' But the sound of Harry's voice fades to nothing in her ears as she looks out over the lake.

'Oh my God,' she whispers.

Near the centre of the dark water a body bobs, rain, like steel rods, pounding against it and the surrounding water, ripples spreading never to return.

'Life imitating art.' A chill slices through her. 'Like the doll in the tree.'

Harry turns and, peering at the body through trembling fingers, says, 'Oh God, please tell me that's not Xander.'

* * *

Tara

Tara dashes through the reception door and into her apartment, Marsha and Janice close behind.

She spins on the spot when she reaches the lounge. 'Where are they?' she cries. She dives into the bedroom, then the kitchen, the bathroom, the home cinema – and that's where she stops, eyes fixed on the giant screen where a film is playing. It's a grainy black and white film, but it's clear who it is. It's Polly in the shower, soap suds running off her hair, her body naked.

Suddenly, Marsha and Janice are behind her. 'What's this?' Marsha says. 'What the hell?'

'Who put it in the player?' Janice says.

'More like, who filmed it?' Marsha says. 'It doesn't look as though Polly's aware of the camera.' She turns to Tara. 'Did Xander film this? Is he secretly filming his guests?'

'No! God, no, of course not.' She moves closer to the screen. Her husband isn't perfect, but he would never do this. 'This wasn't taken at Lakeside.'

'Then where did it come from?' Janice covers her face with her hands and peers through her fingers. 'This man – Beatrice's boyfriend – we know nothing about him. Do you think—?'

'You think he brought a film of Polly in the shower with him?' Tara says. 'That makes no sense at all.'

They return to the lounge. 'Is that his rucksack?' Marsha asks, approaching the sofa and reaching for it.

'Yes.' Tara follows. 'But he was unconscious last time I saw him. He couldn't have got up and put a film in the DVD player.'

'You're sure about that?' Marsha sounds peeved. As though Tara shouldn't have left the man alone with Beatrice.

Tara looks about her. 'Oh God!' A piece of paper has been ripped from her sketchpad and rests on the low table by the sofa. The words are written in large black letters.

Now you are mine.

Janice spots it. 'What does it mean?'

'I shouldn't have left her alone with him,' Tara cries. But she'd gone with her caring instincts. And he seemed nice. She had no reason to think he was faking.

Marsha unzips his rucksack, drags out a reel of duct tape, some cable ties. 'What the hell?'

'Beatrice said he kept contacting her, didn't she?' Marsha says. 'She made excuses for him, insisting he wasn't possessive, but what if he was, what if—?'

'But what has any of this got to do with Polly?' Janice says. 'How did he film her in the shower? I mean, do any of us know how long Beatrice has known the man?'

'Her husband died a year ago, so I'm guessing not long,' Tara says.

'She would have been an easy target.' Janice shakes her head. 'Vulnerable.'

'But it doesn't make any sense, why wait until she's at the retreat?' Tara wonders if this man is responsible for everything that's been happening at Lakeside. If he's been there in the background all along. 'I swear he looked so pale, so helpless, how did he fake that? And the blood, it looked so real.'

'It may have been,' Marsha says. 'But was it his?'

'Hopefully Harry and Polly have found Xander by now. Let's get back to them,' Tara says, picking up the note. 'And we need to let Ralph and Lorcan know what's happened, wherever they are. We all need to stay together.'

'And call the police,' Marsha says. 'Now! Things have gotten completely out of hand. We could all be in danger.'

* * *

Polly

After a short, intense debate with Harry about their mutual lack of rowing skills, Polly had dived into the lake. Rain hammered her body, the wind on her side as she swam, trying to control her panic, knowing it must be Xander floating face down in the water.

Now she turns him over and lets out a gasp. She didn't much like the man, but the sight of him, life drained from his handsome face, is unbearable and she's engulfed in sadness.

With sheer determination she manages to get him across the lake, and with Harry's help she drags him onto the grass bank, where she drops to her knees. And, after checking for a pulse, Harry begins CPR.

'He's not responding,' Harry cries. 'Oh God, how did this happen?'

He continues CPR as Polly crouches beside him, shivering, rain pounding her back. And then she sees it. Blood seeping from the back of his head, mingling with the rain, giving it a pink hue. She presses her fingers against his neck, still unable to find a pulse. Tries his wrist. Nothing.

Suddenly Tara, Janice and Marsha appear, racing through the rain towards them.

'Oh God, what's happened?' Tara says, picking up speed. 'Is that Xander? Please say it isn't Xander!'

'He's gone, I'm so sorry,' Polly says, looking up at Tara, her voice breaking.

Letting out an agonising cry, Tara drops to her knees by Xander's side and sobs.

'It's this place,' Janice whispers, just loud enough for Polly to hear. 'This is all about this awful place. Nobody will ever be happy here. Ever.'

31

ESME

Twenty-Six Years Ago

'She's gone.' I spin round, the note clasped in my hand. A letter from my girl, my beautiful daughter. 'Lila's gone!'

Stephen doesn't look up. He's on the computer in the corner of the kitchen, back straight, shoulders wide, the trill sound of the modem dialling up grinding on my nerves. He's ignoring my distress, as he always does. *I hate him. He hates me.*

The printer behind him chugs out yet another price list, or perhaps photos of medals or Nazi uniform or something – something he'll spend his fortune on, frittering it away.

'Don't you care?' Inside I'm yelling, but my voice is a whisper. 'Don't you care that our daughter has left?'

He gets up, and panic pours into me as his nostrils flare. Bruises barely turn purple before they're freshened by his fist, and I'm afraid of him, there's no doubting that. If only I had more courage. If only I'd protected my Lila.

He goes to the printer. Picks up the slices of paper it's puked out. 'You want my honest answer?' he says, not looking my way, his back to me.

I shake my head. I don't want his cruel honesty. I already know it. He wanted a boy – never had time for a girl, unless he was yelling at her. I should have stopped him hitting her, mentally destroying her. *I hope you're OK, my baby girl.*

'She's a hussy, a tramp. Hanging out with that Elijah Lovell. We're better off without her.'

His words slam against me, rupturing my emotions. How could he be so cruel?

'Where could she have gone?' I say through my tears, as much to myself as to Stephen. 'I need to find her, bring her home.'

With his back still to me, he says, 'It's your fault she left, Esme. She's gone to get away from your constant swaddling.'

'No.' I won't let that idea into my head. I love my girl. 'She's gone because she's frightened of *you*,' I say. 'You terrified her.'

He turns, hooded eyes flashing with anger, his fists clenching, and I feel sick, dizzy, my emotions like a Catherine wheel spinning inside me, chaotic, sparks flying. My girl has gone. My precious girl has gone. I've lost another baby. 'I hate you!' I scream at Stephen. 'This is your doing! It's all your fault.'

I've never confronted him like this before – too afraid of the backlash – but at this moment in time I don't care. Let him do his worst.

He steps towards me with long strides. 'Bitch!' he yells as I reach for the frying pan on the hob, seizing the handle with shaking hands.

32

POLLY

The guests congregate in the lounge. Silent. Unable to grip and keep hold of what's happened to Xander, the handsome artist and entrepreneur. Drowned in Lake Kendalmere at his own luxury retreat.

Lorcan and Harry had carried Xander's body to the house. Laid him on the floor in a spare bedroom and covered him with a blanket, though not before they'd studied the wound on the back of his head. Had someone hit him? Or had he fallen?

Polly, accompanied by Marsha as she didn't want to be alone, had hurried to her room, desperate to shower off the musty, fishy stench of the lake from her skin, strip free of her soaking, sludgy clothes.

When Polly and Marsha return, Tara is still crying, her eyes red, her face blotchy. She's the only one seated in the vast room, elbows on her knees, head cradled in her hands. The others stand about, keeping their distance from each other. Could one of them be a killer?

Ralph appears in the doorway and races over to Tara, sits down beside her.

'Oh, God, you poor girl.' He takes hold of her hand and pats it affectionally. 'I'm so sorry.'

She lifts her head to look up at him, blots her face with a screwed-up tissue, but says nothing.

'What made him go out in this awful weather?' he asks her.

'He said he needed space.' Her voice is weak, tearful. She moves closer to Ralph, and he loops his arm around her shoulder, pulls her to him in a comforting fashion, like a father would a daughter.

Everyone is quiet for what feels like forever, before Marsha walks towards the French doors and stares out at the ravaging storm.

'It was my fault,' she says. 'I asked him to meet me at the pods before two. Told him I needed to talk.' She shakes her head. 'But I didn't go in the end, decided against it. It wasn't the right time.' She turns to meet Tara's narrowing gaze.

'Right time for what?' Tara asks.

'I didn't kill him, Tara. That's all you need to know, for now.'

'Who says anyone killed him?' Janice says, dropping into an armchair and tugging at the sleeves of her jumper. 'The ground is slippery, I almost went down on my bottom out there, and the wind is strong. He could have fallen, bumped his head and slipped into the water.'

'But Xander's a great swimmer.' Tara's voice cracks. '*Was* a great swimmer.'

'You can't swim if you're unconscious,' Janice says.

'Oh God, I can't believe what's happening.'

'Maybe whoever killed him thought he was someone else.' Harry's looking directly at Polly. 'Your painting was vandalised, and he had the same rain jacket as you.'

'You've got to be kidding.' Polly swallows hard. 'Why would anyone want to kill *me*?'

'You tell me, Polly... You're the one here under false pretences. That's what you told me earlier, wasn't it?'

All eyes turn to Polly, and she squirms under their gaze. She's angry at Harry. She'd wanted to tell everyone in her own time.

'Wait a minute,' she says, raising a hand, but there's no strength in her words. She looks at each of the guests in turn. Was someone aware she was here to dig up her past? Is someone afraid of what she might discover? Is this what it's all about?

'Before you say anything, Polly,' Marsha says. 'There's something you all need to know.' She explains how Beatrice's boyfriend turned up, how Beatrice and the boyfriend have gone missing. She places the note they found on the table along with the cable ties and duct tape they'd found in his rucksack.

'Then what are we doing sitting around here?' Polly says. 'We need to find her, for Christ's sake!'

'Hang on,' Marsha says, staring at Polly. 'There's something else. I think Harry's right – this has something to do with you. There was a film playing in the small cinema in Tara and Xander's apartment. It was of you taking a shower, Polly.'

Polly covers her mouth, tears stinging her eyes. Did everything go back to the stalker? Someone spoiled her painting, hung a doll in the tree, and someone had been in the basement that day. 'Oh God,' is all she can muster.

She picks up the note.

Now you are mine.

It's the same writing that was on the note luring her down to the basement.

Marsha gets to her feet. 'We need to find Beatrice.' Her voice is firm. 'Be proactive. Let's split up, search the house and grounds.'

Polly can't move, frozen in fear, the note clasped in her hands. The voices of the other guests echoing around her.

'We need to call the police,' Marsha says. 'Has anyone got a signal on their phone?'

Everyone pulls out their phones and, one by one, shake their heads.

'What about a landline?' Marsha asks. 'Tara?'

'I'll go.' Ralph rises. Races into the reception area. He's back within moments, shaking his head, his face serious. 'The line's been cut.'

Everyone starts talking at once.

'Silence!' Marsha yells. 'If my military training taught me one thing, it's that organisation is key. Wherever he's taken Beatrice, it can't be far. As Polly told us, the roads are blocked. Have you got a flashlight, Tara?'

Polly's mind swims. She's not convinced Beatrice's abduction has anything to do with the stalker who made her life hell in Oxford. Someone else is here tormenting her. But for now, she must support the others, help to find Beatrice.

Tara rummages weakly in the drawer of a unit, hands Marsha a torch.

'Great,' Marsha says, flicking it off and on again. 'Janice and Lorcan, you take the house and basement. Tara, are you up to going with them?'

'I... I don't think so,' Tara says. 'What with Xander... and my head's throbbing.' She buries her face in Ralph's shoulder. 'The keys to every room are behind the counter if you need them,' she manages before she begins to cry once more.

'OK, fine, but you shouldn't be here alone. And we'll need Ralph as one of the search party, since he knows the place. Harry, you stay with Tara.'

'But what if he killed Xander?' Ralph says.

'I can assure you I did not,' Harry says. 'And who's to say it wasn't you?'

Marsha thrusts a hand on her hip. 'Christ's sake, you British are so...' She stops, as though realising she's in the minority. 'OK. Janice and Lorcan, you search the house and basement. Ralph, Polly and I will go outside and search the grounds.' She gives a sweep of their faces, her own serious. 'A man's dead and a young woman is missing, not to mention William taking off and all the other weird goings-on here at Lakeside. Let's take control before anything else happens. Tara and Harry, you can either help Janice and Lorcan search the premises, or stay here, it's up to you.' And with that she grabs her rain jacket, flicks on the torch and hurries out through the French doors. Polly, finding strength from somewhere, and Ralph follow close behind.

33

ESME

Twenty-Six Years Ago

It's been almost a week since Lila's note and since Stephen squeezed my wrist so hard that the frying pan fell from my grip, hitting the floor with a clatter. I can still see the bruises. He laughed loud and harsh that day, throwing his head back, his temper shifting to amusement.

'You're pathetic, woman,' he said, pushing past me so I slammed against the worktop.

Now I hear his car start, the noise of tyres on cobbles, glad he's going out, not caring where to.

My wrist still hurts, though the once purple bruises are turning green. I was lucky, I suppose – he's capable of so much worse. I race upstairs, take my romance novel from beneath the mattress and lie down, stroking my stomach. The baby has gone now.

I read a couple of chapters, rise, and make my way towards the window. Someone is heading for the house, dipping in and out of view as they weave their way through the trees. My stomach churns as I move to the side of the window, making my body small so I can't be seen.

They're not the first person to come snooping since Lila left. I've hidden from Cathy a couple of times, ignored her calls and messages. I feel bad about that. She's been a good friend through the years, but I can't face her. I can't face anyone any more.

When I lost Edward, Lila's twin, the pain that followed was immeasurable. It was only tiny Lila who kept me going, gave me something to live for. The love I felt for my child, the way her eyes followed me round the room as a baby, that first smile just for me, kept me afloat when Stephen was trying to drown me.

But now my girl has gone, and swirling black clouds hover above me, getting lower and lower, waiting to consume me. I don't blame Lila for leaving. I would get away from here, too, if I had the strength.

The figure gets closer: a handsome, dark-haired boy in his teens. I know who it is. It's Perdita's lad, Elijah. The fair must be in Marplethorpe. I smile. To think I once thought the boy was mine. That Perdita had taken him from me. Cathy convinced me I was wrong – that he belonged to Perdita.

As he approaches through the trees, I see he's wearing a long army style coat over skinny jeans. He's confident, shoulders back, a swagger in his step. No wonder my Lila has a crush on him. She says it's love, but she's far too young to be in love. Far too young to be making love.

What do you want, Elijah?

He knocks – a soft, apprehensive knock. I move, watch him through thick nets as he steps from foot to foot, darting looks about him – searching. Searching for Lila? *She's gone, Elijah. She's not coming back.*

I creep down the stairs and edge towards the door. 'What do

you want?' I call through the door, my voice high, croaky from not talking very much, well, apart from to myself, over and over.

'Mrs Frampton?' he calls, a slight hesitation in his voice. 'I'm looking for Lila. I haven't seen her in a while. Is she OK?'

I'm surprised by his courage. He knows I don't approve of my daughter sneaking into Marplethorpe when the fair is in the village, and he must know that Stephen will beat him if he sees him here. He doesn't know the boy got her pregnant. If he did, he would skin him alive.

He knocks on the door again. 'Please, Mrs Frampton.'

I guess it wouldn't hurt to open up the door, I tell myself. Talk to the boy. *Would it?* Stephen isn't here. And it would be comforting to have a young presence in the house.

I place my hand on the doorknob, twist it and gingerly open the door.

'Elijah,' I say, seeing him there. Noticing the shape of a cigarette packet in his pocket, a smiley face on his coat sleeve.

Pain twists my stomach. It isn't real. It's simply the memory of the twins' birth. It's always there, waiting. What would my boy look like now, had he lived?

It's not fair. It's not fair. It's not fair, a voice inside my head I can't seem to control tells me. But it speaks the truth. It's not fair. It's not fair that Perdita has her son when she didn't save mine. And now my girl has gone too, and I'm left with empty arms, heartbroken.

'Come in, son.' I step back for the boy to enter. He smells of fairgrounds: toffee apples, candyfloss, dodgem cars. 'Take your coat off. Would you like some cake? You look like you need building up a bit.'

34

POLLY

'Are you sure this is a good idea?' Polly says, racing to catch Marsha up, rain battering her face.

'Damn right it is.' Marsha's swinging her arms, splashing boots through puddles as she hurries onwards, Ralph close behind. 'Every second counts.'

Polly stops, takes a deep breath. And Ralph throws her a sympathetic smile. 'She's pretty scary, isn't she?' he says. 'It's her training, I think. She's in full army mode right now.'

'She really is.' Polly knows she needs to woman up and help find Beatrice and her boyfriend. And she knows, too, she shouldn't be alone. She glances back at the building, the amber lights of the lounge brightening the patio. Truth is, if she was to run back to her room, lock the door and barricade herself in, would she be any safer than she is out here with Ralph and Marsha?

'Are you coming?' Ralph says, glancing back as he heads onwards. 'Safety in numbers, aye?'

She runs to catch up, skidding on the slick path and almost toppling.

'Woah!' Ralph catches her arm. 'Steady there.'

By the time the three of them reach the jetty, Marsha brandishing the torch into the dismal dark day, they are soaked through.

'This is ridiculous,' Polly says, fed up with being wet. 'I wouldn't be able to see anyone through this rain if they jumped out in front of me brandishing a knife.' The thought turns her stomach.

'Then who's that?' Marsha holds her torch high, pointing it towards the other side of the lake, where a figure sits on the ground. Whoever it is, they're hard to make out, but she's right, there's someone there.

Polly's mind races. Could it be Beatrice? Her boyfriend? The stalker? She thinks of Perdita Lovell trespassing the other night—

'We need to get over there,' Marsha says, as the figure gets to their feet and disappears into the trees. 'Ralph, have you got the keys to the motorboat?'

Ralph shakes his head. 'Sorry, didn't think.'

'Then we need to use the rowing boat.'

'I'm still not over my swim from earlier,' Polly says, shivering at the memory, rain trickling down her face.

Ralph and Marsha head down the jetty towards the boat, Marsha glancing back. 'You're better off coming with us, Polly.'

The whole area has an eerie feel – she certainly doesn't want to be left alone. 'Fine,' she says, catching them up as they clamber into the rowing boat, Marsha taking the oars.

Despite the choppy water, the speed with which they get across the lake – the way Marsha cuts the oars through the water like knives through butter – tells Polly that the woman has strength. And it's not just physical; she is determined, and Polly wonders for the first time why she wanted to meet Xander earlier. Was she the person he was arguing with, threatening with eviction? Did she kill him?

Once they reach the other side, Ralph moors the boat, and they scramble out and stand on the boggy bank in silence. Apart from the rustle of wildlife and the rain hammering against the water, it's chillingly quiet.

'Where do we start looking?' Polly edges towards the trees and hedgerows, stepping over deep muddy puddles.

'Hang on,' Ralph calls, and Polly stops. 'We don't know who this person is. What they're capable of. Let's keep together.'

There's a rustle, and bushes move. Someone is heading their way, getting closer. Ralph grabs Polly's arm and pulls her to him.

'Christ!' he cries, as a figure appears through the greenery. He steps back, taking Polly with him. 'Where the fu—?'

'Why not put the gun down?' Marsha says to the person standing in front of them, her breath raspy. 'We mean you no harm.'

Polly's seen the pistol before. It was the one in the old photograph in William's room. Once part of Stephen Frampton's Nazi memorabilia. The gun that Marsha said is worth millions.

35

ELIJAH

Twenty-Six Years Ago

Esme Frampton is wearing a black loose-fitting dress and flip-flap furry slippers – her hair is a sort of mousey grey, cut straight to her earlobes. She seems kind, but she's also a total weirdo. She's plied me with a large slice of carrot cake and a glass of orange squash, and as we sit in the lounge at Lakeside House, like I'm a little kid and she's my mum or aunt or teacher or whatever, she tells me over and over what a truly lovely boy I am. That I remind her of her son. But I know her son died at birth – that's what Lila told me – so how can I remind her of him? Yeah, she's pretty crackers if you ask me, and I should probably get out of here.

I put the chipped plate down on a scratched antique-looking side table. The room is dark and dingy, the wallpaper peeling in places, damp in others. There's a bad smell I can't make out, a bit like when Mum cooks broccoli in the caravan and doesn't open the window.

'Your tattoo is impressive,' Esme says, and I run my hand across the escaping carousel horse painted on my arm. I upset my dad, having it done. He's got a Ferris wheel on his upper arm – so proud of the fair – and wanted me to have something similar. But I can't help that I've lost interest, that I want to live my own life. My future is with Lila now, and the tattoo was my way of saying I want out.

'Will Lila be long?' I ask, sensing something is wrong. The house is so quiet.

'Not long now.' She rises, touches my arm. 'Dear me, there's not an ounce of fat on you,' she says. 'More cake?'

I shake my head, feeling as though I'm stranded in a fairy tale, and if I don't keep my wits about me, she'll stuff me in the oven. I need to go home and say sorry to Mum. I told her I was leaving the fair, but I didn't mean to make her cry – she's the best. But Lila's pregnant with my baby. I love her, want to make a go of it, my parents have to understand that. And I want to paint too. Mum has always liked my drawings but says there's no money in it – that's why Dad gave up. And if I want to do my best by Lila, I need to earn money. I haven't told her Lila's pregnant, not yet. Lila is desperate that her father doesn't find out.

'Where's Lila?' I ask, getting to my feet and moving towards the window.

'I told you. She won't be long.'

I'm not too great at reading people, but the feeling that Esme is a tiny bit crazy is growing in strength. Lila's told me all about her home life. The way her father bullies her mum, hits her. And I've experienced Stephen Frampton first hand. If I'm honest, the man scares the crap out of me. He came to the fairground once. OK, so I'm not totally innocent. I've got into trouble in my time. Pinched things from those who could afford it – like Robin Hood, though me and me mum are like the poor. I took a Jag out once for a joyride. I've been cautioned a few times. The time I met Stephen I was with some mates. We'd taken a car from the pub's car park –

only took it out for a spin, no more than that, wasn't going to smash it up nor nothing. When we brought it back – we always brought the cars back, we're not bad lads – Stephen saw us. It was his friend's car, Giles something-or-other. He was fecking furious, swearing, waving his fists. We ran, me mates and me, but he'd clocked me, looked right into my eyes. Later he came up to the fair looking for me. Gave me a right beating. *'If I ever catch you doing something like this again,'* he said. *'I'll kill you.'* Mum lunged at him with clenched fists, but the fecker threw her to the floor. *'You've been warned, Elijah Lovell.'*

I vowed never to go near him again, but here I am, in love with his daughter, who's carrying my baby, sitting having carrot cake with his wife. *What the fuck am I thinking?*

'Where's Mr Frampton?' I ask, turning from the window.

'Out. He won't be back for a while.'

I'm an idiot. I shouldn't be here. I need to leave now. I was just so desperate to speak to Lila, to make plans. I didn't think.

I go to step towards the door, but Esme grips my wrist with clammy fingers, and I notice bruises on her arms.

'You should get away from him,' I say, shaking my arm free.

I notice an old-fashioned gun on a dusty sideboard. Would Esme hold me against my will? Draw the gun on me? Or maybe she poisoned the cake. No, I'm being ridiculous. Plus, I'm not sure the pistol even works. It looks about a hundred years old.

'You'll stay for dinner, won't you?' she says.

'I really should go, Mrs Frampton. Mum will be worried.'

'Don't be silly. Perdita owes me this, sweetheart. It was her fault I lost Lila's twin.' She claps twice, and I startle. 'I've made some steak and mushroom pies. They'll be very tasty with a bit of mash and thick gravy.' She turns and steps towards the door, glancing back once to where I'm standing, unable to move. 'I'll go and pop them in the oven,' she adds. 'Do you like carrots?'

I shake my head, watching her leave before turning back to face the window. I dash across the room, try to open it, but it's painted closed. I look towards the door. I'm being stupid – I can just walk out, this woman isn't holding me against my will, and even if she was, she would be no match for me. I race into the hallway.

'Where do you think you're going?' It's Esme, appearing from the kitchen, a knife in her hand, looking close to tears. 'I'm making your dinner.'

'I really should go home, Mrs Frampton.'

'Yes,' she says, as if she's just woken up. 'Your mum will be worried. I'm not sure what I was thinking. Go, darling boy.'

I rush past her towards the front door, glancing back. 'Tell Lila I called round.'

She fumbles in her pocket, brings out an envelope. 'She's gone, Elijah, but I found this addressed to you. I haven't opened it. It might tell you where she is.'

'Thank you, Mrs Frampton,' I say, taking it from her.

'It was nice talking to you, Elijah. Your mum must be so proud.' Esme turns the handle and pushes the door open, lifts down my coat from the hook, holds it to her, sniffs the fabric.

It's then that I see a car pull up, and two men get out. A surge of fear rises inside of me. I know that even if I bolted, they would catch me. My visit to Lakeside House is far from over.

'What the hell are you doing here?' Stephen strides towards me, seizes the scruff of my T-shirt. 'We don't like your sort around here do we, Giles?'

Both men are heavily built, wearing dark grey suits. They're swaying slightly, a whiff of alcohol on their breath.

'No, we don't.' Giles moves forward and slaps me on the cheek once, twice, three times. It stings my flesh, but I clench my jaw, determined he won't see me cry. 'We don't like your sort at all.'

Stephen snatches the letter from my tight fist. 'What have we got here, then?' he says, ripping open the envelope, his eyes stretching wide as he reads. He looks at me then, his face rigid, his eyes dark as death itself.

'You got Lila pregnant?' he says, and though his voice is no more than a whisper, I hear the flames igniting under them. And I know that to walk away from Lakeside House alive now will be a miracle.

36

TARA

Harry stands by the French doors, arms folded. He's been there, his back to Tara curled up on the sofa, since everyone left. He hasn't spoken. Not a single word. Not that Tara wants him to. In fact, she is so deep in her own thoughts, she's not sure she would hear him anyway. Her head is pounding, and she feels nauseous. Xander is dead. Her husband is dead. And the painful blend of gut-wrenching grief and overwhelming relief is killing her. She never wished him dead. Of course she didn't. But she prayed so many times that she could be free of him. And now she is. But the torment is so strong, wrapping itself around her, squeezing the life from her. She lets out a sob, and Harry turns, narrows his eyes. There's something about him – the way he's standing so rigid – that makes him seem familiar; she'd thought it when she first saw him. And now she's sure she knows him from somewhere. A shard of fear stabs into her. There's a killer at Lakeside. Could it be Harry? Could Beatrice's abduction have nothing to do with Xander's death? She looks towards the double doors into reception. Would Janice and Lorcan hear her from upstairs if she screamed?

'You OK?' Harry says, though he doesn't move.

She wipes away a stray tear. 'What do you think?' She regrets the snap in her voice. She needs a cigarette, and the thought that Xander wouldn't be here to stop her hits her afresh. 'Sorry, I'm just not coping too well.'

'Not surprising really.' He glances back towards the window. Lightning flashes across the sky. 'I know what you are going through. It was much the same when my father died. The combination of relief and grief can be toxic.'

'Christ, that's an awful thing to say. I loved Xander. We were happy.'

'But I've watched you, Tara. You feared him, just as I feared my father.'

Tara doesn't reply, despite Harry being right. She doesn't know this man, and he has no right to intrude on her grief. She touches her throat self-consciously. Why couldn't Ralph have stayed with her instead of Harry? He's always been so kind to her – the father she never had. He knew what Xander was like, saw it for himself. Once, he caught Xander with his hand around Tara's throat, pressing her hard up against the wall. Xander released her when he saw Ralph. But Ralph looked angry that day, his hands balled into fists. Xander somehow bluffed his way out of it. But when he was gone Ralph stared into her eyes and said, 'Do you want me to kill him for you?' A joke perhaps. Though she was never quite sure.

'There's something you should know,' Harry says, turning and walking towards her and dropping into an armchair, crossing his long legs. 'It's about Polly.'

'Polly? What about her?'

He waggles his leg up and down, flicks back his fringe and opens his mouth to speak just as voices drift through from reception. 'Maybe I should wait for Janice and Lorcan. Everyone needs to know what she told me. It could be important.'

Janice appears, followed by Lorcan. 'There's nobody about,' Janice says. 'Not inside the property anyway.'

'Are you sure?' Tara's voice is a wobble. 'They could be hiding—'

'Pretty sure we covered everywhere.' Lorcan sits down next to Tara on the sofa. 'Though we couldn't get into Polly's room. There wasn't a key behind the counter.'

'No,' Tara says. 'Sorry, I forgot, I gave her the spare as she lost hers. There's another set in my apartment. Shall I go and get them?' She rises to her feet, blood rushing to her head, feeling dizzy.

'Good idea.' Harry pushes his glasses up the bridge of his nose. 'But not on your own. I'll come with you.' He pauses for a moment. 'Has anyone checked out the basement?'

Janice shakes her head. 'Not yet.'

'Well, we need to—'

'Let's wait for Ralph and co to return, shall we?' Lorcan says. 'Then a few of us can go down the basement, and the rest can find the key to Polly's room. There's someone here who is as mad as a box of frogs, a killer perhaps, and we need to stay together as much as possible.'

'But we're wasting precious time,' Janice says. 'Beatrice could be in danger.'

A noise outside. 'Christ! Was that a gunshot?' Tara cries, jumping to her feet.

They look towards the window.

'Thunder, that's all,' Harry says. 'Calm down, Tara. Deep breaths.'

Lorcan rises to his feet. 'OK, let's the four of us go down to the basement to check it out, then we'll collect the keys and check Polly's room.'

'No,' Harry says. 'You three go, I'll stay here and wait for the others.'

'Alone?' Janice asks, her forehead crinkling.

'Alone.' He flicks back his fringe. 'Now go, for Christ's sake.'

* * *

Polly

'What's this all about, William?' Marsha places her palms together as though praying. She's already tried being assertive, which just made the man angry, to the point where he'd fired a shot up towards the deep grey sky, clipping a tree, clearly trying to prove he wasn't afraid to use the gun, that he wasn't bluffing. 'Please, you don't have to do this,' she continues.

Polly's vision is impaired by zigzag visuals, her head throbs: a migraine that's quickly growing in strength. She feels utterly useless. A gun is pointed their way, and yet this throbbing head is taking control of her body.

William's arm is shaking, the gun hovering from Marsha to Ralph as Polly stands a few steps behind them, blood coursing through her veins at an alarming rate.

'Where have you been, mate?' Ralph asks, taking on a fake friendly tone. 'You've been gone for days. We were worried.'

'Not worried enough, it seems. Nobody tried to find me. And I have one of you to blame for all of this. One of you idiots locked me in a ruddy World War II bunker.' He's twitchy, his knees sagging as though he's all out of energy, his eyes darting about him like a crazy man.

'Are you OK?' Marsha says, her voice sympathetic, though her fists are tight balls, her jaw clenched. She couldn't care less if he's OK.

'Take me to the other side of the lake. I need to get back to Marplethorpe,' William says, his voice raspy. 'In that.' He cocks his bearded chin towards the moored rowing boat. 'Now move.' He waves the gun, and they all turn and head towards the lake, William staggering behind, the pistol pointed at their backs.

William sits at the rear of the boat, slumped to one side. Marsha and Polly sit opposite each other, Polly's elbows on her knees, her head in her hands, as Ralph rows.

'Why didn't you tell anyone you're really William Alderman?' Polly says, and his bloodshot eyes widen. Marsha and Ralph look at Polly, confusion in their eyes.

'Alderman?' Marsha says.

'Yes, this is William Alderman. He owns the company who cleared out Lakeside House.' She looks straight at the man. 'You came here because you found a photo of the Luger pistol amongst the Framptons' belongings, am I right?'

William doesn't reply.

'Who locked you in the bunker?' Marsha asks.

William shakes his head. His twitching lips are dry and cracked, his skin grey. 'I've no idea, and to be honest it doesn't matter now. But I'll tell you one thing, whoever it was, they were moving bones.'

'Bones?' Polly can barely see through the blurs and zigzags dancing across her eyes, but she recalls the bone she found by the lake – the bone Xander slung into the water – and the sighting of someone with a wheelbarrow, throwing something in the lake.

'Yes. I was down there, looking for...' He waves the pistol. 'Well... this. At first, I couldn't find it, but I came across two skeletons. Suspect it's the remains of Esme and Stephen Frampton.'

There's a collective gasp, and Polly trembles at the thought of her grandparents taking their own lives in the bunker, their bodies left to rot for years.

'There's something else,' William says. 'Both skeletons have bullet holes. One has two in the rib cage, the other one in the skull.'

'They were *murdered*?'

'Looks like it.'

'But who would want them dead? Why?' Polly pushes her fingertips into her temples.

'Well, let me see,' William says, rubbing his chin. 'Just about everyone hated Stephen. Before my father took off with his fancy woman, he hung out with the man a lot, so, although I never met the Framptons, I knew all about them. Stephen was a nasty bit of work, and my father wasn't any better.'

'So, you found the pistol eventually,' Marsha says. 'Down in the bunker.'

'As I say, I didn't find it the first time I looked, but I came back later for a more thorough look, and one of the skeletons had gone. It was as I was searching down there that I heard someone coming down the steps. They must have heard me too, because they bolted, shut the hatch with me inside.'

'But you got out?'

'Whoever it was came back, threw a bottle of water down – obviously they didn't want me to die. But they made the mistake of not quite latching the hatch.'

They reach the jetty, and Ralph jumps out and ties the boat.

'Listen,' William says, once they're back on dry land, stroking a hand across his bald head. 'I'm not a killer. Yes, I was an arse in my teens, and I'm not ashamed to say I like money. I came here to find the gun, is all, and I now need to get out of here. So, I'm going to take off. But if any of you follow, I promise you, I *will* use this.'

'You won't get far,' Marsha says. 'Everywhere is flooded. And we know who you are. You're being a fool.' But before she can say another word, he takes off, disappearing into the trees.

The basement gives Tara chills. In fact, in the eighteen months she's been at Lakeside, she's rarely ventured down here. Put off when she overheard a couple of women discussing Lakeside's renovations in the bakery in Marplethorpe. *'Wouldn't be surprised if they discover the Framptons buried in the basement,'* one said. *'And if Stephen Frampton's ghost haunts the place, God help the new residents.'*

'Apparently, there are tunnels leading all the way to Marplethorpe,' said another. *'Anyone could be lurking down there.'*

Tara takes a deep breath and follows Lorcan and Janice down the steps, Lorcan flicking a light switch as he goes. A weak bulb below struggles to life, flickering and buzzing, then fading to a dim amber glow.

'Hello?' Lorcan calls as they reach the bottom, as though whoever's been prowling Lakeside will respond. 'Hello?'

'Do we have to do this?' Tara says. 'I can't imagine Beatrice being dragged down here. It's much more likely they've left the premises.'

'But none of the cars have gone. I checked. They have to be

here somewhere,' Lorcan says. 'We have to check everywhere. We'd never forgive ourselves if she's down here.'

The three of them are silent for a moment, Tara turning on the spot, taking in the racks of wine bottles, the pools of water on the concrete floor, some areas deep, where rain has got in. It smells damp and mouldy down here.

They search every corner, Janice darting towards the wine racks, her sudden speed making Tara jump and clutch her chest. She peers behind them. 'There's nobody here,' she says. 'We should probably get back to Harry. We shouldn't have left him alone.'

'Sounds good to me.' Tara wades through the puddles, water seeping through the fabric of her trainers as she heads towards the steps. She begins climbing, not looking back.

'Shouldn't we check the tunnels?' Lorcan says. 'Wasn't that the plan? Why we came down here? I mean it has to be said, I don't fancy it much myself, but if he's got Beatrice trapped down here...'

Tara pauses halfway up the steps and sighs. She's liked Lorcan from the moment he arrived a few weeks back for an interview – always a sucker for an Irish accent. And he's been friendly, charming, but who's to say he isn't somehow involved in Beatrice's disappearance? He could be in cahoots with her boyfriend, or maybe he has another agenda. *Did he kill Xander? Send the letters?* She hates that she's so paranoid, so quick to see the villain in people, but then it's hardly surprising after everything that's happened.

'It was Harry's choice to stay, if that's what you're worried about,' Lorcan goes on. 'He isn't our priority right now.'

Tara sighs, climbs back down the steps. 'Fine.'

Lorcan leads the way. There are two directions they can take, and Lorcan, without consulting the women, takes the left one, his phone torch lighting the tunnel as they wade through more puddles.

It isn't long before they come to a stop. The route is bricked up.

'Let's turn back,' says Janice. She seems agitated, keeps tugging at the sleeves of her jumper. 'To be honest, I've come over a bit odd.' She rests her hand against the wall, lowers her forehead into her free hand. 'I've never been great with closed-in spaces – and I'm not as young as I was. In fact, I'm not sure what help I'd be if we came across...'

Before she's finished speaking, Lorcan begins retracing their footsteps, and the women look at each other before following. They finally reach the entrance to the other tunnel.

'I'm afraid I'm going to have to get out of here.' Janice's voice is tense. 'As I say, I've come over most peculiar.' Before Lorcan or Tara can respond, she dashes towards the steps. 'I'll send Harry down, shall I?' she calls.

'Should we go after her?' Tara asks Lorcan.

'No. We need to check the other tunnel, I really don't want to do it alone.'

She waits a moment, waving her phone torch across the damp walls, catching sight of a spider scurrying across a web. Lorcan heads into the tunnel and, as he takes a bend, she loses sight of him. 'Lorcan!' she calls, wondering if someone could be crouched in the shadows waiting to pounce. Chills race down her spine.

'Lorcan,' she calls once more. 'Please. Wait for me.'

* * *

Polly

Polly's head's still pounding as she crosses the patio behind Ralph and Marsha, their bodies a blur. It's the kind of unbearable migraine that if someone offered to chop off her head, she just might agree to it. She needs her medication, can barely see in front of her for flashing zigzags.

Marsha throws open the French door, and, heavy footed and leaving muddy prints, she makes her way to the nearest sofa and flops down.

'Where is everybody?' Ralph says, looking about the stark empty room.

Polly sinks into an armchair and pushes her head into her hands, pummelling her temples once more.

'Tara and Lorcan are searching the basement.' It's Janice, standing in the doorway, holding a steaming mug. 'I came over quite peculiar down there, so had to leave them to it. I've always suffered a bit with claustrophobia.'

'We found William,' Marsha says.

Janice's eyes widen as she bites down on her lower lip. 'You did?' She looks towards the windows. 'Is he OK? Where is he?'

'He took off. Someone had locked him down a World War II bunker.'

Janice presses her hand against her chest. 'How awful.'

'And there's more,' Ralph says. 'It seems the bodies of the Framptons were down there.'

'Oh, my word. Can this day get any worse?'

'I doubt it. Where's Harry?' Ralph asks.

'We left him alone here – he insisted – and when I got back, he was gone.'

Polly looks up, so close to tears they're burning her eyes. She wants to tell them again that Beatrice's boyfriend isn't the only danger at Lakeside, but she's struggling to form words.

'Are you OK, Polly?' Janice says. 'You look very pale, dear.'

'Just a migraine,' she whimpers.

'*Just* a migraine? My dear girl, I had them in my younger days, and they are incredibly debilitating. Have you any medication?'

Polly goes to nod and freezes, the pain jarring. 'In my room...'

'Then let's go get you some painkillers—'

'We should all go,' Marsha says, as though she suspects Janice.

'Of course, yes.' Janice puts down her drink, tea splashing onto the table. 'Safety in numbers, that's what they say, isn't it? The more the merrier.' She chuckles, taking hold of Polly's hand. 'So, I'm guessing you haven't found Beatrice,' she says, almost like an afterthought.

* * *

Tara

'Christ! Lorcan!' Tara yells, as he slips on the slime that lies in patches and drips from walls, and tumbles to the ground.

It happens so quickly. Seconds. One minute he's on his feet, the next on his back.

Tara drops to her knees. 'Oh God, are you OK?'

He pulls himself up against the wall, crying out in pain. 'It's my ankle, I think it's broken.'

She looks up and down the tunnel. 'We need to get you back.'

'Not a chance.'

'What if I lift you?'

'You can try, but—'

Tara puts Lorcan's arm around her shoulder, pulls him to his feet, but he lets out such a bloodcurdling cry, she lets him slowly sink back to the ground. He's going nowhere.

'You go,' he says, breathless. 'Get help.'

She looks again at the tunnel they've just come down and back at Lorcan, whose head is buried against clenched fists.

'OK,' she says, but her stomach is churning. There's only one thing worse than worrying she shouldn't be alone with only Lorcan, and that's being completely alone.

* * *

Polly

Polly turns the key and pushes open her bedroom door with her shoulder.

Inside she flicks on the light, the brightness hurting her eyes, and Ralph, Marsha and Janice follow her in. It all feels a bit claustrophobic in the room – too many people, like bodyguards hovering around her. But she knows it's for the best. While they're together, the stalker can't strike.

She's about to make her way across the room towards her case, desperate to take a couple of painkillers, when from the corner of her eye she sees something propped against her pillow.

'What the hell is that?' Marsha says, spotting it too and striding towards it.

Polly follows. It's a doll, but not the one she'd seen hanging from the tree. This isn't made of plastic: it's primitive, looks hand-made out of some sort of sacking, its mouth a straight line of stitching, eyes made from buttons, a red triangle for a nose, wool for hair. It's creepy – like something you'd find in a haunted house or an eerie attic.

Nausea rises. She needs her painkillers – and quickly. She rummages in the side pocket of her case, grabbing the box and pinging two tablets from the foil casing. Once swallowed, she makes her way to Marsha's side. Pinned to the doll's patched raggedy dress is a piece of paper, but Polly can't make out what it says through the blurs in her eyes. 'Read it,' she says to Marsha. 'Please.'

Marsha picks up the doll, looks down at the words and begins. '"Miss Polly had a dolly who was sick, sick, sick. So, she called for the doctor to be quick, quick, quick. The doctor came with his bag and his hat. And knocked on the door with a rat a tat tat."' She swallows hard then looks at Polly. '"He found Miss Polly to be dead, dead, dead. Which serves her right, he said, said, said."'

Polly covers her mouth, holding in a gasp. 'Why?' she whimpers. 'Why me?'

'We need to get away from Lakeside,' Janice says. 'It's not safe. We're all in danger.' She drops down onto the edge of the bed, knocking the bedside cabinet. Something falls to the floor. She bends to pick it up. 'Where did you get this?' she says to Polly.

It's the framed photo of Lila.

'It's my mother,' she says, sounding defeated. Everyone will know soon enough, especially as Harry has already wormed it out of her. 'My grandparents were the Framptons.'

38

TARA

Out of breath, Tara staggers through the heavy rain, her feet slashing the puddles under her feet, heading towards the French doors. She throws them open, and steps into the lounge.

Inside it's eerily quiet. 'Ralph?' she calls. 'Janice? Harry?'

She drags her soaked hair away from her face and makes her way towards reception.

Immediately, she sees Ralph, Marsha, Janice and Polly as silent as spectres, making their way down the stairs in single file.

'Lorcan's hurt!' Tara cries through tears. 'His ankle. He thinks it's broken. He's stranded down in that awful tunnel. This is all too much, I'm not sure I can take any more.'

'It's OK,' Marsha says. 'We'll—'

'How is any of this OK, Marsha?' Tara's eyes move from Marsha to Janice to Ralph, then Polly. 'Where's Harry?'

'No idea,' Marsha says. 'He's gone AWOL.'

Tara's eyes land on the doll in Polly's hands. 'Oh God,' she whimpers, a chill racing down her spine. 'That's bloody freaky.'

'It was on Polly's bed,' Janice says.

'Really not helping.'

'Polly is the Framptons' granddaughter,' Marsha says, her voice calm and assertive. 'She could be being targeted because of that.'

'You're related to the Framptons?' Tara says, with a sniff.

Polly nods. 'But I don't think this doll, or the additions to the pictures, or the film of me in the shower...' Her eyes fill with tears, her hands shaking. Janice takes the doll from her, lays it on the sofa. 'I just don't think it has anything to do with the Framptons or Beatrice going missing,' Polly goes on. 'I believe someone followed me here.'

'Followed you?' Tara rubs a hand around the back of her neck.

'My friend and I were stalked recently.'

'And you think that the stalker's here at Lakeside?' Tara says.

'Yes.'

'And you don't think it has anything to do with Beatrice going missing? Her boyfriend?'

Polly shakes her head. 'I really don't know any more.' She shakes her head again, tears streaming down her face. 'The film of me in the shower... only the stalker could have a copy of that.'

Janice moves closer, puts her arm round Polly, lowers her onto the sofa, then sits down next to her. 'It will all be OK,' she whispers. 'Everything will be OK.'

'Look, I'm so sorry this is happening to you, Polly,' Tara says. 'To all of us, but I think we need to get Lorcan out of that tunnel – he's alone down there, in a lot of pain.'

'Yes, go,' Polly says. 'I'll stay here.'

'I'll stay with you,' Janice whispers. And, looking up at the others, adds, 'She'll be safe with me.'

* * *

Polly

Ralph and Tara leave immediately, but Marsha hovers, her eyes on Polly.

'Go,' Janice says to her, flicking her away with her hand. 'I said I'll take care of her. Ralph won't be able to lift Lorcan alone, and I'm sure Tara would break if she tried.'

'Yes. Yes, you're right. Well, keep strong.' Marsha, seeming less like an army officer now, ruffles Polly's curls like she's a dog – which doesn't help her migraine. 'We'll get to the damn root of all of this, you'll see.' And with that she turns and marches after Tara and Ralph.

Polly holds her palms against her temples, trying to control the nausea, the only sound for several moments is the rain hammering against the window.

'So, you're related to the Framptons?' Janice says, rising to her feet and looking out of a side window at the drive. 'How do you know that?'

'The photo you saw in my room of my mother, well, it turns out she was Lila Frampton, Esme and Stephen's daughter. She died giving birth to me, and it was her only possession when she died.'

Janice keeps her back to Polly. 'Your mother is dead?'

'My biological mother, yes. I traced the photo to Lakeside. But—'

'Oh God.' Janice ducks down. 'There's someone out there.'

'Where?' Polly gets to her feet and looks through the window – the flashes on her eyes are improving a little, but she can't see anyone. 'Perhaps it's Harry.'

'Whoever it is, they could have Beatrice,' Janice says, hurrying to the door.

'We're not exactly a dream team, Janice. I've got a supermigraine, and you're—' She stops herself – had been about to say 'ditzy' and thought better of it. 'We need to wait for the others.'

But Janice is already in the porch, grabbing an umbrella like a weapon and throwing open the front door.

Despite her thumping head, Polly can't let her do this alone. She takes a deep breath and follows, grabs an umbrella too.

The rain has eased to a fine drizzle, but the grey clouds are heavy, darkening the area. There's no doubt it's only a reprieve from the onslaught.

Janice steps out towards the garages, brandishing her umbrella like a sword, but Polly's attention is drawn to the old Volkswagen camper. The checked curtains that had been tied back with ribbons when she arrived are closed across the windows. Is someone in there? She goes round to the driver's side, but the windows are blacked out and it's impossible to see inside. She props the brolly against the van and makes her way round to the sliding side door and tries it. Her stomach lurches as the door opens easily.

She gasps, stepping backwards, her ankle twisting. Inside, her blue dress with white daisies – the one taken from her and Nicky's apartment – is laid out. Displayed as though whoever put it there expected Polly to see it. A piece of material has been cut from it: the fabric used for the doll's dress.

'Oh God,' she whispers, covering her mouth. She's about to move when she hears fast approaching footsteps from behind.

Before she can swing round, the pain in the back of her head is intolerable.

'Why?' she whispers, as she crashes to the ground, her world turning to darkness. *Why?*

39

TARA

'He's just down here.' Tara's voice quivers with uncertainty as she leads the way through the eerie tunnel to where she last saw Lorcan. 'Just round this bend, I think.'

'Where is he then?' Ralph says, as Tara stops and throws the beam of her torch across the ground.

She freezes. He's gone. 'I don't understand, I... He was here. He couldn't have gone far. He was in agony.'

'Lorcan!' Ralph's desperate cry reverberates around the damp, enclosed space. 'Lorcan, where the hell are you, mate?' The echo of his voice lingers in the oppressive air. 'Lorcan!'

'He may have heard something, crawled further along the tunnel trying to reach Beatrice,' Marsha says.

'Surely not.' Tara shakes her head. 'He was injured, he wouldn't have been able to get far.'

'What do we really know about Lorcan?' Marsha says. 'He hasn't been here long, has he?'

'You think he's involved?' Tara shudders, wondering who she can actually trust. 'Surely not, he seems such a nice man, and we checked out his CV. He worked as a chef in London. Michelin star rated. Originally from Ireland, though I only know that because of his accent. Never married. No children. He's a great cook... and seems so genuine. I can't imagine—'

'Well, let's be on the safe side, shall we?' Marsha whips out a knife from her sling bag.

'Oh my God!' Tara steps back, falling against the slimy wall.

'Let's go,' Marsha says, continuing down the tunnel, the knife glinting in her torchlight. 'I may be in my late fifties, but no one gets one over on Marsha Jarvis. Absolutely no one.'

* * *

Polly

Polly opens her eyes, the throbbing in her head and blurs in her vision made worse by a rocking movement – the ferocious wind is swaying the vehicle she's in the back of. Cable ties cut into her wrists and ankles. In the gloom she recognises the checked curtains, the dress by her side. It's the camper van. Rain hammers the roof and tyres splash through puddles. She twists her neck, can just make out the driver's dark hair resting against a black collar. There's someone in the passenger seat too, she's sure of it, though whoever it is, they're just a shadow, out of her line of sight.

Swinging from the rear-view mirror is the friendship necklace Nicky bought her that went missing from her room at Lakeside.

'Who are you?' she cries, her voice cracking. 'What do you want?'

The driver doesn't speak. Keeps their head facing forward. They begin to slow, puddles splashing the side of the van as they swerve to a stop. There's a thud, thud, thud: flat hands banging against the steering wheel, once, twice, three times, frustration in every strike.

'The roads are flooded!' Polly yells. She's afraid, her body trembling, but she's angry too. 'You'll never get away with this.'

The driver is eerily still. Moments feel like forever. Then they jerk forward, press Play on the CD player. A whimsical child's voice begins to sing:

'Little Polly Flinders sat among the cinders, warming her pretty little toes. Her mother came and caught her, and whipped her little daughter, for spoiling her nice new clothes.'

The recording ends, and a toxic silence creeps around the camper van.

'What do you want?' Polly wiggles violently, attempting to free herself, the movement making her feel sick. But it's no good. She's trapped. And she's certain whoever's sitting in the driver's seat wants her dead.

Tara

'Lorcan!' Ralph's frantic call echoes through the darkness. 'Where the hell are you?'

'Here!' A haunting voice responds, coming from the depths of the tunnel, and Ralph, Tara and Marsha pick up speed, their shadows dancing on the walls. They spot Lorcan propped up against the wall where the tunnel is blocked off. Ending abruptly, a wooden box on his lap.

Marsha slips her knife slowly back into her bag.

'Why didn't you stay where I left you?' Tara says, crouching down beside him.

'Because I'm an eejit. I thought I heard movement, but it must have been a rat.'

'And what would you have done if it was something more dangerous?' Ralph says. 'In that state.'

'I know, I know. As I say, I'm an eejit. Now can you quit with your nagging? The point is, I found this.' He taps the wooden box. 'I'll warn you, it's pretty grotesque, and I've no idea what it means. Or why it's down here.'

Marsha holds out her hand. 'I can do grotesque. My stomach's pretty strong,' she says, and he hands the box to her.

Tara hovers behind her, looking on as she opens it. 'Oh my God!' she cries, turning away and heaving when she sees what's inside. 'Oh God, oh God, oh God! Who does it belong to? Why would someone chop off someone's finger?'

'Calm down, Tara. It's fake,' Lorcan says.

'Fake!' She folds her arms tight across her beating heart. 'Jesus, Lorcan, you could have led with that.'

Lorcan throws her an apologetic smile. 'Sorry.'

'It's so lifelike.' Marsha picks it up with thumb and forefinger and studies it. 'The blood looks so real,' she says. 'And what about the ring?'

Tara studies the gold band with the green gem that's wedged on the finger, trying not to focus on the blood – or whatever it is – dripping onto Marsha's hand. She presses her palm against her mouth, trying desperately not to throw up.

'You're right. It is fake.' Marsha drops the finger back into the box. 'But the question is, what the hell is it doing in the basement? And who the hell put it here? It doesn't make any sense.'

'Seriously, we need to get out of here,' Tara says. 'Now.'

As Ralph and Marsha lift Lorcan to his feet, he asks, 'Where's everyone else?'

'To be honest, I've lost track of them,' Ralph says.

'Well, Harry took off alone,' Tara volunteers.

'And Janice and Polly are together,' Marsha adds. 'And we

found William. He'd been locked in a bunker, and now he's taken off. He mentioned he found skeletons down there.'

'The Framptons?'

'Possibly.'

'Jesus, Mary and Joseph, this is one twisted place. Any sign of Beatrice?'

They all shake their heads.

'Christ, the poor woman must be petrified.'

Polly

Polly knows her abduction has nothing to do with the history of Lakeside and everything to do with the stalker. She's sure that whoever is sitting silently in the driver's seat is the person who put the cameras up in her apartment and filmed her in the shower. And she's certain, too, they're the person who stole her daisy-print dress and strung up the doll, the person who messed with her painting. Maybe even killed Xander.

'It's no good, Polly.' The figure doesn't turn round, but Polly knows the voice, and realisation sends shockwaves through her body. 'I now know Nicky cares more about you than me. In fact, I couldn't believe it when he arrived here, looking for you. Worried you were in danger. He's got a thing for you.' She laughs. 'Did you know?'

'Nicky's at *Lakeside*?' Polly's stomach lurches. 'Where? Where is he?'

The driver throws open the car door and steps out. Within moments the side door slides open, and Polly blinks the figure into focus.

Tendrils of red hair fly wildly, the wig gripped in one of her hands like a dead squirrel. A knife is clenched in her other. Rain splatters her short dark hair.

'Beatrice.' Polly feels as though she's choking, as though someone is squeezing life from her, her heart pounds against her ribs. 'Oh God, why?'

'Because you ruined everything, pretty Polly. And now it's time to pay.'

40

TARA

Lorcan sits on the sofa in the lounge, leg balanced on the coffee table in front of him. They've removed his boot, and his trouser leg is rolled up to reveal his swollen, purple ankle. Tara has supplied him with painkillers but, frankly, he looks terrible – at least ten years older than his sixty years. His face is creased in pain – being lugged up the basement steps by Ralph and Marsha couldn't have helped.

'This is all too awful,' Tara says through a lump in her throat, unsure how she's still standing after everything that's happened. 'We should get the hell out of here, take our chances on the roads.'

'No.' Marsha gets a pile of books and elevates Lorcan's leg, which is a little too close to the box with the fake severed finger. 'We're safer here. If we all stay together—'

'But we're not all together, are we?' Tara cries. 'Beatrice has gone missing with whoever that awful man was, and I've no idea where Janice and Polly are' – she flicks her hand dismissively – 'and Xander...' She holds back tears, swallows hard. 'And Harry—'

'Is here.' They turn to see Harry striding through the door, a wad of papers tucked under his arm, looking far less frazzled than the rest of them.

'Where the hell have you been?'

'It's good to see you too, Tara.' He flumps down in a chair. 'There was something I needed to check, is all. I'm here now. What's been happening?'

'Xander has been murdered, Beatrice abducted, and you decide there's something you need to check. Are you crazy?' Tara drags slim fingers through her hair, her eyes full of tears. She sounds hysterical. 'What was so important that you had to take off?'

'Calm down, Tara,' Ralph says. 'It's OK. We're safe here together. Everything's going to be just fine.'

'Is it? Is it really?'

Marsha gets to her feet. 'We need to check on Polly and Janice. Is anyone with me? Sticking together is the name of the game.' She goes to walk towards the door, and the others follow.

'Hey!' Lorcan says, raising a hand and wincing. 'Pretty sure I shouldn't stay here alone. I'm not a coward, but I don't fancy my chances in this state if an axe-wielding murderer passes through.'

Tara's heart pounds at the thought. 'Oh God, Lorcan, please don't.'

'He's right,' Ralph says. 'OK, Tara and I will look for Janice and Polly. Harry and Marsha, you stay here with Lorcan.'

'Who put you in charge?' Harry says, lips twisting. 'But fine. I need to look through these papers anyway.'

'I would prefer to come with you guys,' Marsha says.

'No. Stay, Marsha. Lorcan needs you both here.'

'I'm not his bodyguard. Just because I was in the forces, it—'

'Christ's sake, Marsha!' Ralph grabs Tara and pulls her towards the door. 'Just stay. We won't be long.'

* * *

Polly

It's been over ten minutes since Beatrice cut the cables on Polly's ankles and dragged her from the van, forced her to walk into the woods, and Polly wonders now if there ever was a second person in the van.

Polly's hands are still tied behind her back, and she keeps stumbling, losing her balance on the slick, muddy earth, her legs now splattered with murky puddle-water. Her hair, wet from the mizzling rain, clings to her skull.

Beatrice is right behind her, and several times she's felt the knife pressed against her back. Pushing her onwards.

Her heart pounds. Beatrice saying nothing is unbearable.

'Where are you taking me?' Polly says, finally.

But still Beatrice is silent.

The harsh chattering of a magpie on a branch above them startles Polly.

'One for sorrow,' Beatrice whispers in her ear. 'Shame.'

They trudge on, brambles scratching Polly's arms. 'Please...' she says, but her words disappear on her tongue. This woman won't listen.

They finally come to an open area, a wooden cabin coming into view.

'It's not where I planned to take you,' Beatrice says. 'I'd found a wonderful abandoned house a few miles down the road, but the stupid floods put paid to that idea. So, I'll have to make do with Ralph's cabin. *A cabin in the woods,* next best thing, don't you think?' She lets out a fake laugh.

'You're taking me to Ralph's cabin?' Polly recalls how he told her about it. 'Is Ralph—?'

'A bad guy? Well, there's a question.' A pause. 'Do you think Ralph is capable of murder? Did he kill Xander to protect his precious Tara?' She pulls a face. 'What do you think is going on there? I mean, Ralph might be a good-looking guy, but he's got to be sixty, and Tara's so much younger. Do you think it's a sex thing? Do you think Ralph's got the hots for her? And maybe Tara needs a daddy figure as, apparently, she grew up in care homes. My eyes glazed over when she told me that, but she was so self-absorbed she didn't even notice.' She shakes her head. 'No, I don't think anything's going on with those two. They haven't got that chemistry, that buzz, that uncontrollable passion.' A beat. 'The kind Nicky and I had, until you ruined everything.' She presses the knife into Polly's back. If she was to push a fraction harder...

'Faster!' Like a wild animal, Beatrice kicks Polly's leg and cracks a hand across the back of her head. 'I haven't got all fucking day.'

* * *

Tara

'Janice!' Tara races across the drive and crouches next to the woman lying on the grass near the garages. She's soaked through, blood trickling from a head wound, an umbrella by her side. 'Hey, hey,' she says, picking up Janice's hand and tapping it. 'Janice! It's me, Tara. Please wake up.'

Ralph is suddenly beside her, taking the woman's pulse. 'She's alive.'

'Thank God!'

'Janice, wake up. Please. It's Ralph.'

Janice stirs, her eyes flickering open. 'Polly?' she says. 'Where's Polly?'

Tara looks around. There's no sign of her. But Marsha is heading towards them, hood up against the rain. 'What's happened?' she cries.

'Christ, Marsha,' Ralph says, 'what part of "stay with Lorcan" didn't you understand?'

Marsha folds her arms. 'Nobody – not even you, Ralph – tells me what to do.'

'I saw someone from the window. We came out to see who it was,' Janice says, bringing everyone's attention back to her. 'Polly was looking around the camper van.' She attempts to move, grabs her head, winces in pain. 'I heard footsteps behind me, and then whack, a flash of white, before everything went black.'

'Where is it?' Tara says, looking towards the row of parked cars. 'Where's the camper van now?'

'It was here. I swear it.' Janice pulls herself to a sitting position with Ralph's help. 'It was there when—'

'Who does it belong to?' Ralph asks, as he and Tara help Janice to her feet.

'Beatrice,' Tara says. 'Do you think Beatrice's boyfriend took it? Abducted Beatrice *and* Polly?'

'No,' Janice says. 'Beatrice took her.'

'Beatrice?' Tara says. 'How can you be sure?'

'Just before she hit me, I smelt her perfume. I'd noticed how unusual it was a few days ago.' She rubs her temples. 'Have we got everything back to front? What if Beatrice's boyfriend – if that's who he is – didn't abduct her? What if she abducted him? And now she's got Polly too.' A tear runs down her face.

'Or maybe Beatrice and her boyfriend are in it together.' Tara's voice is shaky.

'Well, whatever's going on, I have to find her,' Janice says. 'I need to save that dear sweet girl. It's the least I can do.'

41

ESME

Twenty-Six Years Ago

I can't move. Frozen on the doorstep: paralysed, petrified. Stephen's face has morphed into the monster he is. A face I've seen so many times before. A face that's told me time and time again that I should run for the hills and never come back to this awful place. A face that trapped me here like a helpless animal, afraid to stay but more afraid to leave.

Stephen takes out a lighter, flicks it several times before a flame catches Lila's letter to Elijah, turning it soot black within moments. The flames reach his fingers, and he drops the singed paper. Smiles as it floats to the ground. Lila's last hope dying, turning to ash.

I feel helpless, blame myself that I kept the boy here at Lakeside for my own indulgence – that I've put him in danger.

'You got my daughter fucking pregnant?' Stephen says, stepping closer to Elijah. He's not shouting, but there's a tense menace in his voice that turns my stomach.

I let out a gasp, trying to fool Stephen that I wasn't aware of it –

that I had no idea Lila was having a baby. If he has any idea I knew, he'll do something truly awful.

Stephen seizes the boy by his neck and throws him to the ground, slams a booted foot into his stomach. Elijah lets out a painful cry and curls up like a foetus, whispering he's not sorry, that he loves her. That he loves Lila and he'll care for the baby.

'I warned you, Elijah Lovell,' Stephen yells, dragging him by his hair onto the grass, where the boy swings punches into the air, attempting to fight back. He's no coward, but the tears streaming down his face tell me he's frightened – scared out of his wits. And who wouldn't be, with a monster like Stephen gunning for you?

'I warned you if we ever caught you again, I would kill you,' Stephen spits. 'And now I hear you raped my daughter.'

'No, no, no. I—'

'What? You're saying my daughter's a slut? That she' – he scowls down at the boy – '*agreed* to sleep with the likes of you?'

'I love her, Mr Frampton. I came here looking for her. We're going to get married.'

Another strike with Stephen's foot. Elijah screams, cowering on the ground, blocking his face with his arms and trying to shuffle away as Giles aims a kick at his head.

Stephen stares down at the boy, his jaw tight, fists clenched. 'Do you hear that, Giles?' he says and, putting on a whiney voice, adds, 'He was looking for Lila. He wants to marry her.'

Giles lets out a loud fake laugh. 'He really thinks he's good enough for her.'

'The boy's delusional. Your William is far more suitable for Lila. Fine son you have there, Giles. Going places.'

'Let me go.' Elijah's blue eyes are wide and terrified. I have to do something. I have to. 'Please, I want to go home,' he cries. 'Me mum will be worried.'

'No can do, I'm afraid,' Stephen says with a sneer. 'Your days are over, you piece of shit.' He smirks. 'We're going to kill you, but first we're going to make you suffer for what you did to my girl.'

'Stephen, please. Stop!' I cry. He won't, I know he won't, so I race inside, dash into the lounge and pick up the Luger. I won't use it. I just need to give the boy a chance to get away.

Back at the front door, I see Elijah's still on the ground, Stephen and Giles towering over him.

'Stop!' I yell, pointing the gun at Stephen, my hand wobbling. I'm not even sure how to use the thing. If it even works.

He laughs. 'Get back in the house, you stupid woman.'

'Let the boy go.' I stand my ground, an inner strength to protect this boy rising inside me. If only I'd found it earlier, saved my daughter from Stephen's tyranny.

Elijah uses the distraction, scrambles to his feet.

'Run!' I shout. However much I blame Perdita for the loss of baby Edward, I don't want her to lose her son too. There is nothing worse than losing a child. 'Run, Elijah!' I yell again. 'And never stop running.'

He looks my way, stares at the gun in my trembling hands.

'Go, for goodness' sake. Now!'

But before the boy can take off, Stephen grabs him by the neck. Squeezes. Hard. And suddenly Giles is right beside him, egging him on, as if they're the Kray twins. They look demented. The look of enjoyment on their faces as they watch life drain from Elijah makes me physically sick. They're evil. Unafraid of the gun I'm holding.

But they should be.

One shot to Stephen's head brings him down, two bullets in Giles's chest and he collapses.

Elijah drops to the ground too, and I race over to him, take hold of his hand. He's unconscious, his face purple. I check his wrist for a pulse, relieved to find one. I need to get him to the nearest hospital.

'Wake up!' I cry. 'Wake up, please.'

His eyelids flutter open to reveal glazed eyes. 'Who are you?' he whispers, his voice croaky. He presses his fingers to the red bruises appearing on his neck, attempts to swallow. 'Where am I?'

It takes barely a moment to realise the boy's mind has gone, brought on by the strangulation and lack of oxygen, I suspect. My mind spins. I can't be sure if it's short term or long term, but I seize the moment with both hands.

'My name...' I pause then. Is it fair that I should get this new start – a chance to have my son back? *You're crazy, Esme. Crazy.* I look at the bodies of Giles and Stephen, their blood spilling onto the driveway. There's no doubting they're dead, killed with a Nazi gun. I've committed murder or, at a push, manslaughter. Either way I will go to prison. There's no doubting that.

I can't stay here. I need to get away. And Elijah will come with me. I'll take good care of him. It will make up for everything I've lost. I run a shaky hand over my flat stomach. If Stephen noticed I'd lost another baby, he never mentioned it.

I run a gentle hand over Elijah's cheek. This is a gift from God. Yes, it's God's way of saying he's sorry for what he's put me through.

'My name is Janice,' I say to Elijah. It's the name of a character in the latest book I'm reading. The first name that comes into my head. I lift Elijah to his feet and guide him to the passenger seat of Stephen's car, trying not to let him see the bodies lying spreadeagled on the driveway, the blood clotting on the cobbles. Once he's seated, I stroke his battered face gently. 'And you are Edward, my son.' And at that moment I almost believe my own lies. 'I'm going to take good care of you, sweet boy. I'll be here for you always.'

* * *

Sheer adrenalin enables me to lift Stephen's body into the waiting wheelbarrow and wheel it round the inky lake. His arm, as though trying to stop me from moving forward, flops from the barrow and drags along the hard earth. But the wind is on my side, pushing against my back, whispering, *They deserved to die. They brought this on themselves.*

After a long walk, I drop his corpse into the World War II bunker. He lands face down, arms and legs bent awkwardly at the bottom of the steps, like one of those murder-victim outlines you see on TV. I throw the gun down too, then wait some moments, catching my breath, before heading back for the second body.

And then the process begins again.

Back at the house I rest, taking deep breaths, my hair clinging to my skull, damp patches under my arms, wondering if I'm doing the right thing. I could report what happened – the police may understand. No, it's too late for that.

I scrub blood from the driveway and the wheelbarrow, my odour none too pleasant. Breathing erratically, I go into the house and type a suicide note, print it off, pin it to the front door against the flaking paint. It will be a while before anyone comes here. Visitors are rare at Lakeside House. But if they come, they'll believe the suicide note, of course they will. *The couple were odd,* they will say.

In time, the house will become derelict. Nobody will know what happened here.

Dashing towards the car, where Elijah is waiting in the passenger seat, I glance back just once, sickness churning my stomach, bile at the back of my throat threatening to choke me. Yes, the whispering wind is right: they deserved to die. They brought this on themselves.

42

POLLY

Hanging baskets overflowing with flowers swing in the wind. A cushioned rocking chair clatters back and forth.

'I overheard Ralph telling you he never locks the place,' Beatrice says, dragging Polly across the veranda and opening the cabin door, pushing her inside. 'Such trust.'

Through a sheen of tears, Polly tries to take in her surroundings: the paintings of lakes covering the wall, pine furniture, a butler sink.

'Don't let the cuteness of the place fool you,' Beatrice says, shoving Polly further into the room. 'This isn't Center Parcs.' She laughs. 'Sit!'

Polly lowers herself onto one of the pine chairs. She doesn't speak, afraid of giving away how terrified she is.

The sick tension intensifies as Beatrice lays the knife on a low table and takes two cable ties from her pocket. She binds Polly's ankles to the chair's sturdy legs, then with one hand scrapes a stool across the wooden floorboards, positioning herself two feet away from her. She drags on the straggly wet wig – slightly crooked – which, in another situation, may cause a laugh, but right now, accompanied by the streaks of mascara on her cheeks, the smudges of black around her eyes makes Beatrice look truly terrifying.

'And now I'm going to tell you everything,' she says, her voice low and commanding as she picks up the knife once more. 'Your deathtime story, if you like.' She jolts forward, runs the flat side of the blade down Polly's cheek. 'And then' – she grins – 'we take a walk.'

The pulse in Polly's neck thuds as the woman twists a tendril of the red wig tight around a finger, the tip turning white. Her eyes are vacant – there's nothing there, no hint of emotion. Polly had thought Beatrice wasn't fully happy, perhaps still grieving her husband's death, despite her apparent new relationship. She'd tried to be there for her, thought she needed a friend. She never dreamt—

'So, how far back should I go?' Beatrice taps the knife against her lips. 'I'm guessing we haven't got all day. Those wannabe artists will find Janice unconscious soon enough. At least I hope she's unconscious. I gave her a pretty hard whack on the back of her head. Let's hope it didn't kill her.' She shuffles the stool closer, and Polly pulls herself back against the chair, flinching at the sound of the woman's voice.

'I rather like Janice,' Beatrice goes on. 'There's something about her that says she's suffered in the same way I have. I can't put my finger on how I know that. Maybe we're kindred spirits.'

'Did you kill Xander?' Polly whispers.

'Yes, yes, I did. But only because I thought it was you. If I can give you some fashion advice, Polly: that green rain jacket of yours doesn't do you any favours. Far too manly.'

Polly struggles to take in Beatrice's words as she tugs against the cables, the plastic cutting into her wrists and ankles.

Beatrice laughs again. 'Seriously? You really think you can escape when I'm sitting right here with a bloody great knife?' She waves it in front of Polly's eyes.

'You don't have to do this.'

'Oh, but I do, pretty Polly.' She pauses for a moment, looks towards the wooden ceiling. 'Now, where was I?'

'Please, Beatrice. I thought we were friends.'

'Friends!' she yells. 'You stole my boyfriend! Friends don't steal each other's boyfriends.'

But he wasn't your boyfriend.

'I saw you on the cameras, always flirting with him, waltzing around with next to nothing on, trying to excite him.'

'No, you've got it wrong.' Polly curses the tremble in her voice. OK, yes, she would walk round the apartment in her PJs, but she'd always felt so comfortable with Nicky. 'He's my friend, that's all.' But Polly wonders, not for the first time, if Nicky had taken things further, if he'd shown signs of wanting to be more than friends, if she would have gone with it.

'Where is he? What have you done with him?'

Beatrice is silent for some time before beginning again, her voice calmer, all on one level. 'I had a loveless upbringing,' she says, ignoring Polly's question. 'My mother died giving birth to me, and my father blamed me for that. Don't get me wrong, he provided for me. He was rich, you see. Inherited my mother's fortune. I had live-in nannies, some better than others, but what I craved was the love of my father. Something I never got, right up to the day I killed him.' She narrows her eyes, looking hard at Polly, as though seeking a reaction. She can't see the churning of Polly's stomach, hear the thud of her heart. The voice in her head shouting, *Help me, someone, please.*

'That was eighteen months ago. He had a weak heart, was on medication. There was no autopsy – no reason for one. Which was a relief as they would have found *Digitalis purpurea*.' She pauses for a moment.

'Purple foxglove,' Polly whispers, recalling how her mother would teach her the Latin names for plants when she was a child.

'Clever girl.'

'You murdered your own father?'

'You make me sound quite evil.'

'You killed him! How is that not evil? You—'

'Enough!' She leans forward, inches from Polly. 'You're hardly in a position to judge me.'

Polly closes her eyes. Tries telling herself this is all a dream – a terrible nightmare. That none of this is real. *Wake up! Wake up!*

'My father didn't approve of David, you see.' Beatrice straightens on the stool. 'The one man I thought finally loved me for who I am – and Daddy thought he was after the family money. He said if I insisted on marrying him, he would cut me out of his will. So, you see, I had to kill him before he could. You do see that, Polly, don't you? I had no choice.'

Sudden heavy rain hammers against the windows, rattling the glass. 'Perfect weather for ducks. And dying,' Beatrice says, with a laugh.

How did I miss how deranged this woman is?

'David and I were married a month after the funeral,' Beatrice continues, raising her voice against the rain. 'I even got a stupid tattoo with his initial. He wouldn't get a *B*. Maybe I should have known then, because guess what? My father was right.' She runs the knife over her tattoo, nicks her skin, making it bleed. There's no reaction. She shows no pain. 'David started seeing someone else, would you believe? I still have no idea who she was – but I will find her once I'm done here. We'd been married five months when he said he wanted a divorce, insisted he hadn't planned to leave me, but hadn't realised how obsessive I was. He called me twisted, said he hated that I always needed to know exactly where he was, hated that I picked out his clothes, chose what he ate.

'I had no idea what he was referring to. I was the perfect wife. I loved him. It was clear to me then that he must have married me for my money, and the problem was I hadn't even put a prenuptial in place. I was just so besotted by him, trusted him.' She lowers her head, and, despite there being the slight crack in her voice, there are no tears. 'More fool me.'

'So, you killed him too?' A clap of thunder cracks the sky. Simultaneously, a burst of lightning illuminates the dimly lit cabin.

Beatrice looks up, nods. 'I did. Yes. Of course, the official story is he fell down the stairs. Poisoning wouldn't have worked as he had a healthy heart, there would have been an autopsy.' A beat. 'He let me down, Polly.' It's as though she wants her approval. 'He was going to take half my inheritance, leave me for someone else.'

'And then you met Nicky?'

'That was a long time later. For months I locked myself away in that big house I grew up in, saw nobody but the ghosts of my mother, father, David.' She pauses for a moment. 'Do you believe in ghosts, Polly?'

Polly shakes her head, shudders.

'I don't mean the spectral kind, though sometimes the faces that appear in the night seem so real, back to haunt me. Sometimes I'm scared to open my eyes for fear of seeing them. I thought I was going mad at one point, couldn't face the outside. I had nobody. I barely ate. Got so thin.' It's clear at this moment Beatrice feels incredibly sorry for herself. Is this a chance for Polly to sympathise?

'I'm so sorry,' she says, but she knows she doesn't sound sincere. 'It must have been so hard for you.'

Beatrice cracks a smile, which disappears as quickly as it came.

'I know what you're doing, Polly.' She leans forward, presses the edge of the knife to Polly's throat. 'But the truth is I don't give a crap what you think, because I'm the one with the knife, and you're the one tied to a chair.'

43

ESME/JANICE

Now

I look in the rear-view mirror of my Vauxhall Corsa at Ralph and Tara in the back, Tara gripping the seat. I'd argued that I would drive, despite their concerns about my head injury. I insisted. Gave them no choice. I have to be the one to save Polly.

It's all going to come out. Everything. There's no way out now. Polly needs to know who I am.

'I can't believe I actually confided in Beatrice,' Marsha says from the passenger seat. 'She seemed so sincere, if a little vulnerable.'

I stay quiet. I don't want to know what Marsha confided in Beatrice. I've no room in my head for other people's problems. Not right now. All I care about is Polly. My granddaughter. But will she understand? Will she forgive me?

It was easy enough to register on the course. I've been Janice Hardacre for over twenty years. But now I wish I'd never come back to Lakeside. Before I came here, the chances of being found were slim to none, hiding in plain sight in the bustling city of

Edinburgh: a new name, a new identity, which was easier to come by back then.

But I had to return. Get rid of the evidence. I couldn't take a chance on Stephen's and Giles's remains being found once the Caldwells took over Lakeside. My DNA would be all over the bones.

But I never dreamt things would become so tragically messed up. And now my granddaughter, Lila's daughter, is missing. Beatrice has taken her, and I have no idea why, or what she is capable of.

Tyres splash through deep puddles, wipers doing their best to batter away the rain, and my mind flashes back to the day I left Lakeside. The day I killed my husband and his awful friend to protect Elijah. The day I took all the cash Stephen had stashed in the house for his black-market buys: hundreds of thousands – enough to set us up.

'My name is Janice,' I told the boy that awful day, realising immediately that Stephen's attempt at strangulation had wiped the boy's memory, though for how long I could never be sure. 'And you are Edward, my son.' It was a wicked thing to do to Perdita, to Elijah, but I wasn't in my own mind at the time. I'd murdered two men. My daughter had left me. And the trauma of the years I'd spent with a man who bullied me mentally and physically had played havoc with my mind. I think I still believed on some level that Elijah was Edward, that Perdita had stolen my baby that freezing day forty-two years ago. By the time I came to my senses, realised what an awful thing I'd done – taking the boy from his parents, leaving Perdita to live her life wondering what happened to him – it was far too late.

'Watch out, Janice!' It's Marsha, yanking me from my thoughts. A fallen tree lies across the road. I slam on the brakes, skidding to a stop.

'You need to reverse,' Ralph says from the rear of the car. 'I saw another turning a way back.'

'But how do we even know this is the route Beatrice took?' Tara's voice trembles with tears. 'We're wasting our time. We have no idea where she's taken Polly.'

I reverse at speed into a layby. Stop. Pull on the handbrake. Kill the engine. 'So what do you suggest?' Anger rises inside me. 'Should we leave the poor girl in the hands of a psychopath? At the very least Beatrice knocked me out and abducted Polly. She may have even killed Xander.'

'OK. OK.' Tara bashes a tear from her eye. 'Do whatever you want.'

'To be honest,' Ralph chimes in. 'I'm with Tara on this. The roads are treacherous, and the wind is fierce.' As he speaks a gust wobbles the car and tree debris falls onto the windscreen. 'We'll never find her in this, not without dying trying.'

'We need to turn back, Janice,' Marsha says, touching my arm. 'I think you know that.'

I want to tell them who I really am. That I came to Lakeside because I'd heard about the further plans for the house. That I tried to stop the original extension – though my efforts had failed. Xander was never afraid of my letters from The Stranger, even if Tara was.

Another gust of wind rattles the car. 'Janice, please,' Tara whimpers. 'We need to get back to the house.'

'OK, yes,' I say. 'But we should check our phones for a signal while we're out here. See if we can get hold of the police.' I pull my phone from my pocket, and the others do the same. 'I haven't got a signal. Has anyone else?'

'A few bars.' Ralph jabs 999 into his phone's keypad.

'Thank God,' Tara says.

As Ralph explains to the police everything that's happened, everyone holds a collective breath.

'They're going to try to get to us,' Ralph says, once he's ended the call. 'They're not sure if a vehicle can get this far, and while the wind is this severe, they can't send a helicopter. They suggested we try to get back to the house and stay together.'

'But we can't leave Polly.' Tears fill my eyes. I let Lila down, and, as God's my witness, I won't let her daughter down. I press the ignition, and the car bursts to life. 'We have to find her. I will find her.'

Suddenly Ralph flings open the back door and jumps out, and before I can thrust the car into gear and release the handbrake, he's opened the front door and is leaning over me, releasing the seatbelt, pulling me, crying and yelling, from the car. I try to fight him, but I don't stand a chance.

For a moment he holds me tight in his arms, rain and wind whipping round us, like a mini hurricane. I realise he's not angry, that he's trying to calm me.

'Please, Janice,' he says, his face wet with rain. 'You know we shouldn't be out here. The chances of finding Polly in this... well, it's impossible. We're putting ourselves in danger.'

I look at Tara and Marsha peering from the rain-splattered car windows as a branch crashes to the ground inches from the car.

'OK,' I say, and Ralph releases me. I head towards the back door, still ajar from when Ralph jumped out, and pull it open.

Ralph climbs into the front seat, and as he pulls on the seatbelt, I slam the back door closed. And then I run.

44

TARA

'Should we go after her?' Tara says, watching Janice – a streak of yellow in her long raincoat – disappearing through a clump of trees, the wind battering her body. 'She doesn't stand a chance of finding Polly in this.'

'She'll struggle to win a battle with this wind,' Marsha agrees. 'What was the woman thinking?'

Tara releases her seat belt. But as she opens the car door a gust of wind snatches it, almost ripping it from its hinges.

'Close it!' Ralph yells above the howling wind, and Tara, her hair tossing across her face, leans out and, with difficulty, drags the door closed.

'We need to get back to the house,' Ralph says, starting the engine. 'There's no point in us all risking our lives.' And without waiting for a response, he pulls away from the layby and heads back to Lakeside.

* * *

'Thank God, you're back,' Lorcan says from the sofa, his leg still propped on the pile of books. 'I thought I'd been abandoned.'

'Where's Harry gone now?' Tara says, leading the way into the lounge.

Lorcan shrugs. 'He said he wanted to find you guys. I told him to stay put, but no, he wouldn't listen. Off he went. To tell the truth, I wasn't sure he was being completely honest. He grabbed those folders, and I reckon he was attempting to leave.'

'He'll be hard pushed,' Ralph says. 'It's hell on earth out there.'

Tara glances back into the reception area. 'We didn't see him on the way in, or on the road. Though he could have taken a different route, I guess.'

'It was a while ago he left.' Lorcan screws up his face. 'Anyone else think there's something not right about him? I've thought it since the off. All those weird paintings—'

'To be fair,' Marsha cuts in, 'I thought his paintings were incredible—'

'Disturbed mind,' Lorcan goes on. He shudders. 'Creepy, if you ask me. And those papers he had. I got a sneaky look at them, and I'm pretty sure they were the extension plans to this place. What would he want with those?'

'Perhaps he wants to stop any more work being done,' Marsha says. 'He's passionate about the environment.'

'When he first arrived,' Tara says, her voice anxious. 'I had a feeling I'd seen him before. We had some protesters up here a while back, and I wondered if he was one of those, but I can't be sure.' She shakes her head, and everyone falls silent. 'So, what the hell do we do now?'

'Don't you Brits normally make a pot of hot, sweet tea right about now?' Marsha laughs, but it's fake, forced, and her face is drained of colour. She drops down into an armchair. 'Though I'd much prefer a double vodka on the rocks.'

'So, where are Janice and Polly?' Lorcan asks, as though he's just noticed their absence. 'Any luck finding Beatrice?'

Tara moves towards the window. The storm is getting worse, the doors rattling in the wind, the sky dark. 'We don't know where they are.' She turns, meets his eyes. 'We discovered Janice unconscious outside—'

'Jesus!' Lorcan hitches himself up, winces. 'Is she OK?'

'She was, but she took off searching for Polly.'

'Polly?'

'We think Beatrice abducted her.'

'What? But I thought—'

'We've called the police, Lorcan,' Ralph says, knocking his entwined fingers against his chin. 'But to be honest, I can't just sit around doing nothing.'

'But you were the one insisting we should return,' Tara says, widening her eyes.

'I know. It's just there's a young woman out there in danger, and even though I thought I could, I can't ignore it. I need to go back out there. Now.'

Polly

'Ooh, I meant to ask,' Beatrice says, as though she and Polly are friends chatting over a glass of wine. 'Did you like the dolls?' She's still seated, dangling the knife between her knees. 'The blonde one in the tree is a Pollyanna doll, apparently. They were popular yonks ago. I found it on eBay and thought how much it looked like you. Cost me a bit, but it was worth it to see your face when you noticed it swinging from the tree. The other one, the one in your room, was called Polly Prim. I got her on Etsy, creepy, right?'

'So, that was all you?' Polly isn't surprised. Who else could it have been? 'The paintings too? You added the—'

'Corpses, yes, that was me.' She looks so proud of herself. 'I wanted to scare you, Polly. It entertained me. Silly stuff, really: knocking on your bedroom door – it helped that your room was opposite mine – and playing the nursery rhyme. And the time I lured you down into the basement was so much fun. I had a real treat in store for you down there to freak you out: a wooden box with a grisly fake finger inside and Nicky's ring that I took from your apartment. It would have been hilarious to see your face. Imagine the thoughts running through your mind. Such a shame you never found it.'

'And the letters from The Stranger. Was that you?'

'The Stranger?' Beatrice looks puzzled for a moment, then dismisses Polly's words as though she hasn't spoken. She rises, paces the cabin, the wooden floorboards creaking under her feet, her eyes scanning the paintings on the walls. 'I wonder if Xander painted these?' she says. 'Pretty good, I guess.' She spins round, glares at Polly. 'Bet you didn't know Xander never painted *New York in Spring*? He stole it from some poor sap who died in a fire at a studio in the US where they'd both been working on their paintings.'

Polly's heart's thudding, her head still muzzy from the dregs of her migraine. 'Who told you that?'

Beatrice shakes her head. 'Not my place to say.' She grins. 'Oh God, this is so much fun, don't you think?' She spins on the spot like an excited child, waving the knife like a baton. 'I'm going to enjoy killing you, Polly, and Nicky—'

'Tell me where he is, please.' Polly's stomach churns – a surge of sickness rising. Her best friend came here fearing she was in danger, and now she has no idea where he is. 'What have you done with him?' she yells, heat flushing through her body.

Beatrice laughs. 'You know what? I couldn't believe my eyes when he turned up at the retreat to save you. But it all went so well for me. Fate, I suppose. Tara thought he was my boyfriend after seeing the photo of him on my bedside table. And, let's face it, he would be my boyfriend if it wasn't for you.'

'You're delusional!' Polly cries. 'Crazy. You won't get away with this.'

'Shut. The. Fuck. Up!' White-hot anger explodes from Beatrice as she lunges forward and presses the knife once more against Polly's throat and grabs a handful of her curls, pulling hard, laughing as Polly cries out in pain. 'Now apologise, you stupid bitch.' She rams the knife closer. Polly feels the sharp edge pushing into her flesh.

'Sorry,' she whimpers.

'Louder!'

'Sorry. I'm sorry, OK?'

'So, whose fault is this? Who broke me and Nicky up?'

Polly sucks in a breath. 'I did.'

'That's right. You've got it.' She drops backwards onto the chair, dangling the knife between her knees once more. 'This is all your fault, Polly. And by God, you're going to pay.'

A tap, tap, tap against the window and Beatrice shoots a look over her shoulder. A tree waves in the wind, branches bashing against the glass. Her eyes swing back to Polly. 'When Nicky appeared at Lakeside, Tara came to get me. He nearly had a heart attack when he saw me. Tara left us to it, didn't hear him call out to her when he opened his eyes and saw me standing there, and he was in no state to retaliate when I shoved cable ties into his rucksack to make him look guilty.'

'Where is he? What the hell have you done to him?'

'I tied his hands. Covered his mouth with duct tape. He was so weak, bless him.' She grins.

Polly tugs on the tight ties around her own wrists, the chair moving, scraping across the floor. But it's no good. There's no escape.

'OK... If you must know, he's cooking in the kiln. Should be about done by now. Roast Nicky with cranberry sauce, now doesn't that sound delicious?'

'Oh my God!' Tears fall as the pain of her words hits.

Beatrice lets out a sigh. 'I gave him a chance, Polly. I said I would come back to him, that we could get married, have children, even a couple of cats. But he told me I was...' She places a finger against her lips. 'Now, what were his exact words? "A crazy bitch, who needs certifying." Well, as you can imagine, I saw red, and as far as I'm concerned, our relationship is dead. Of course the irony is, so is he.'

'You killed him? You killed Nicky?'

'That's right. You've got it. Your precious Nicky has been roasted alive, and, after the way he treated me, I couldn't be happier.'

45

ESME/JANICE

Now

Rain slants from the dark sky, its relentless assault pummelling the earth. I struggle through bushes, not sure where to begin searching for Polly, wind whipping around me, howling like something supernatural.

I have no idea where Beatrice would take my precious granddaughter. There was no sign of the camper van on the road. They could be miles away by now. But I struggle onwards, clinging to the fact the police can't get to us, so surely Beatrice couldn't have got far. They must be here somewhere.

I push back brambles, a thorn scraping my palm, making it bleed. This all feels so impossible. I mean, what happens if I do find Polly? What then? Beatrice is deranged, possibly homicidal. Would I even stand a chance of rescuing her from a psychopath?

The moment I saw the photograph of Lila in Polly's room I knew. How hadn't I seen it before? How hadn't I noticed how Polly's eyes are so like Lila's? What kind of parent doesn't see such a resemblance?

Tears burn my eyes, and I want to scream, sink to the ground and sob. But I have to keep going. I must find Polly. Attempt to make up for everything I've done.

The stinging rain hammering against my face makes it difficult to see through my glasses. I remove them, shove them into my pocket and continue through slushy puddles, mud speckling my raincoat, the path in front of me slightly out of focus but clearer than it was.

My thoughts turn to Edward. He needs to know the truth. That he has a daughter. That I'm not his real mother. He needs to meet Perdita. That woman has been through hell because of me, and the guilt I've blocked out for years is now weighing me down, crushing me.

I wonder, as I often have through the years, if Edward will ever fully recall those days when he was Elijah Lovell: the young fairground boy who was so in love with Lila, crushed at the hands of Stephen and his evil friend Giles. He's had moments of clarity over the years, often quizzed me about the tattoo of the carousel horse on his arm. And his memories often come through in his art. A few years back he asked if we went to the funfair when he was a child. He was having recurring dreams of a fairground. *I'm always working on the bumper cars,* he would say. But it was never enough for him to wonder if his life as my son was no more than a façade.

I reach the end of a winding path, coming out at the edge of the lake, struggling to get my bearings. I spot Lakeside House in the far distance on the other side of the lake, amber lights burning in the downstairs windows. In the other direction I see the roof of a small building. It's the old cabin. Stephen used to go there with Giles. I sometimes wondered what they did there. It wasn't where Stephen kept his valuable memorabilia – that was kept in the World War II bunker – but I never allowed myself to think too deeply about their strange relationship, always simply relieved they weren't in the house with Lila and me.

I pick up pace, heading towards the cabin. I need to shelter from the storm for a short while, attempt to catch my breath. Try to cobble together some sort of plan. Wandering aimlessly isn't going to find Polly, the grounds are too big.

It's as I round the edge of the lake that I see something – no, some*one* – lying in the mud near the water. I run towards them, splashing through puddles, water seeping through my shoes, soaking my socks.

I reach the body, my heart thudding as I put on my glasses.

'William?' I cry, crouching down beside him, shaking him, trying to stir him.

His eyes flicker open. 'Janice,' he says, rubbing his head, blood and mud mingling on his flesh.

'William, what happened?'

'A falling branch... That's the last I remember. I must have blacked out.' He shivers. Soaked through. His face a creamy white. He stares up at me for some moments, and a cloud of guilt settles on my shoulders. I trapped this man in the bunker. *I had no choice,* I tell myself. *He'd seen the bones.*

'Have you seen Polly? Beatrice?' I ask.

He shakes his head, reaches out a hand. 'Can you help me up? I've ended up getting lost. Going round in circles.'

I'm about to take his hand when I spot a pistol half-hidden in the mud beside him. The Nazi Luger. The gun I used to kill Stephen and Giles. 'Is that what you were searching for? Down in the bunker,' I say, before I can think it through.

He attempts to shuffle away from me, as though he fears what I might do. '*You.* You locked me down there?'

'But you got out.'

'I saw the skeletons, Janice. I know you were moving them.

What was the plan? Were you going to leave me down there to die?'

'No, of course not. I threw a bottle of water down to you, remember?' But the truth is I hadn't thought it through. Would I have let him die down there? But it doesn't matter now. It's all going to come out, and I want it to. I'm sick of living a lie. I shake my head. 'I'm Esme Frampton,' I say, close to his ear to make myself heard above the storm.

'What? Christ. I thought you were long dead.'

'Most people do.' I stand. The rain is easing, though the wind continues to howl like some sort of phantom. 'But here I am, right back where I started.'

He drags a hand across his soaked face. 'What the hell are you doing here after all these years? What's going on?' He screws up his face, narrowing his eyes. 'The bones? I thought they were you and Stephen. But here you are. Did you kill someone? Your husband?'

I nod. 'Yes. He deserved to die.'

'There were two skeletons?'

I need to begin as I mean to go on: confess my sins. 'The other man was his friend Giles Alderman.'

William presses his palms against his forehead, clear shock radiating across his face. 'You killed my father?'

I mirror his shock. 'Your father?' I stare at the man caked in mud, saturated by the rain. Shivering. 'I will pay for what I've done, William, but for now I must find Polly. She's in danger.'

He doesn't seem to hear me, his eyes far away. 'Christ,' he mutters. 'I thought he took off when I was in my teens.' His tone is calmer than I would have expected. His initial shock wavering. 'Mum said he was having an affair, that he'd left us for his mistress. It messed me up for a while – he never wrote – never visited. And now I know why.' He meets my eye. 'This might surprise you, but I don't care that he's dead. He wasn't a good man. I knew that. OK, so I thought I wanted to be like him for a while – I guess I wanted to impress him, but when he took me up to the fairground caravans, told me to burn one down, not knowing who was inside, I admit I ran, and never looked at him the same way again. Of course, he still burnt the caravan to the ground.' He shakes his head. 'I was relieved when he left.'

I feel for this man who was controlled by his father – a father who, even after death, has left an indelible mark on the man he's become – but I need to get away from him, continue my search for Polly.

'He talked about the bunker when I was a kid,' William goes on. 'The Nazi collection. The Luger being worth a small fortune. When Lakeside was renovated, it seemed like the right time to try to find it. Owning the emporium meant I was in the perfect position... I confess, despite hating my father, I'm more like him than I want to be.'

I reach out my hand, pull him to his feet. 'You need to get back to the house,' I say. 'You look pretty rough.'

He stumbles and I catch his arm, keeping one eye on the gun half buried in the mud. If I can grab it, I will at least have a chance against Beatrice.

'I can't help you back,' I say, releasing him. 'I have to find Polly and Beatrice.'

He attempts to steady himself. 'What's going on with them?'

I shake my head. 'If I'm honest, I don't know for sure. I just know Polly's in danger.'

He doesn't push me further, seems slightly disorientated, and as he walks away, shoulders rounded, I can tell he's defeated.

'Careful as you go, OK?' I call, but he doesn't look back. Seems to have forgotten the gun.

Once he disappears round a bend, I dip down and take the gun from the mud, and slipping it into my pocket, I continue towards the cabin.

* * *

It's a good five minutes before I see the wooden shack clearly, amber lights beaming from the window.

Wind battering against me, I reach the pretty veranda. A rocking chair creaks to and fro, hanging baskets brimming with flowers swing hard, barely hanging on to their wrought iron hooks.

The front door is ajar. I take a breath, the gun shaky in my hand, and ease it open.

46

ESME / JANICE

Now

It takes less than a moment to see there's nobody in the cabin. But they've been here. Two cut cable ties lie discarded on the floor, and Beatrice's perfume lingers in the air.

I take a few deep breaths and perch on the edge of a chair, resting my head in my hands. 'Please be OK, Polly,' I whisper, the memory of Lila's departure smacking into my consciousness. The words in the note she left swirling around my head. *I can't have my baby growing up here, Mum,* it said. *I don't want my child going through what I've been through.*

I rise and drift towards the window, attempting to see through the darkness. A flicker of light – a pinprick on velvet – a torch, I suspect, darting across the night. I race back onto the veranda, where the hanging baskets squeak as they sway. I track the light with my gaze, it's getting further away. It must be Beatrice and Polly heading towards the water. I grip the gun and step once more into the stormy night, determined to save my granddaughter.

* * *

Polly

They're heading towards the lake. Beatrice nudging Polly from behind each time she slows.

'Move!' she yells above the wind. 'I'm bored now. I need this to be over.'

Polly's hands are still tied behind her back and, with the slippery, slidey ground, it's difficult to keep her balance. She's run out of words now. Not accepted her fate, exactly, but is almost numb to it. Beatrice intends to drown her. That's what she said as she dragged her from the cabin. *I'm going to hold you under until your life passes before your eyes.'* Yes. That's what she said. And then she laughed.

They're almost at the water when suddenly Janice appears as if from nowhere, wielding a pistol in their direction.

'Let her go, Beatrice,' the woman yells. 'I've killed before, and I'm not afraid to kill again.'

Beatrice grips Polly's arm. Presses the knife tip against her stomach. 'Well, if it isn't ditzy Janice, in head to toe yellow,' she says with a twisted smile. 'I certainly never saw *you* as Polly's saviour.'

* * *

Esme/Janice

My hand trembles, but I have to hold my nerve. 'Get away from her!' I cry. 'Get away from Polly.'

I move closer, but Beatrice doesn't seem to fear me. She's

pushing Polly towards the water as though I'm not here. 'Stop! I will kill you.'

'On your knees,' Beatrice yells at Polly as they reach the lake, and as Polly drops down, I run towards them, continuing to point the gun.

'Leave her alone, Beatrice. I *will* use this.'

'Get away from us,' Beatrice yells, her eyes wide and vacant. 'This is Polly's fate. Just go. I don't want to have to kill you too.'

Tears burn behind my eyes, my heart thuds. But I won't let her win. I won't. 'I don't care if you do. In fact, take me instead of Polly.'

'I'll give you to the count of three,' Beatrice says, 'and if you're still here when I get to three, I will stick this knife deep into Polly's stomach. One... two...'

I aim the pistol at Beatrice's forehead, attempt to pull the trigger. But it won't budge. Nothing. I try again and again, and I hear her laugh and laugh, and it's as though the evil in her is being whipped up by the wind, surrounding me, suffocating me.

I stare down at the gun. Mud must have clogged the mechanics, jammed it.

Before I can return my eyes to the scene in front of me, she's here, inches from me. The sudden pain in my stomach is searing. I look down to see the blade has punctured my raincoat, blood spilling, and know the knife is deep in my flesh. I drop the gun, see it sink into the boggy earth. Crying out, I slump to the ground. The last thing I hear before everything turns black is the piercing sound of Polly's scream.

47

POLLY

'Calm the fuck down, Polly.' Beatrice yanks the knife from Janice's stomach, stands up and stares – smiling as blood trickles down the blade.

'No!' Polly cries. 'You're not meant to pull it—'

'SHUT UP!' Beatrice spins round, her glare menacing. 'She's not dead. Pretty sure I didn't hit any organs. But then I'm no expert.' Beatrice takes several cable ties from her pocket and ties Janice's ankles together, the surplus ties falling to the ground. 'Just in case she springs up and makes a run for it,' she says with a giggle. Her mood changes are chilling.

Tears stream down Polly's cheeks, her body jerking with sobs. Still on her knees, so close to the water, she stares at Janice, bleeding, mizzling rain mingling with red. Why had the woman risked her life in an attempt to save her?

Her eyes scan the darkness, and she wonders, not for the first time, if she could make a bolt for it. But it's no good. Although her ankles aren't tied, she's weak and the plastic cables cutting into her wrists would throw her off balance. She knows, too, that Beatrice's hatred of her gives her incredible power. She wouldn't stand a chance.

'I'll call an ambulance for Janice soon,' Beatrice says, matter of fact. 'If she's not dead when I've finished with you.'

'We need to put pressure on her wound,' Polly says through tears. 'Get her back to Lakeside.'

Beatrice laughs again, throwing her head back. She seems to find this all hilarious. '*We?*' she says. 'In a few minutes there will be no *we.*'

'You need help, Beatrice. Someone to work with you, help you through your—'

'My what, Polly? My pain? My pain at losing David? My father? Nicky?' Beatrice's eyes gleam before she lunges forward and seizes Polly's hair in a cruel grip. She hauls her to the lake's edge. Within seconds she plunges her head under the water. Holds her down.

Freezing water stings Polly's flesh, her lungs burning as she gasps for breath. Her instinct is to use her arms, but they're trapped by the tight cable ties. She's helpless, even thrashing her legs is useless. Any attempt to get back to the surface is futile. She's going to die. *I'm going to die.*

With a strong hand, Beatrice pulls her out. Dripping strands of hair cling to Polly's face, her head, as she coughs and splutters. Once Polly can focus, she sees the manic glint in Beatrice's eyes. She's laughing once more. The woman is insane.

Beatrice drops Polly face down in the mud, and it's though it's melting under her. She's sinking. Lakeside is pulling her under. But she has no strength to save herself. It's claiming her. This awful place.

She drags her head up. Sees a pair of hollow eyes staring at her through the reeds.

Beatrice sees them too. 'Oh my God, a skull!' she yells, flapping her hands like an excited teen. 'You couldn't make it up.'

Polly knows it's from the bunker. That it could be one of her grandparents staring right at her. But none of that matters now. She's going to die.

'Please stop,' she whimpers.

'Do you know what it was like to have your first date with someone ruined by him going on and on about his fantastic flat-mate?' Beatrice says. She's sitting cross-legged now, the skull on her lap, staring at Polly. 'He seemed oblivious to how much he loved you, but I knew he would realise eventually. That I would have to take you out of the picture if we were ever to be happy.' Any brightness in her voice has gone. Her face now serious.

Polly's fingers are numb, her body shaking. 'You won't get away with this.'

Beatrice shrugs, rubs her hands over her face, smearing more mascara. 'Of course I will. I got away with killing David, and my father. I'll get away with killing you.'

The unmistakeable sound of slow footsteps reaches Polly's ears. Her breath catches as she glimpses a shadowy figure lurking in the darkness.

Beatrice whirls around, her torch slashing through the shadows. 'What was that?'

Polly, heart pounding, forces a shaky response. 'An animal, a deer perhaps.' But truth is, she's sure someone's out there. The question is, are they here to help her, or to support Beatrice with her crazy plan?

Beatrice slams her hand against the back of Polly's head, drags her up by her hair, and once again shoves her deep under the water.

It feels like forever that Polly attempts to hold her breath, but it could only be twenty seconds before she starts swallowing water. The burning sensation of liquid entering her windpipe is intolerable. Water slaps against her ear drums, but she's sure she hears voices above her, feels the loosening of Beatrice's hand holding her under. But still she gasps, losing her battle with the lake – with Beatrice – her mind floating away from her, travelling through time, before everything goes black.

48

POLLY

A dark figure kneels beside Polly as she splutters and chokes, water spraying from her mouth.

'Thank God,' he says.

It takes a moment for her to realise this man, who she can't quite make out in the torchlight, saved her life, and a moment more to see Beatrice lying unconscious a few feet away. 'What's...?'

'She would have killed you.'

Polly attempts to sit up, and he helps, but it's no good; she's weak and falls back to the sodden ground.

'Here,' he says, taking off his red jacket and placing it over her. She attempts once more to pull herself up.

'Easy,' he says, picking up Beatrice's torch from where it lies on the ground. 'Give yourself a minute.'

She knows his voice. Spots a blooded rock lying by Beatrice. Sees his face clearly now: *Harry.* 'You saved me.'

He's balling up his silk scarf, pressing it against Janice's wound. 'I'm not proud of knocking her out,' he says, his voice shaky, 'but I couldn't think what else to do.'

'Is she going to be OK?' Polly's not sure why she cares. If he's killed her, she will be free of the woman.

'She's alive.' His eyes shimmer in the torchlight. 'We need to get you both somewhere safe. My car is back on the road.'

A sudden flash of light whips across the surrounding trees, a voice yells out, 'Polly! Janice!'

'Ralph?' Harry calls, continuing to press against Janice's wound. 'Over here. By the lake.'

Hurried footsteps stomp towards them and Ralph appears, eyes landing on Polly. 'Oh God. Are you OK?'

'Beatrice tried to drown her,' Harry says, looking over his shoulder at him.

'I would have died if...' Polly's throat tightens, her voice croaky.

Ralph looks at the cable ties still holding Polly's wrists together, takes a pen knife from his pocket, flicks it open and, crouching, releases her.

'Thanks,' she says, rubbing her sore, red wrists.

As he rises, Ralph's eyes fall on Beatrice lying face down in the mud. 'Christ! Is she dead?'

'Unconscious,' Harry says.

Ralph looks towards Janice, where Harry is still holding his scarf against her stomach. 'What happened to her?'

'Beatrice stabbed her.' Polly's words sound wrong on her tongue. How had she ended up in this awful nightmare? 'We need to save Nicky.'

'Nicky?' Ralph drops down on one knee, takes Janice's pulse.

'The blood flow is slowing,' Harry says. 'A good sign, right? We should get her and Polly back to the house.' He turns to Polly. 'Do you think you can walk?'

'Didn't you hear me?' Polly cries. 'We have to get back to the house.'

'We will, Polly,' Harry says. 'Ralph, you and I can carry Janice.'

Ralph shakes his head. 'I'm not sure we should move her. We could make her worse. And what about Beatrice? We can't leave her. Risk her waking and taking off.'

'So, what do you suggest? We haven't many options.'

'Stay here and wait for the police,' Ralph says. 'They've been called.'

'No!' Polly cries, trying to get to her feet but failing. 'We have to get back to the house,' she chokes out. 'Beatrice said she's put Nicky in the kiln.'

'Christ!' Ralph looks horrified. 'She really is one whack-job.'

'OK. We need to get back now,' Harry says. 'We can't wait for the police. Even if they get through the floods, it could be ages before they find us.' He casts his eyes across the darkness. 'And the grounds are huge.'

'I'll stay with Janice,' Ralph says urgently. 'Keep putting pressure on her wound. It doesn't look like the knife has punctured any vital organs, as her breathing seems regular. She'll be better off staying put. You two go, and when the police turn up at Lakeside House, let them know where we are.' He pulls out his phone. 'Actually, I've got a weak signal. I'll call 999 again, tell them everything that's happened and where we are.'

'And Beatrice?' Polly says, looking at the woman on the ground, still zonked to the world. 'What if she wakes?'

Ralph looks about him, spots a cable tie on the ground and binds her wrists together. 'Then I'll be ready for her,' he says, picking up the bloody knife and clenching his fist around the handle. 'Now go!'

49

POLLY

Harry had helped Polly to her feet, and as she'd struggled for breath, her clothes soaked, her body heavy, eyes stinging, he'd led her through bushes and brambles. And although the wind was no longer gusting so violently and the rain had stopped, it had been a struggle to get to where his Fiat 500 was parked at the side of the road.

'How did you know where I was?' Polly says now – still shivering and holding Harry's coat tightly round her as he drives through deep puddles on their way back to Lakeside House.

'I confess, I was taking off, escaping Lakeside, hoping to find a way through the floods. I have what I came for.' He throws a glance over his shoulder, and Polly looks back to see a pile of folders on the back seat. 'But when I saw Beatrice's camper van in a layby I had a prick of conscience. I know I can be a bit of an arse at times – even my mother says so – but I'm not a bad person.

'Anyway, I parked up, got out and looked round her van. It looked abandoned. Not that I could see much: the curtains were closed, the front windows blacked out. So, I took off into the woods, thinking at the time I was looking for her. We all thought

she'd been abducted.' He seems different to the aloof environmentalist who painted alarming but brilliant Gothic pictures. He turns
to meet her eye. 'I knew, whatever was going on, I had to do
something.'

'I'm grateful you did,' she says, as Beatrice's words flash
through her mind and tears roll down her cheeks. *He's cooking in
the kiln. Should be about done by now. Roast Nicky with cranberry
sauce, now doesn't that sound delicious?*' 'Can you go any faster? I'm
so worried about Nicky,' she says.

'I get that, but the roads are treacherous, Polly.' Harry has
returned his gaze to the road ahead, is picking up speed, swerving
round a corner. 'So, do you know this man? This Nicky?'

'He's my best friend,' Polly says, wiping a tear with the back of
her hand.

Harry turns to look at her and then back at the road. 'We're
almost there,' he says.

They are silent for a time, the tyres splashing through puddles
and trees cracking and rustling in the tormented wind the only
sounds.

'The folders?' Polly says eventually, her voice weak.

'Details of the extensions that the Caldwells plan to do – I'm
guessing, now Xander's dead, Tara will still hope to go ahead,
though they haven't been submitted yet. I believe they want to
build on a conservation area. I had to do something before it's too
late.'

'I get it, you know, your desire to save the world. If it wasn't for
people like you—'

'Thanks,' he says, pulling onto the drive and coming to a stop
in front of the house.

Polly wastes no time swinging open the door and jumping out.
'Thanks, Harry,' she says before slamming the door and making
her way into the house.

As she enters reception, her feet squelching on the marble flooring, her body aching, Tara and Marsha appear through the lounge doorway.

'Polly! Thank God you're OK,' Tara says.

Polly clambers down the stairs towards the art studio, almost tumbling, Harry's jacket falling from her shoulders. 'Nicky's in the kiln!' she yells. 'Beatrice put him in there.'

'What? Nicky? What are you talking...'

Tara's words fade as Polly stumbles along the hallway and into the art studio, past the pottery wheels, and out through the glass door into the garden where the brick kiln stands. It doesn't take a moment to see that the kiln is on.

She turns it off and grabs the handle of the heavy metal door.

'No!' Tara cries, racing up behind her, followed by Marsha and Harry. 'The heat will be intolerable,' she goes on, dragging Polly away from the kiln. 'Depending how long it's been on, it could be over a thousand degrees in there.'

Polly's eyes burn with tears. The only man she's ever really loved – and it's not just a friendship, she knows that now – is being swallowed by flames. 'We have to get him out. We can't let him die.'

'It's too late, Polly. I'm so sorry.' Tara shakes her head, her eyes welling with tears. 'There's no way anyone could survive in there.'

Marsha takes Polly into her arms and hugs her close. But Polly doesn't want to be held. She wants to get inside the kiln and save Nicky. 'Beatrice put him in there,' she cries, tears streaming her cheeks as she sinks down to the floor and buries her head in her hands. 'She killed Nicky.'

* * *

Back in the lounge ten minutes later Lorcan, Marsha, Tara and Harry are all frantically trying to make themselves heard as they attempt to work out what to do now, only stopping to listen as Harry explains what's happened to Janice and Beatrice, that Ralph is with them, that he's called the police again.

But the only thing Polly can think about is Nicky being burnt alive. She's in shock, shaking, her head full of dancing flames, so much so she can almost feel their heat burning her from the inside out.

A loud bang on the French doors stuns everyone into silence. Two muddy palms are pressed against the glass, slowly slipping down. Polly jumps to her feet as Marsha races towards the door and throws it open.

Someone lies crumpled on the patio, wet and bedraggled, gasping for breath.

'Good God, William,' Marsha says, and with Harry's help she hoists the man up, lifts him across the lounge and onto a sofa. 'I thought we'd seen the last of you. I hope you're not going to draw a gun on us again.'

But the man doesn't respond. He just closes his eyes. Slips into unconsciousness.

'So, what now?' Marsha presses her hands against her hips. 'We can't just do nothing. Ralph and Janice are still out there with a killer.'

But before anyone can reply there's a thump on the front door.

* * *

They hadn't heard any sirens. But two police officers – DS Davies, a woman of around forty, and PC Raven, a tall thin man in his twenties – now stand in the lounge.

'We've had an update from someone called Ralph,' PC Raven

tells everyone. 'We know his location and everything that's happened since your first call.'

'Not everything, I'm sure,' Marsha says, glancing at Polly. 'I'm Marsha Jarvis, ex-military. We believe Beatrice Fuller murdered a man called Nicky.'

'Nicholas Falmer,' Polly says, her voice cracking. 'He's...' She can't go on, unable to believe what's happened to her friend.

'Beatrice told Polly that Nicky is in the kiln,' Marsha says. 'When we went to the kiln, it was on.'

'Did you turn it off?' PC Raven asks.

'Yes. Of course we did,' Tara says. 'But it will be some time before it's cooled down enough to go inside.'

The officers look at each other for a moment. 'And you're sure Nicholas Falmer is in there?'

Marsha nods, glancing again at Polly, throwing her a caring look. 'It seems likely, yes. Beatrice said she put him in there.'

Tara rubs a hand around the back of her neck. 'And it shouldn't have been on, so...'

'Get a forensics team down here,' the DS says to the PC. 'In the meantime, the wind has dropped and an air ambulance is on its way to the injured women out by the lake. Further officers are on their way here and to the lake.' She nods at William, whose eyes have flickered open. 'You OK, sir?'

William nods, grimaces. 'Been better.'

'An ambulance crew has been called.' She turns her attention to the rest of the guests. 'In the meantime, we would like to ask you all some questions about Xander Caldwell's death. We understand he drowned in the lake.'

'Yes.' Tara covers her mouth, sniffs. 'Which I still can't understand. He was an incredible swimmer.' She lets out a sob. 'How the hell is this happening? What did we do to deserve this?'

'The bump,' Marsha says. 'The bump on Xander's head. My

expertise doesn't cover forensic pathology, but there's a lump on the back of the man's head the size of a golf ball. It looks as though he could have been struck.'

'Where is the body?' the sergeant asks. 'We'll need to get forensics to take a look. And then we need to take a look at this kiln. Tape off the area. It's potentially a crime scene.'

Their words fade as Polly edges her way towards the door.

Once alone in reception, she takes the steps once more towards the art studio, where she throws open the door to the garden.

She needs to get inside the kiln.

'Don't open it, Polly.' It's Harry. 'The heat will still be intense.'

'I don't care!' she yells, tears streaming down her face. She covers her nose and mouth with one arm, ready to launch herself inside, whatever the consequences. 'I must save him.' She reaches out to grab the handle, but Harry takes hold of her arm, pulls her away.

'Can you hear yourself, Polly? If he's in that kiln, he's gone.'

'I need to see for myself. I need to know.' She's sobbing now, arms flailing as she tries to get away from him.

'Listen! There's usually a peephole, used for checking the pottery.' Harry scans the kiln, keeping hold of Polly. 'There,' he says, finally releasing her. 'Look through that, if you have to.'

She races over, puts her eye to it. A pile of black ash sits in the middle of the kiln, the sight of it breaking her. She drops to her knees, sobbing into her hands. The shock intolerable. Yes, she was told he was dead, but she'd hoped... she'd prayed.

Harry moves his eye to the peephole. 'Polly, there's no way that was once your friend.'

Polly stops crying, rises to her feet once more.

'For a start, there's nowhere near enough ash, and I can't see any bone fragments. Whatever was burnt in there, I'm sure it was plastic. Can't you smell it?'

Polly's silent for a moment as she returns her eye to the peephole. Harry's right, there's no way there's enough ash for it to be Nicky's body, and the relief is immeasurable. She picks up on the cloying smell. 'The doll?' she whispers. 'She must have burnt the doll. Why would she do that?'

'Because she's crazy?'

Polly's mind swims to Beatrice. Why had she said Nicky was in the kiln? What was the point if she was about to drown her? But then nothing makes sense with Beatrice. Perhaps she simply wanted Polly to go to her grave believing Nicky was dead.

'But if he isn't in the kiln,' she says, as Harry places an arm round her shoulder. It feels oddly right there. 'Where the hell is he? We have to find him.'

It's moments later, as they make their way up the stairs towards reception, that the sound of a helicopter overhead echoes throughout the house.

50

RALPH

Ralph looks up at the helicopter navigating the dark sky, the lights beaming down almost blinding him.

Janice is alive, just. Though it doesn't look good.

The roar of the helicopter landing in the field is deafening, the power of the backdraught from the propellers almost reaching him. When the blades finally stop whirring, paramedics disembark, carrying portable stretchers and equipment, racing towards him.

Their main concern is Janice. They get her onto a stretcher, place an oxygen mask over her mouth and nose.

Ralph turns to one of the paramedics. 'Will the police be long? Because the woman who did this has taken off.'

'We need to get the patient to hospital,' one of them says, a woman with a round, flushed face and kind eyes. 'But I'll get onto the police again and make sure they know how urgent this is.'

Just as she finishes speaking, Ralph sees blue lights flashing through the trees. Next, four police officers appear, heading towards him as the paramedics carry Janice away.

The officers get closer and closer and his heart thuds, guilt swirling. 'Ralph?' one of them says.

'Yes,' he says, and without preamble he lets it all out. 'Beatrice grabbed the knife.' He raises his voice above the sound of the helicopter blades turning. 'She took off that way.' He points towards the trees. 'About half hour ago.'

One of the officers turns his back and talks into his radio, another steps closer. 'Are you hurt?'

Ralph shakes his head. 'Listen, do you need me right now? I'm exhausted, could do with an hour or so to freshen up.' He's covered in Janice's blood and soaked through. He needs time. Time to regroup his thoughts.

'We'll need to speak to you, I'm afraid.'

They move away, leaving him sitting on the soggy earth with no energy to rise. He scrubs his face, rubs his head, thoughts of the last hour playing out in his mind. The thought of blood from his hands now smeared across his face turning his stomach.

They will find Beatrice. He knows they will. It's unlikely they'll let her disappear without doing a thorough search of the grounds, including the lake.

Beatrice told him, when she came round, that if he'd been through the hell she had been through, he would understand why she needed to destroy Polly. She told him how her father, her husband and then Nicky had let her down. How Polly had to pay for that. And he listened. And then told her that he got her pain. How his son had disappeared when he was sixteen. How it sent his wife crazy. How he had to leave Marplethorpe for years to clear his brain. He had no idea what made him confide in her; she was the last person on earth he should have been spilling his heart to. *Perhaps that's why he chose her.*

'Tragedy steals a part of you that you never get back,' he said and found himself crying.

And then she laughed.

Told him he was pathetic.

Ralph brings his thoughts back to the moment and scans the faces of the police officers.

Should he tell them she's in the lake? That she'd goaded him, making him flip. That he'd leapt to his feet, threatened her with the knife – that she'd continued to laugh, stepping backwards – one, two, three steps, slipping, tumbling backwards into the water, her hands still bound with cable ties.

That she'd began kicking and screaming then, struggling to keep her head above the water, yelling that he was a fucking bastard, that she couldn't swim. It was shallow near the edge, though still deep enough that she disappeared under the water. He'd made no attempt to save her.

Once dead, he'd cut the cable ties, and pushed her out into the deeper water. *No, I won't tell them she's in the lake.*

'Right, Mr Lovell,' one of the officers says, reaching out a hand to help him up, as though he can tell he's sinking. 'We're happy for you to clean yourself up a bit and pick up anything you might need, and then we'll take you down to the station, ask you a few questions.'

As he walks through the bushes and brambles, he thinks of Janice. How she came round just as Beatrice disappeared under the water. She was disorientated, confused, but the words coming from her were her buried truths. She told him her name was Esme Frampton and then rambled regrets at taking Elijah – *his son!* – how she hoped Perdita would forgive her, that Polly would understand. Should he tell the police officers how he didn't return any pressure to her wound after that? How anger took over and he hoped she would die too?

No, he thinks, as he makes his way towards the cabin, *nobody needs to know. They both deserved to die.*

51

POLLY

The Following Day

'You look awful,' Polly says, approaching the hospital bed, trying for a smile.

'Thanks for that.' Nicky mirrors her smile, as she kisses his cheek. How had she not seen how much she cares about this man? *Loves* him. 'You don't look so great yourself.'

'Almost drowning can do that to a person.' She laughs, but she knows the trauma is here to stay.

'Have you been checked out by a doc?'

She nods, sits down and takes hold of his hand. He was found in the passenger seat of Beatrice's camper van, drugged with *Digitalis purpurea*: purple foxglove. The dose hadn't been fatal, but whether Beatrice had planned it to be, they may never know.

'Why the hell did you turn up at Lakeside?' she says.

'I saw Beatrice in one of the photos you sent me. She must have followed you. I knew it was her, the woman who'd stalked me.' He sighs, attempts to haul himself up the bed. 'I tried to call you, but couldn't get through, so I decided to be your knight in shining armour.' He sighs. 'But the roads were awful and I ended up abandoning the car, and the rest is history, as they say.'

'Thanks for trying.' Polly's eyes fill with tears, her words catching in her throat. 'And thanks for not dying on me.'

'You're very welcome,' he says, squeezing her hand.

52

POLLY

A Week Later

Elijah's military coat hangs over Polly's arm as she follows Ralph and Perdita along the landing towards the Edinburgh apartment he'd shared with Janice – Esme, as they now know her – for over twenty years.

Polly's still coming to terms with the fact that the eccentric woman who painted dogs in jumpers was really Esme Frampton, her biological grandmother, and that she'll never really get to know her now. She died a few days after reaching the hospital, but not before confessing to what happened that day twenty-six years ago, when Elijah suffered at Stephen and Giles's hands.

'They were attacking him,' she told the police. 'I had no choice.'

She told them how Elijah's memory was shot, how his brain was affected by the injuries. That he's now Edward Hardacre, living in Edinburgh. She told them how, with the cash Stephen had left about the place, she'd managed to get new identities for her and the boy – *'it was easier back then'*.

She confessed how, when she heard about further development on the property, she came to Lakeside intending to get rid of
the skeletal remains of the two men, how she'd sent letters to
Xander and Tara from The Stranger trying to scare them away.

'I couldn't go to prison,' she said. 'Who would look after
Edward?'

Her final words were a plea to be forgiven by Ralph and
Perdita, but especially Elijah. But the truth is, Ralph and Perdita
will never forgive her for taking their son, and Elijah is in a poor
way mentally, unable to understand where Janice – the woman he
thought was his mother – has gone.

Polly wept when she realised her biological grandmother had
died. She couldn't put her finger on why. Was she crying for Janice,
the woman who seemed quaint and, although irritating at times,
innocently likeable, or the woman who was connected to her by
blood? The woman capable of murder. Had Janice, with her ditzy
personality, been real or an invention? Polly suspected Esme
Frampton was far darker. She killed two men and took a young lad
from his loving parents. She'd been tormented and bullied by a
violent man. Lost her brother when she was young and her baby
son while stranded alone at Lakeside – something Polly suspects
she never got over.

Ralph knocks on the front door of the apartment, his face
etched with anxiety. This is the first time Polly's seen him and
Perdita since that awful day at Lakeside. These people are her
grandparents too, but she feels no connection. There's nothing to
bind them together except tragedy. She doesn't doubt Ralph is a
good man. She likes him, but no more than she might like a
pleasant waiter or a friendly midwife. And Perdita hasn't regis-
tered that Polly is her granddaughter, anyway – her own mental
health still fragile, despite Ralph getting her help.

Sarah, a smiling woman in her fifties, beckons them into a

small, cramped hallway. She's been Edward's carer for twenty-six years, and now she's staying at the apartment full-time. She tells them to be prepared that Edward's confused and unable to understand where Janice has gone.

'He's in there,' she says, pointing to the door in front of them. 'Please go in.' She grips hold of Perdita's arm. 'And please take it slow.'

The man sitting on the sofa watching TV is handsome, dressed in jeans and a T-shirt with Matt Smith and Karen Gillan on the front, and a pair of bootie slippers. The room is small. Cosy. There's a framed picture of a poodle in a jumper on the wall signed Janice Hardacre – perhaps the only part of her life that was genuine. Photos and ornaments jostle for space on dated furniture, romantic novels fill an MDF bookshelf.

'Edward,' Sarah says. 'You have visitors, love. Turn off the TV.'

He looks up. Reaches for the remote. Snaps off the television. Smiles.

'This is Perdita, Ralph and Polly. They've come to see you.'

A lump rises in Polly's throat as she battles with tears. She hadn't expected to feel emotional. <i>This is my father.</i>

'Hi,' Edward says. It's hard to believe he's in his forties; he looks much younger, not childlike exactly, but there's something vulnerable about him. 'Do you want to sit down?'

'Cheers, mate,' Ralph says, taking the armchair, and Perdita drops down beside her son, her eyes shimmering with tears. She looks better than when Polly last saw her, her hair tied back, her nails clean. Polly prays she doesn't move too fast and bewilder him.

They've been told the injury he suffered all those years ago wiped his memory. Though he's had moments of clarity. Recurring dreams through the years taking him back to the fairground days, but he's never been able to hold on to anything. His traumatic brain injury also affects him in other ways – headaches, mood swings and confusion – though Polly wonders if Janice throwing him into a whole new life when he was sixteen played a major part in that.

Sarah brings through mugs of tea on a tray, and they sit in silence for a moment. They all know what the plan is: Elijah will get to know his father and mother slowly, while Sarah continues to care for him in Edinburgh. Polly's not sure how they will make this man in front of them, who has always believed he's Janice's son, Edward, understand. He seems settled here, waiting for his mother.

'Nobody will tell me where me mum is,' he says, as though reading Polly's mind. 'I've tried calling her.'

Perdita grips his hand, tears falling down her pale face. 'There's things you need to know, my dear boy.'

Sarah jumps to her feet. 'Slowly,' she tells Perdita. 'Please.'

Polly sits down on the floor, places Elijah's coat across her knees, the musty smell of it oddly comforting.

'Who are you all?' Edward says, furrowing his forehead as his gaze flitters across their faces. 'Why are you here?'

'These people care about you, Edward,' Sarah says. 'They're here to help.'

Ralph has opened a sketchpad on the coffee table in front of him. 'Did you draw these?' he asks, looking over at his son. 'They're really good.'

'Thanks,' Edward says. 'I like drawing.'

'Me too. I paint landscapes, mainly.' *So the paintings in the cabin had been his.* He flicks another page over, coming to a drawing of a Ferris wheel, and tears fill his eyes. 'Wow,' he says, and he rolls up the sleeve of his jumper to reveal a tattoo. 'It's like mine.'

'Wow. Cool.' Edward pulls his hand from Perdita's. Gets to his feet and steps towards Polly. Looking down at her he says, 'Who are you? You look so familiar. Your eyes.' He sinks to his knees, his gaze on the coat. 'This is great,' he says, running his hand over the smiley face sewn on the arm. 'It's mine, isn't it?' He stares into Polly's eyes. 'I lost it a long time ago.'

* * *

'They found Beatrice in the lake,' Polly tells her mum over FaceTime that evening. Her mum is sitting on the veranda of their house in Provence, and Polly can almost smell the beautiful flowers in their late summer garden.

'Hang on for your father,' her mum says. 'He'll want to be in on this call. I still can't believe all you've been through, and you didn't let us know a thing.'

'I wanted to. It's just... well you're living your best life out there. I didn't want to worry you.'

'Yes, and I'm cross about that.' Her mum scoops her blonde bob behind her ears, peers closer at the screen. 'We would have been over on the first plane.'

'I know. And I'm grateful. But everything's OK now.' She's not sure it is. She's been having recurring nightmares, and some days she doesn't want to leave the house. Post-traumatic stress disorder, that's what the doctor called it.

'Hello, Polly Longstocking.' It's her father, puffy cushions beneath his eyes. It's clear he hasn't been sleeping, and she blames herself for that.

'I was telling Mum how they found Beatrice's body in the lake. It's been ruled accidental.'

'Good riddance to bad rubbish, that's what I say.' He's trying to sound upbeat, but she hears the angry undertone.

'Clifford. Stop that!' Her mum says.

'Well, the woman was evil, Angela. She could have killed our Polly. No, I won't "stop that". I'd have topped her myself, if I could.'

'So, you said in your message that they're putting Xander Caldwell's death down to Beatrice too?' Angela says.

'That's right. She told me she'd killed him because she thought he was me. We had the same jacket.'

'Oh, my word, Polly. This is all too awful.' She runs a hand over her chin. 'And you said Esme Frampton died?'

'Yes, she confessed to killing Stephen Frampton and Giles Alderman. She also had something to do with William's short disappearance. Apparently when she was trying to move the bones from the bunker, William was down there, so she attempted to lock him in. I have to say I should have been a bit sharper. Janice lied when she said she'd seen him leave in a taxi from her window. She had one of the rooms looking out over the lake. Even waved at me from it. There was no way she could have seen him leave.'

Polly's mum's chin crinkles, a look of concern in her eyes. She clears her throat. 'Well, we'll be with you in two days, love,' she says, trying to sound upbeat. 'When we'll give you the biggest hug.'

'Thanks, Mum.'

'I hope your brother's taking good care of you.'

'He's being brilliant. I don't know what I'd do without him.' She pauses for a moment. 'Oh, I spoke to Giles Alderman's widow yesterday.'

'Now, who was he?' Clifford asks. 'Was he the one who pinched the pistol?'

'No, that was his son, William. Giles was Stephen Frampton's friend – the one Esme shot.'

'Ah yes.'

'Mrs Alderman thought her husband had taken off – left her and her son. It seems Giles was gay but refused to come out. She thought he'd finally accepted who he was and met someone, was glad to see the back of him. She'd always hated him and his ideologies, and how he influenced William.'

'So, what was William doing at Lakeside?'

'He was after the Luger, which has now disappeared. The last time I saw it, Janice – I mean Esme – was brandishing it, threatening to shoot Beatrice. As far as I know nobody's found it. William's back working at the emporium, keeping his head down – he certainly hasn't become a millionaire overnight.'

'And Nicky?' her mum asks. 'How is he?'

'Getting there. He's living with his parents at the moment. I'm going to see him next week.'

'You have a sparkle in your eye when you talk about him, Polly,' her mum says.

'He's a good friend.'

'And that's all?'

Polly smiles. 'Listen, I'd better go. I'll see you in a couple of days.'

'I can't wait,' her mum says. 'And in the meantime, make sure you take good care of yourself.'

'I will. Thanks, Mum. Love you. Love you, Dad.'

'Love you too, darling,' her parents say in stereo, before disappearing from the screen.

53

POLLY

Twelve Months Later

It feels odd that a whole year has gone by since I stayed at Lakeside. On a bad day, or a nightmare-fuelled night, it seems like it was only yesterday. Other times it's as though it happened in another lifetime, to someone else.

I've been keeping this diary for a year now. A private journal that's gone some way in helping me come to terms with everything that happened.

It still feels bizarre that, in a few short days, I was almost killed, I thought Nicky had been roasted alive and Xander was murdered. It was like something out of a horror story, and all because of Beatrice's obsession with Nicky – her deep-rooted desperation to be loved.

I'm not saying I'm glad Beatrice is dead. I wouldn't wish anyone dead. But I'm glad she's not out there somewhere, that I'm not having to look over my shoulder.

I think the main thing I'm still coming to terms with is my identity. I love my parents, and I know they love me. (In fact, I'm packing now, moving to France to be near them for a while.) But when it comes to my biological family, I struggle. My birth mother is dead, and so are my grandparents, Esme and Stephen. My grandfather was cruel and evil, my grandmother a killer who took another woman's teenage child. Am I happier that I know all of this? The answer is of course not. Ironic, given that my stay at Lakeside was all because I wanted to find out more.

And then there's my grandparents Perdita and Ralph, and my father Elijah. It still blows my mind. But this isn't some TV show, set up to jerk the viewer to tears. This is my life. And despite feeling emotional when I met Elijah, I haven't allowed myself to get to know him. Perhaps if things had been different, who knows? But, as it is, he will never understand who I am.

My family are Angela and Clifford Ashton, my brother, and my grandparents – the people who were there for me when I was growing up. The parents who cared for me, dried my eyes when I cried as a child if I woke from a nightmare or fell and grazed my knee. My brother is the once lanky schoolboy who saved me from bullies, the teenager who taught me how to play all the best computer games, and the man who took me in when Beatrice put cameras up in my apartment and later after everything that happened at Lakeside. He's always been there when I needed him most. My family aren't those characters who played a part in the worst five days of my life; my family are the people who have loved me for over twenty-seven years.

I haven't seen anything of Ralph, Perdita or Elijah for over six months, but Ralph keeps in touch via email. Perdita's mental health is improving, and Elijah's memories are coming back gradually. Though Ralph thinks his son will always believe his name is Edward. He's OK with that. Ralph has moved to Marplethorpe, deciding to leave the cabin even though the new owners said he could still rent it. The place held too many dark memories, he said.

He does gardening for the locals, but his main priority is taking the two-and-a-half-hour drive to Edinburgh in an attempt to bond with his son.

He regrets walking out on Perdita two years after Elijah went missing, but he couldn't take the pain of losing his boy and watching the woman he loved lose her mind. He knows now he should have supported her and is ashamed it took him so long to return. He'd made a few attempts to talk to Perdita over the months before the retreat opened. It had broken his heart all over again when she didn't recognise him. But now, with her mental health improving after finding her son, and with Ralph's support, she is returning slowly to the Perdita he fell in love with.

The money that had lain dormant in the bank for so long came to me as Esme's next of kin, but ownership of Lakeside House wasn't affected as Xander bought the place in good faith and invested millions in its development. He'd bought it at rock-bottom price anyway due to its condition and the fact the place had a dark past. Xander left the house and his art gallery to Tara. She's moved back to London and is concentrating on her art – seems happy, going by her social media updates. She's sold Lakeside, and the new owners are going to turn it into a writing retreat. A condition of the sale was that no new buildings will be built on the property, which has pleased Harry. Lorcan has stayed on at Lakeside as the chef.

I am friends with Marsha on Facebook, and there have been big celebrations in the US that she's finally proved *New York in Spring* was painted by her late husband, and not Xander. I saw an interview with her on TV recently.

'I knew as soon as the painting turned up two years ago that it was James's work,' she'd said. *'Not only was it his art style, but he also always signed his paintings with a distinctive X because he couldn't read or write. I recognised it immediately, even though Xander had added a,*

n, d, e, r *and the rest of his name. Did Xander really think if he kept the painting hidden for twenty-three years, I wouldn't recognise it? Though perhaps he had no idea how much it would sell for at the time.'*

It turns out Xander had grown up in the US and taken Marsha's husband's painting from the burning studio, leaving James to die in the flames. It was something she'd hoped to prove – trolling him at first on social media as @NYIS222 before arriving at Lakeside. Xander had threatened to evict her, but she hadn't backed down. Her late husband's other paintings are now selling for millions.

I follow Harry on Instagram. He's saved several habitats in the last year. And sold several paintings. He'd been at Lakeside attempting to stop further development and was part of the crowd who went there waving protest banners before the retreat opened, which must have been why Tara thought he looked familiar when we first arrived at the retreat.

I've almost finished packing ready to move to France. Though I was upset yesterday when I dropped my framed photograph of Lila and cracked the glass. It was as I reframed it that I found a sealed envelope addressed to 'My dearest baby'. I haven't opened it yet. I can't bring myself to. A letter from my biological mother just before she died will make traumatic reading. I will wait until I get to France, until I'm settled.

Nicky is at the front door, so I'll finish this entry quickly. He's been practising his French for when we leave and keeps saying, '*Je t'aime*, Polly.'

I told him I have no idea what he's talking about, that my French is pretty rubbish, but of course I do, and I love him too. Realising that incredible fact was probably the only good thing that came out of Lakeside.

EPILOGUE

My dearest baby,

My name is Lila Frampton, and I am your mother. Your father's name is Elijah Lovell.

I'm writing this for you to find as I fear I may not survive your birth. I've been living on the streets of London for some time now, and my health is poor – my ankles are swollen like balloons, and I've been suffering with terrible headaches, flashing lights on my eyes. I know enough to suspect it's pre-eclampsia. That I should see a doctor. That I'm putting both our lives in danger. But the crushing thought that they'll take you away from me, or worse, send us back to Lakeside, stops me. I don't want you to suffer the same life I had, my darling.

My hope is we both survive your birth, and you will never read this letter. That I turn out to be the mum I so want to be – a good one, unlike my own.

I had hoped that my mother would pass on my letter to Elijah telling him where I'd gone. That he would follow me, and we would set up home together, give you the perfect life, but he never came, and I'm certain now that my mother never gave him the letter. He would never let us down.

On good days, I dream of holding you in my arms, of us searching together for Elijah. And that we will all be together. We'll work hard. Find a house with a garden, and you will have a slide and a swing and everything I never had. But most of all, you will have so much love. Because, tiny one growing inside me, I love you already.

But, should I die, I've hidden this letter in the photo frame with a wish that it's passed on to you, my child.

And if you find this letter, never be afraid to find your father, Elijah – you will adore him, and he will adore you. And his mother, Perdita, is loving and caring and so full of life.

But I want you to promise me, my little one, that you'll never set foot in Lakeside House. That you will never try to find your grandparents.

And you need to know why.

Stephen, your grandfather is a violent, cruel man, and Esme, your grandmother, is troubled. You might say, if you knew everything she'd been through – the loss of her brother when she was young, the loss of my twin, the torment my father put her through – that it's not surprising she lost her mind.

But it was when I discovered I was pregnant and confided in her that things reached their lowest. She said I shouldn't have been rude out of wedlock, that my father would go crazy when he found out, and insisted on pretending she was pregnant, and that I was never to say I was. I went along with it at first, fearing my father. But I wanted you so badly, and the thought of my mother taking you from me and calling my baby her own sent me crazy. You are mine.

Mother started talking about wanting a boy, that she would call him Edward and care for him always. She stuffed a pillow up her jumper, would say things like 'the baby's kicking'. Pretended to have morning sickness. It was all too much.

I didn't hate my mother. She'd had an awful time of it. And some might say her plan to call my baby her own was a sacrifice. But if it was, it was a sacrifice I didn't want her to make. I knew I had to get away. I didn't want you to be brought up in that awful house, to have the life I'd suffered.

I'm not telling you this to scare you, my dear child. This is simply to ask you to stay away. Stay safe. And I hope, if I don't survive, that you will find this letter before you ever contemplate looking into your past and travelling to Lakeside.

All my love forever, Your Mummy x

ACKNOWLEDGEMENTS

Huge thanks to Francesca Best. It's been an absolute joy working on *Now You Are Mine* with such an incredibly talented editor.

A big thank you to the wonderful team at Boldwood. With special thanks to Nia Beynon and Marcela Torres for all their support.

Big thanks too, to Helen Woodhouse, for her excellent copy-edit, and Paul Martin for a brilliant proofread. And I'm thrilled with the wonderful cover design, thank you Jane Dixon-Smith.

To my lovely friends Karen Clarke and Joanne Duncan, thank you so much for your unfailing support.

Thanks to everyone on Facebook, X, Instagram, and, of course in real life, for being there and cheering me on. I appreciate every single one of you.

I'm so grateful to all my readers, and the bloggers and reviewers who take the time to give such wonderful reviews.

Thank you to all the lovely members of the Socially Distanced Book Club, with special thanks to Lisa Bedford, Teresa Nikolic and Trina Dixon. And to all the lovely members of The Book Club Virgins.

Thanks to Hitchin Library for their incredible support of my books.

Thanks also to Jude, Gina and Lynn for their undying support.

And to all my writer friends, with special thanks to Keri Beevis, Rona Halsall and Charley Crocker.

Big thanks to Liam, Daniel, Luke, Lucy and Amy, and, as always, my acknowledgements would never be complete without a mention of my mum, dad and Cheryl – miss you so much.

And last but never least, thank you Kev, for keeping me fed when I'm in my writing cave, and for your continual support.

ABOUT THE AUTHOR

Amanda Brittany is a bestselling author of psychological thrillers including Her Last Lie. She lives in Hertfordshire with her husband and dog.

Sign up to Amanda Brittany's mailing list for news, competitions and updates on future books.

Visit Amanda's websites: www.writingallsorts.blogspot.com and hitchinhertfordshire.blogspot.com

Follow Amanda on social media here:

- facebook.com/amandabrittany2
- x.com/amandajbrittany
- instagram.com/amanda_brittany_author
- bookbub.com/profile/amanda-brittany

THE

Murder

LIST

**THE MURDER LIST IS A NEWSLETTER
DEDICATED TO SPINE-CHILLING FICTION
AND GRIPPING PAGE-TURNERS!**

**SIGN UP TO MAKE SURE YOU'RE ON OUR
HIT LIST FOR EXCLUSIVE DEALS, AUTHOR
CONTENT, AND COMPETITIONS.**

SIGN UP TO OUR
NEWSLETTER

BIT.LY/THEMURDERLISTNEWS

Boldwood

Boldwood Books is an award-winning fiction publishing company seeking out the best stories from around the world.

Find out more at www.boldwoodbooks.com

Join our reader community for brilliant books, competitions and offers!

Follow us
@BoldwoodBooks
@TheBoldBookClub

Sign up to our weekly deals newsletter

https://bit.ly/BoldwoodBNewsletter